The Big Banana

Also by Roberto Quesada

El desertor

El humano y la diosa

The Ships (Los Barcos)

When the Road Is Long, Even Slippers Feel Tight:
A Collection of Latin American Proverbs
(editor)

The Big Banana

Roberto Quesada

Translated by Walter Krochmal

Arte Público Press
Houston, Texas
1999

This volume is made possible through grants from the National Endowment for the Arts (a federal agency), Andrew W. Mellon Foundation, the Lila Wallace-Reader's Digest Fund and the City of Houston through The Cultural Arts Council of Houston, Harris County.

Recovering the past, creating the future

Arte Público Press
University of Houston
Houston, Texas 77204-2174

Cover illustration by Alejandro Romero
Cover design by Giovanni Mora

Quesada, Roberto. 1962-
The big banana : a novel / by Roberto Quesada.
p. cm.
ISBN 1-55885-255-7 (pbk. : alk. paper)
I. Title.
PQ7509.2.Q44B54 1998
863—dc21 98-28333
CIP

∞ The paper used in this publication meets the requirements of the American National Standard for Information Sciences—Permanence of Paper for Printed Library Materials, ANSI Z39.48-1984.

Printed in the United States of America

9 0 1 2 3 4 5 6 7 10 9 8 7 6 5 4 3 2 1

To maestro
Kurt Vonnegut
for his advice and his books

—

and to
Mr. Charlie Cohen
the best Gringo Manhatteño

1

I hate New York Telephone, I hate it, I hate New York Telephone like I've never hated before. I love New York but I hate New York Telephone . . .

He was like a scratched record and a broken-down robot: he paced and cursed up, down, all over the place. He had a moment's peace, but too fleeting. All he had to do was see the phone bill and those four hundred twenty-two dollars and fifty cents rained on his head like a shower of thorns, as if a giant sea urchin had cornered him in a dead-end alleyway and were rattling off bursts of barbs at a steady clip. He swore he'd never call long distance again, he vowed to become the most prolific letter writer the post office had ever known, he screamed it at the top of his lungs, and if someone were to hide in some corner of the apartment to watch, they'd have believed him without a second thought, without the slightest doubt. Sometimes he believed it too, yet all he needed was for his thoughts to betray him for a few seconds, to remember that face and the little voice like a tiny silkworm coming out of the receiver and tickling his eardrums. His inner ear felt like a miniature, snail-shaped, spiral stairway, which the tiny silkworm circled and climbed into gently, caressing it until it slipped inside, to the hilt, to the heart, and once the tiny worm had nestled there, he didn't want it to leave. The bill at the end of the month stopped mattering. He justified it by thinking he'd find a way to pay, he'd look for a loan, get another job, trim expenses, anything for the tiny worm to stay in its nest as long as possible, inside him, with him, on his account and for him. Then, at those moments of insect delirium, he loved New York Telephone more than anything on the face of the Earth, he loved the cables, the satellite link, anything that would transport his tiny worm to him.

Outside, Queens was dressing in white, the frost cutting across the windowpanes as if it had been heaved from a faraway volcano. For some unexplainable reason, he liked the snow. He believed it made him more creative. For some reason he presumed that greater human development in some corners of the earth more than in others was strictly a matter of climatological conditions. He imagined Africa with its searing, suffocating heat—who could think about philosophy or literature, about technology or art, about space or underwater travel in such an arid place? Still, he'd been in the snow for several months already and things weren't working out at all. He'd sworn, yes he had, not to give up his aspirations.

He pulled back from the window, put the phone bill away, popped open a beer and sat on the bed. He grabbed the remote and started channel-surfing. Television wasn't what he needed. He turned it off. It was the depression, which had taken the shape of the remote; it was the sadness of seeing that the objectives he was striving for were nowhere in sight, not even in the distance. For now, at least, he had a job, and to save himself from the monstrous stress, which sometimes announced itself in the shape of the remote, other times in the form of a beer can, he thought about how much better he lived now in Queens than he had a few weeks ago in the South Bronx projects. In an attempt to escape the depression he set out on a trip to the past:

It seemed to him like several centuries' distance between Manhattan and the South Bronx. The week he'd lived in Manhattan, his outlook on life had been optimistic. He walked on Fifth Avenue, up and down Lexington Avenue, and strolled on Broadway tempted by those theaters, those people with heavy fur coats going into this theater or that. It dazzled him: the neon, the gigantic billboards, the New York Newsday building which reports instantly, by way of the link he loved the most—the satellite link—on events in other places on the planet. It wasn't just a thought; he had the feeling that he'd been born to live in a place like Manhattan. Pity it was all fleeting: hours later he faced reality and found himself living in the South Bronx, in Mairena's house, a black man and childhood friend from the Atlantic Coast of Honduras who'd offered him a small room until he found a better situation. He'd already heard about the Bronx, and more than just heard, he'd been rattled by so many films shot in the Bronx with gangs, drug addiction, prostitution; in a nutshell, to judge by the films, it was off limits to someone like him, who'd maybe never associated with anything quite like this vein of the lowest strata on the planet Earth. That, however, wasn't what made him paranoid that he might not make it out alive; it was more the disconcerted look his friend Javier gave him when he told him he'd found living quarters in the South Bronx. He'd looked at him in despair.

Without even hiding his terror, he asked, "Are you sure you want to live there?"

He'd more or less seen it coming and replied, feigning cool, "I don't know, but there's not a lot to choose from. This friend's giving me room and board for three months until I get a handle on my situation . . . I have no choice."

"Do you have the address? I'll drop you off, but I want you to know I don't recommend living there. You can stay here a few days if you need to look for a better place. The Bronx is bad, but the South Bronx is hell."

They took the subway, the number 5, which left them at 149th and Third Avenue. There they had to get a transfer as they left the train to get on the 15X bus, which took them to 174th and Washington. No one had to say a thing, look at history books, interview someone, or even see to believe. It was a matter of extraordinary simplicity; just getting off the bus you feel that whole atmosphere which corners you up against an indestructible, unscalable wall, a wall no alpinist in the Universe dares defy, a wall of discontented faces, disconcerted eyes, hasty steps as if a second of rhythm lost might be enough to bid your life good-bye. There he was getting off that bus, taking in the half-wrecked buildings of an earthen yellow. There were lots of buildings, some close together, all of a single appearance as if they were dressed in uniform. The streets were littered with totaled cars; it was like the scene of a recently ended war. His attention was drawn to the fact that with all this, there were still children playing in the square. Could they still be children, could they have any of the infant left? Maybe they're dwarves who pretend to play to get me to drop my guard, and then they'll eat me.

"What are you thinking about?" Javier asked him.

"No, nothing," he smiled. "If there are children around, it's probably pure fiction about this place being so bad."

"Maybe they'll give you the chance to tell me what this place is really like. I once heard something like there are no bad people here, it's just that air's scarce, the opposite of other parts of the planet, and you're an outsider. What would you do if an outsider came along to breathe your air, knowing it's scarce? You're not likely to hurt him, but you would keep him from breathing at all costs."

He didn't answer; an inner cataclysm kept him from answering.

He popped open the fifth beer and came back from the South Bronx; you could see Queens through the window, still dressing in white. He remembered New York Telephone again. He swore up and down he wouldn't call long distance anymore, and he took a long drink, half the can to wash the vow down. He searched for the phone bill, nodded, picked up the phone and dialed.

"Hello, Mirian dear, it's me. I'm calling to tell you not to expect any more calls from me . . ."

"What's the matter, *cariño*?"

"No, no, it's got nothing to do with us. The bill's too high, you know. I think it's better that we write each other more."

"I agree, *cariño*, I'd already suggested that . . ."

His face became a thing of untold sweetness. It was as if in the course of the conversation he were filling up with something that was revitalizing him.

"Yes. It's better that way. I haven't stopped thinking about the day when we can be together again."

"Yes, that day will be marvelous . . ."

The tiny worm brushed his ear lightly. Now it must slip in and slither down the miniature spiral-shaped stairs, gently, slowly until it reaches the center of the nest.

2

Monday again. Who could have invented Monday? It was Satan most probably; God couldn't be so cruel. Surely God created the week from Tuesday to Sunday and his perpetual enemy conspired, as always, and invented Monday so things wouldn't turn out so nicely for him. Luckily it wasn't January, another Satanic invention.

Eduardo got out of the sleeping bag and the bed, mumbling a complaint. You could see Queens through the window, now all covered in white, like a bride awaiting her fiancé. This time he was the prince in blue who was about to face the snow. But it couldn't be an infernal invention because it was white, and the tradition said, "if the sky isn't white, it's at least a transparent light blue." He was overbundled, but the cold reached deep beyond his bones. While his new quarters in many ways surpassed what he'd had in the South Bronx, it was also true that something fundamental was wrong with his new apartment: you had to walk twenty-five minutes to the train station. He hadn't realized this until now, as the winter harshened and he headed to 74th and Roosevelt in Queens to take the F to Second Avenue, near Chinatown, to the construction company offices. Those twenty-five minutes from the apartment to the subway seemed endless. At times he thought he would not make it in one piece, so as he boarded a subway car, he checked himself to see whether he'd gotten there with both legs still attached, whether there was an arm missing, whether he was still the proprietor of his two ears. After the check-up he could feel at peace and stand there between asleep-and-awake, in the reality-dream, because the train at six in the morning is crammed with people who didn't sleep long enough or comfortably enough, and it's as if those who do manage to grab a seat go from one bed to another, from the beds in their houses to beds on the train, and they let their heads rest against the walls of the subway cars and sleep carefree, unafraid that the subway might leave them at the wrong station. They've learned from habit, with overwhelming precision, how long it takes the train to reach their destination, and they sleep placidly for it. The dream knows where to stop.

Good fortune never was with Eduardo as far as these beds on wheels go. At 74th and Roosevelt in Queens in the morning hours it's impossible to get a seat, and people finish their dreams standing: they hang from the straps like swaying bats.

"Good morning, Mister Eduardo," said Charlie, his boss. "You're late, but don't tell me anything because I know what the *trabajanderos* say, the subway, always the subway to blame for making them late."

"The word is *trabajadores*," he corrected him.

"Trabajanderos," insisted the boss, who didn't allow anyone to correct him, much less a foreigner.

Charlie was an old, tall gringo, not much for talking with the employees. To avoid contact with them he'd get on the telephone and call one place or the other for as long as necessary. He knew how to handle the undocumented worker situation, which gave him the freedom to joke with them, often harshly, and the immigrants took it without complaining because of their circumstances.

The company restored buildings and repaired and painted apartment interiors. Eduardo had come there through a Guatemalan friend, who introduced him to a statesider, who took him to Charlie.

Sometimes they worked outside, meaning out in the ice. Other times they worked in occupied apartments, where, once in a while, the people who lived in them took pity on the workers and offered them coffee or hot chocolate or something to eat. Eduardo had discovered a successful strategy for whenever adversity caught him by surprise, whether it was a matter of the weather, an especially trying job or some unpleasant memory: he'd journey to the past or into the future. That was how he freed himself from being where he was. He demolished a wall and as he hit it with the sledgehammer he traveled to the South

Bronx where he'd surely be worse off, or to the future once he'd made it as an actor, and saw himself in the pages of *The New York Times* and in fanzines. Work time was shrinking so much that Charlie had started to soften up with him, because he was the only employee who had to be reminded when it was quitting time. One time, just to test him, Charlie neglected to let him know that it was quitting time, and Eduardo worked two extra hours painting a wall, until Charlie gave up: "Let's go, you're a good *trabajandero*."

"*Trabajador.*"

"*Trabajandero,*" insisted Charlie.

For several months Eduardo's life was a ghastly routine: job-home, home-job. He had no friends, and the places he aspired to visit were too expensive for him. One day of self-criticism he realized he was resigning himself to a workman's life: work, drink beer, pay the phone bill. All he needed now was to start sending a few dollars back home. He felt he was neglecting his main objective, and as this chaos sunk in, he got busy finding out where plays within reach of his budget were being performed. So he visited the theater at St. Ann's Church in the Bronx. That became his weekend hangout. The *peña* took place every Saturday, and from the time he found out about it he never missed one. The old patrons came to know Eduardo's face, and he came to know their faces and those of some of the artists.

One night out of many, a tall man, who always dressed in a black Mexican poncho, with a beard and a bald spot in the middle of his head, approached him.

"Are you an artist? I've seen you here a lot these days. How about a beer?"

Eduardo agreed. The conversation was drawn out, and after the *peña* they visited Latino bars in the Bronx.

"So where do you live?"

"In Queens, on 74th and Roosevelt."

"And how much do you pay?"

"Three fifty a month."

The big fellow slapped his head. "*Huevón,* you must be a rich man's son. That's very expensive. What amenities do you have?"

"None, matter of fact, the subway's half an hour away."

"In the cold, *huevón*, you're crazy! As if you'd been born in Alaska. Is Honduras that cold?"

Eduardo laughed, "Yes, of course. So cold no one cooks. It's hellishly hot, so hot all our food has to be eaten raw by government decree. It's so hot you strike a match and you set the whole country on fire."

They laughed heartily, which scandalized no one in the Dominican restaurant. Silence isn't exactly one of the virtues of the people of the Caribbean.

"I like you, *huevón.* Look, there's a room available where I live. If you're interested call me, I can talk to the owners so they'll rent it to you. When you call ask for Casagrande. That's me."

3

Mirian was blind to other men. She had eyes for no one. She loved James Bond. She didn't recall where, that is, which film. She only knew that from the moment she first saw him she would live for no one else but for her Agent 007. She knew all his films from beginning to end. On account of him she'd had family disagreements, because the VCR ceased to be of any importance unless it was to show her James Bond skiing, chasing hoodlums down highways at high speed, piloting late-model planes, challenging all obstacles in his way. The only thing she detested about her agent was his promiscuity: he couldn't lay eyes on a plain or pretty woman if it wasn't to take her to bed. When this happened she wept with jealousy, she railed, she cursed the television to such extremes that one day, as James Bond snuggled up against a wall with a woman and searched for something in her mini, she sent a shoe flying so hard the screen shattered in a million pieces, a flash of sparks ignited panic in her family and smoke flooded the living room.

"She needs psychiatric treatment!" yelled the father.

"My poor Mirian!" whined the mother.

And the remaining telespectators hid in their respective bedrooms, fearing future shoe tosses would be aimed not at the screen but at their faces.

Her parents took her to a psychiatrist. She had agreed to go only in exchange for their buying her a television set with a remote control for her room, a VCR and films featuring James, as she casually referred to him.

Her father took it upon himself to explain the situation to the psychiatrist. "It's sensitive," the professional for those with loose screws in the head limited himself to responding. He took the parents aside. He advised them that he would interview the sick one in apparent privacy, showed them the little hidden window from which they could observe their daughter's reactions, and pointed out a red button that they could press in case some of the answers were not true, or if she made any mistakes. The psychiatrist sat down in front of her, using the desk as a foxhole in case she attempted to physically assault him, and began.

"How old are you?"

"Twenty."

"Where were you born?"

"In Tegucigalpa."

"Country?"

"Honduras."

"What's the population in Honduras?"

"Six million, plus those who were born after the census, and minus those who died after the census."

"Are you studying?"

"Yes."

"What is your major?"

"Journalism."

"What's your purpose in studying journalism?"

"To graduate as a journalist."

"Why?"

"So I can stop studying."

"What are you going to do when you're grown up?"

"I'm grown up already."

"I mean, when you're older."

"I am older now, I already menstruate."

"What's your name?"

"Why do you wait until now to ask me? As I understand it, in all life's exchanges the first thing you ask for is a person's name. My name's Mirian."

"Mirian what?"

"What are last names for?"

"I don't know."

"If you don't know why do you ask? Just call me Mirian, and that's that."

"Who's your hero?"

"My papa, and my mama's the heroine."

The physician smiled with satisfaction. Behind the little hidden window the embracing parents smiled, too, for she hadn't responded as they'd all expected her to.

"Why?"

"Because my papa supports me, and my mama protects me. Those are more than enough reasons, don't you think?"

"Do you have a boyfriend?"

"No."

A second smile from the doctor. "Have you ever been in love?"

"Yes, just once. I'm in love right now."

"With whom?"

"With you . . ."

The doctor's third smile was neither affirmative nor negative, simply a nonsensical smile. Behind the little hidden window there were no smiles.

"Why are you in love with me?"

"You're pretty näive, aren't you? I told you that, see, because they say when the patient falls in love with the psychiatrist or psychologist it's because they're healthy, they don't need further treatment. But if falling in love with you makes for the remedy, I think I'll be eternally ill. You're not my type. I'm in love with James."

The doctor forgot he'd ever smiled in his life. Behind the little window the couple embraced even tighter, as if to protect themselves from an incoming missile that had been announced beforehand.

"Which James?"

"James Bond, who else?"

"That's a dream of yours. He only exists on the screen."

"You're so out of touch!"

"No, he's the product of a writer's imagination."

"Introduce me to the writer, maybe I'll trade James in for him."

"No, I don't know if there's only one. I think there are several."

"Are you insinuating I should prostitute myself in an orgy of writers?"

"No, absolutely not. What I'm trying to tell you is that he doesn't exist."

"The writer was only one, Ian Fleming, but after he disappeared John Gardner kept it going, and with great success too. But, aside from that, James Bond is real, he does exist. I am in love with James Bond even though I know that isn't his name."

The doctor smiled again. That was the path to follow, he thought. He deduced that she had a real boyfriend who she disguised as James Bond for fear of her parents. When she wanted to talk about him, she transformed him into Agent 007, which allowed her total freedom to express her passion. Behind the little hidden window the parents rejoiced. They expected the other James to be one of the boys they knew. They'd already whispered to each other that they'd accept him no matter who he was. What mattered the most was their daughter's health.

"And what is your James Bond's real name?"

"You don't know? You're so out of touch! Roger Moore."

4

He would have liked to continue living in Queens: the cold and the high rents prevented him. He was back in the Bronx. Casagrande had spoken to the people in charge of the place: he had lied to them, had told them he'd met Eduardo several years ago in San Francisco. The couple had believed him and took in the new tenant. Casagrande helped him resettle. Once Eduardo's few things, books and clothes, were in place, Casagrande called in the other tenants to welcome him. He uncorked a gallon of wine, some of the cheapest you could find in the world. He left another gallon jug on the table, untouched.

"You already know José and Rosa. Now these two, Mauro and Alfredo, for better or for worse, are neighbors, they rent here."

As they introduced themselves, they shook hands. They listened to music, drank, talked about their countries, and agreed that the next day, Saturday, when no one was working, they would meet with Eduardo to go over each one's duties and rights.

Eduardo wasn't sure whether the racket travelling the length of the hallways was a dream or reality. Midway between dream and reality, he found the din was produced by a seaquake formed in a faraway ocean, and the torrent of water was falling on the city of New York; it was like a whirlpool carrying all sorts of metallic products, and the sound multiplied like a flame over flammable gas and deafened all New Yorkers, who ran, some covering their ears with the palms of their hands; others sticking their index fingers in their ears until they bled; some growing desperate from the intense noise and taking hold of any sharp object, from knives to pieces of things found in the trash, then piercing their ears savagely with them while pleading for immediate deafness. The sound reached his door and finally awakened him. It was a voice yelling, "Up, *huevones*, it's late."

It was Casagrande travelling the length of the hallway from door to door, carrying a pot full of kitchen utensils and banging on the sides with a ladle. Eduardo was annoyed, but it was better to keep quiet and look the other way.

From José's room arose a cry of protest: "*Puta,* Casagrande*, no joda,* let a man sleep. Just because you're a lazy slob who never works."

"Up, *huevón,*" Casagrande bore down on him. "What the hell is the matter with you all, you want to slab till noon?"

Everyone got up audibly cursing Casagrande, with the exception of Eduardo who did so to himself but with much more sincerity. They took turns in the bathroom. Once they were dressed, groomed, impeccable, they met in the large common living room. An enormous jug of coffee and a pitcher of juice, which was beaded from the ice, were there waiting for them.

"Good," said Casagrande, "whoever likes to nurse their hangover with coffee can have coffee, whoever does it with juice can have juice, and whoever wants both, that's fine too."

Eduardo thought that once they'd assembled, there would be protests levelled at Casagrande, whether by the tenants, Mauro and Alfredo, or by those in charge of the apartment. Yet it was as if nothing had happened. Casagrande laughed and talked about all sorts of things without a trace of guilt; the others listened and laughed, showing no sign of having been upset by anything.

"How'd you sleep, *huevón*?" asked Casagrande.

"Very well, very well," replied Eduardo.

"And how did you wake up?" added Casagrande with a laugh so hearty and authentic it infected them all, including Eduardo. *I more than like this guy*, he thought.

As they drank coffee and juice they related or recalled events Eduardo knew nothing about, but which ended up filling him with such happiness he suddenly felt as if he'd already lived with them all before.

"Well," said Casagrande as he stood, "now let's get down to brass tacks. This is for Eduardo, who doesn't know the rules. On weekdays we tenants cook, and on weekends the owners of the house cook. Each one of us has to cook for one week, from Monday to Friday, and another washes dishes. That same week's trash is picked up by those who aren't scheduled to cook. When you use the bathroom you have to leave it clean. Run a mop through it if the shower floods. Something very important: when you come in late don't make noise, and triple-lock and bar the door, which I'll show you later, Eduardo. The telephone: at the end of the month we divide local calls up equally, whether you've made calls or not. Each is responsible for his own long distance calls. And don't forget when you call long distance you have to pay taxes. Well, I think those are the most important things."

José, the subletter, spoke up: "Rent's due every weekend. Don't expect me to come around collecting. By the way, Casagrande, you're two weeks behind."

"Joder. You keep quiet. Didn't I tell you I'd pay you next week all at once plus one in advance?"

"He did tell you already," said Rosa, José's wife. *"Coño*, you love to go around embarrassing folks."

As if none of this concerned him for an instant, Casagrande said, "Well, get some paper and pencil because we're going to make up a new schedule."

"So why did you leave Queens?" asked José.

"The train was too far away for me, a half hour."

"And where do you work?"

"At a construction company."

"Are you legal or illegal?"

"All right," Casagrande interrupted, "what the hell's the matter with you, *huevón*? You sound like a priest or a torturer."

"Yes," added Rosa, "you love to go around embarrassing folks."

"What's it matter," said Eduardo, "the world should belong to everyone. Paperwork and borders were invented by men. As inhabitants of this planet we should be able to live wherever it pleases us most without restrictions."

José gestured like someone being addressed in a dead tongue. Casagrande pointed at Eduardo and wagged his index finger up and down. "There, see, there are a few intelligent *hondureñitos.* Who would have thought a *bananero* could talk like that!"

They all laughed.

"Poor Casagrande," said Rosa, "he thinks all the geniuses in the world come from Chile."

"Gabriela Mistral, Pablo Neruda, and I," Casagrande laughed.

"And Salvador Allende," added Eduardo.

Casagrande agreed."Check out this *bananero* guy. He must be the smartest Honduran of all. And why aren't the rest of you saying anything, did some whore swallow your tongue?" Casagrande yelled, addressing Mauro and Alfredo.

"The thing is we don't know what you're talking about," said Alfredo. "For me there's no place in the world like Guayaquil."

They were magic words. The spell grew and, except for Eduardo, they answered in chorus: *"There's no place like Ecuador."*

"No," said Casagrande, "Ecuador has a long way to go. Chile's the most solvent country in Latin America. We have two Nobel Prize winners and before long we'll have a third."

"Those prizes are nothing, Casagrande," said José, who had no idea what the Nobel prize meant. "Look, Casagrande, just go to Ecuador and see those green mountains . . . those enormous trees . . . besides, I heard it said somewhere that we have a prime location."

"But Chile . . ."

"What Chile?" Rosa interrupted. "Your geography's horrible. Chile's made out of little pieces."

Trying to change the subject, Casagrande provoked Eduardo: "And what does Banana Republic have to say?" he laughed. "In Honduras all they produce are Yankee military bases, right, *huevón*?"

This didn't sit too well with Eduardo, but neither did he have any grounds for a comeback.

"Well," he attempted to smile, "aside from the bases, we produce coffee, cotton . . ."

"Nothing doing," Casagrande interrupted, "those are sent to you from Nicaragua."

There was no delay in the group laughter. Eduardo creased his brow. "Seriously," he continued, "we produce many things, many agricultural products. We also have plenty of creativity, plenty of imagination."

Casagrande guffawed. "Sure, *huevón*, now you're making things up. Aside from what you've mentioned, not counting bananas or pineapples, of course, because they grow there but aren't yours, what else do you produce?"

Eduardo got annoyed and began to whet his reply like a knife that boasts of many enemies. He was eager to wound. Little did he suspect that his answer would actually make Casagrande feel closer than ever to him. Eduardo, his voice dripping with gall, replied: "We're the best producers of semen."

5

Fortunately the psychiatrist didn't prohibit Mirian from continuing to watch James Bond. Now she performed miracles with the remote control: if she liked a scene she rewound it; she played him in slo-mo; and when James slobbered over an actress or made love to her, she fast-forwarded and James and his mate wrapped themselves around each other in ludicrous motions. In a matter of seconds they were in a scene that made her forget the anger and excessive jealousy into which her Agent 007 constantly threw her.

The psychiatrist explained to the parents that, despite the fact that Mirian was twenty years old, her development in the art of loving had come late, and therefore it was normal for her to act like a fourteen-year-old girl falling in love with movie stars. Given some time, and once she'd grown bored of watching her James, she would get over it and fall in love with a real man. She was not to be repressed or reprimanded for that.

At first her parents believed the psychiatrist's theory. Yet when the first semester had gone by and they'd found no positive changes in their daughter—to the contrary, now she was more crazed than ever over her agent and even knew his dialog by heart in impeccable English—they decided to try another approach.

The psychiatrist and the parents hatched a conspiracy. They remembered that Roger Moore wasn't the only one to have played Agent 007, and they got their hands on video tapes featuring previous Agent 007s Sean Connery, George Lazenby and new agents Timothy

Dalton and Pierce Brosnan. They gave them to her gift-wrapped the day of her twenty-first birthday.

When she saw the labels on the cassette case that said James Bond, Agent 007, she cheered up, thinking that she was going to see films featuring her hero which she didn't know about. She suffered a huge disappointment. When she uncovered the hoax, she trashed the videos and scattered the shredded tape all over the house. It cost her more visits to the psychiatrist.

"And why are you treating me so formally now?"

"Because now you're a full-fledged woman—you turned twenty-one."

"You mean before twenty-one one is a man?"

"I wish you wouldn't play the fool."

"And can one speak seriously with a psychiatrist?"

"Why did you destroy the videotapes?"

"That's a pretty elementary question, don't you think? Supposedly I destroyed them because I didn't like them. They're impostors, they're not Agent 007."

"Who do you think is the real 007?"

"Roger Moore, it can't be anyone else."

"Sean Connery came before him, maybe he's the original, or George Lazenby."

"None of them, before or after. Roger Moore's the real one."

"How can you prove that?"

"Who do I have to prove it to? To no one, I would think. It's enough to see him. I can't conceive of an Agent 007 that isn't Roger Moore."

"Others can't conceive of one who isn't Sean Connery."

"That's their problem. I have mine solved."

"Your problem is you're dazzled by fame, celebrity . . ."

"Maybe not; maybe James's intelligence is what turns me on."

"How about his body?"

"Of course, you believe that silly idea the leftists invented about the body not mattering . . . You know, the truth is it wasn't the leftists who invented that, but ugly men and ugly women. Yeah, they're the ones. The body matters, how could it not?"

"You mean you're a narcissist, you consider yourself very beautiful?"

Mirian got on her feet. She drew close to a mirror hanging on the wall. She looked at herself. She stood back a bit and contemplated her face, her neck, and ran her fingers through her hair. She turned to the psychiatrist. "You'd have to be blind not to see I'm gorgeous."

"Not all tastes are the same."

She took off her blouse. He was dumbfounded. Behind the little hidden window, the parents were dumbstruck. She pulled down the zipper on her skirt. The psychiatrist didn't do a thing to stop her. Behind the little hidden window the father was on the brink of yelling or pressing the red button. The mother stopped him, persuading him that these were the techniques of modern psychiatry. Mirian, from her very feminine heels, looked coquettishly at the doctor. There she stood, covered in nothing but a small, transparent bikini, her breasts round and full, quivering as if to scream an invitation. She modelled facing him with hair to one side, then to the other, head tossed back, hair covering her face, hands on her neck, each hand cupping a breast.

She then turned around halfway, ending up with her back to the doctor, and said to him,"What do you say, am I gorgeous, or might you be needing a psychiatrist?"

6

Casagrande was a musician, photographer, singer, mystic, and teacher. Casagrande knew how to develop photos, wash clothes, cook, repair radios and, above all, he knew how to live without working. He didn't have a girlfriend, and didn't need one. Thirty years out of Chile and he didn't think about going back. He felt no nostalgia for his country, nor did he miss any of his countrymen. The only place you could say Casagrande really loved was San Francisco. He loved San Francisco and the sixties. For him the Hippie Generation was not and would never be out of style. Nothing on the face of the Earth before the 1960's or after the 1960's could be of equal importance. In the sixties hippies came on the scene, Marxist revolutions developed in the Third World, man landed on the moon, the Beatles appeared, technology was revolutionized, the Latin American Boom in literature started to show signs of life . . . For Casagrande humanity should have never moved past the decade of the sixties.

Casagrande heard the coffeepot whistling. He turned the burner off, put two empty cups on the table, and knocked on the door to one of the bedrooms.

"Hey, *huevón*, up man, the coffee's ready. It's noon, *huevón*."

Eduardo's *I'm coming* was barely heard, as if it came from a dark, deep well, as if they'd ejected him from a distant dream.

Casagrande had his own timetables for bringing in money. Eduardo was out of a job for a week because his boss sent him to rest when there was no interior work, out of fear that immigration would catch Eduardo and fine the boss. That was why Eduardo and

Casagrande, at ten in the morning on a Monday, were sitting at the dining room table with a huge cup of coffee, deep in conversation.

"So, *huevón*, you want to be a movie star. You must be nuts. You're going to have to come down to Earth a bit," Casagrande laughed.

"You think it's that hard?" he asked näively.

Casagrande laughed loudly. "Ah, *chingado*, it's not difficult, it's impossible. Imagine a *bananero* in Hollywood? Here's El Gran Banana, The Big Banana, The Big Banana in the Big Manzana, The Big Banana in the Big Apple, see how it doesn't rhyme in English? What do you think? Some time later New York will be invaded by The Big Banana? Are you crazy, *huevón*? I imagine you're already dreaming of beautiful women walking down the main avenues of New York with T-shirts that say, I ♥ The Big Banana, or with a little banana and another legend: I don't have The Big . . ."

Eduardo laughed too.

"Yes, I guess you're right. I must be crazy. The thing is, Casa, it's not that I'm bent on this one thing. I could devote myself to being and doing anything else, but first I want to try, that is, first I want to fail in my ambition to become a movie actor. And later on maybe I can work and study here, or stay here to live, make my stay legal."

"You're better off that way, that's more down-to-earth. Still, you ought to start looking at your studies right now. Your ambitions to fail will come quicker than you think."

"Don't you ever give people a speck of hope?"

"No, not when there's none."

"It's that impossible?"

"Look, *huevón*, let's not say impossible, maybe not. But think about it. How many people are there in New York, between native-born and foreigners, who want to be movie stars? How many painters, out to make it in this city, settle in the Village every day? How many authors with books that will never see the light of day, and so many of them dreaming not of becoming a bestseller, but at least of getting published, even if only in plain, limited editions?"

"You're right. Still, out of all those you named some will make it."

"How many? One in a million."

"Maybe I'm the one."

"Look, *huevón*, if you're going to conquer some woman out there, don't give her that dribble. I guarantee you'll get nothing for it. You're better off telling her you dream of being a respected mason in the Bronx, that's more down-to-earth, and maybe even more erotic."

Casagrande couldn't stop laughing or drinking coffee. Eduardo was mortified; Casagrande's fifty-two years, and thirty of them living in the United States, didn't speak for nothing: he'd probably uttered the greatest truth on the planet. Eduardo didn't continue talking, but took refuge in his self-escape by attempting a journey to the future or the past, but at that moment he couldn't travel to the future because Casagrande had made it out to be more uncertain than ever. New York is like Casagrande said it is: full of all kinds of people who want to make it in business, in the arts or literature. Out of those millions many would not make it; they would fall behind to become good audiences for good films, to become art connoisseurs or wise readers or simply writers for their own enjoyment.

In his trip to the past he saw himself the day he arrived in the Big Apple.

He was scared of something: not of the distance or the farewell or the new territory. He feared the morning. It was twelve noon sharp, his wake-up time, and there was total silence, a fact. The silence that no one had told him might exist in the city of New York. He had arrived the night before and from the little window of the American Airlines plane he had seen the lights of New York, the interminable car lights, the neon scrambling every which way. He was now in the largest airport his eyes had ever seen. He got lost looking for his luggage. He was saved by his almost perfect English, otherwise he would have been lost without a clue, luggage and all.

The taxi driver turned on the meter, and he allowed his eyes to roam and crash into the skyscrapers, the streets clogged with cars and people, the billboards that reminded him he was a new arrival, the bridges made of small hanging lights, the trains running overhead, the airplanes taking no notice of the night sky . . . He heard the insults his taxi driver shot out and fielded for coming too close or not driving at the required speed. He felt the foreign air laughing in his face, the horns blasting him from all angles. The cumulative noise, the collective haste frightened him.

He arrived at an apartment where no one was waiting for him, just a note and the key to the front door, which the building super had given him. In the note, Javier welcomed him and told him they'd see each other the next day, because it was a sin to stay at home on a Saturday in New York. There was so much to do, so much to experience, so much of everything that if he wanted, he could go out and walk along the nearby streets, taking care not to get lost. He preferred to go up to the ninth floor, lock himself in, open a window and take in that New York they'd told him so much about and which he'd admired time and time again in any film it was featured in. Where could Broadway be? he wondered, moving his eyes in a little fiddle-stroking motion, which made him feel dizzy. He opened the refrigerator and popped open a can of beer. After an overdose, he slept like someone at home in New York.

It was twelve noon on the dot and New York was not the same as last night. The silence could be felt, heard, sensed. He didn't dare draw open the curtain; an unexplainable fear held him captive. He couldn't believe silence existed in that city, above all on a Sunday. It was impossible for him to believe it in the city that never sleeps, the city that stays up, the all-nighter, the insomniac. After a quick shower he decided to go downstairs and track down clues as to the why behind the New York silence. He thought of the building super, who seemed like "good people" and spoke his language. He walked out of the elevator, but in the lobby last night's super wasn't the same as the morning one. This one was another color and was sprawled face down on his desk, on his arms, sleeping as if after a battle. He walked along making his heels click with the importunate purpose of waking up the watchman: mission impossible, the watchman was a statue in cast iron from the last century. He found the silence worse down there. He headed out cautiously to the street. He staggered. He shivered, body and soul, before what he saw: the square in front of his building was strewn with fallen people. You couldn't take a step: men fallen on the ground, beautiful women, some lying there, others doubled over themselves, a few face down across some monument, others flat between the steps, men who seemed to have fallen as they attempted some heroic feat. Eduardo's breath was cut short. How did this all happen? he asked himself. Completely taken aback, he began falling slowly as in a 20th Century Fox reel, onto his knees. He pounded the cement floor with his fists and cursed and cursed again. He was in pain: Not for the gringos, *or the Europeans or the Asians or the Australians or the Arabs or the Blacks or the Latinos but for all of it, in pain for all that breathes life. The bitterness choked him like the New York traffic. He continued pounding the ground helplessly and crying like someone returning from space only to find nothing on the Earth but the ex-Statue of Liberty's crown.*

On his knees and in a Niagara of tears, he asked himself how he hadn't found out earlier about such an enormous tragedy. How had it happened that humanity finally had to come to such a cataclysm, the Third and last World War? He had the evidence, he was right in the middle of that lifeless multitude with buildings and other material things intact, as if nothing had happened. It was just like the scientists had predicted the atomic war would be. How could it have happened if the Cold War was over? Could it have been by mistake? he asked himself in a freeze of his Niagara, the waterfall drenching him again as he thought: What the hell good does it do to know that now? And he thought of his Central Americans who at that time, as by custom, might be coming to their death in small groups and last in line as well, breathing the foul air blown in from the north, their blood coming to a standstill inside, as if all hearts were on a sit-down strike. He cursed and cursed again for having abandoned his people with humanity so near its end. He was left there, curled up in a ball, not like a seashell but like a devout follower of Gandhi in mid-prayer, ready to die of dehydration, for his eyes had turned into gushing pipes. Once he'd resigned himself to meeting the rest of them in the great beyond, to raising the banner of united citizens of the world, he felt a hand touch his left shoulder, which didn't amaze him in the least. And without breaking his Gandhiistic position he said, "I was waiting for you. I already knew you would come for me. Didn't it satisfy you to take away so very many already?"

He fell mute until the voice at his shoulder said to him, "What's the matter, Eduardo, are you kidding around or did New York drive you crazy?"

He heard the deep voice, the voice of a man, and got up in a single jerking motion. "I don't know why—I've always thought death is a woman."

Javier looked at him in amazement. "What's the matter with you, are you delirious?"

The ex-Gandhi follower crossed Javier with his gaze. "Tell me all this isn't true?" Eduardo said and pointed at the crowd sprawled in the square. "This pile of people the final holocaust has left for us."

Javier laughed because he understood nothing. At that precise moment a woman—slow as a fainted one's coming to—tossed her yellow hair.

"She moved," Eduardo yelled.

"Well, yes," Javier replied, "and in bed she probably moves even better. The thing is all these gringos are alike. When they sunbathe, this laziness comes over them and, well, look at them, they look like they're dead."

"Come on, *huevón*," said Casagrande, "snap out of it now. You're thinking about it too much, don't take it so hard. Who knows, maybe you are that one in a million."

"Could be, what do we know?" Eduardo smiled.

Casagrande poured himself the fourth cup of coffee. "What was it you were thinking about, *huevón*, that gave you back your sense of humor?"

"About things that can only happen to me. Once I cried over the Third and final World War. I made a mistake and thought I was the only one left on the planet. I cried for everyone, even for you, Casagrande."

"You are crazy! Hey, since you want to be a movie star, do you have any experience, have you done theater in your country?"

Eduardo smiled. He nodded. "A little. My best performance was once when I had to play the role of James Bond, Agent 007."

"What a horror, what a country, what lack of imagination! They put James Bond on stage in Honduras! That's outrageous, Banana Republic!"

7

The idea of walking in Tegucigalpa is distasteful not only for Mirian, but for many others, especially the chronically lazy, because its topography of uphills and downhills, of hills without plateaus, of stairs and more stairs, is exhausting, even for the hardiest walker in the world. Still, walking in Tegucigalpa can be great therapy when you're bored, on the edge of depression or low on cash. You're likely to see the most outlandish sights. Mirian had no desire to walk out of depression or boredom, but simply for the sake of wandering.

She passed the cathedral. She thought of sticking around to watch how many citizens genuflected. After a few minutes it seemed to her that humanity was losing the faith. She continued walking past the monument to Francisco Morazán, lingered before it and thought about how if Morazán were alive now, she might turn James Bond in for him. She recalled a bit of history, as if she were living a movie: she imagined Morazán the revolutionary in the pitch of combat, his sword glinting and flushing the enemy out, wielding weapons and ideas to convert Central America into a single nation, large, powerful and respectable in the eyes of the world. She blew the statue a kiss and asked herself if Morazán's dream of a united Central America, including Panama and Belize, could come true now. After saying good-bye to Morazán, she started walking on the pedestrian mall. She got lost among the hundreds of people at noon who run from diner to office, among students going home or to school, among the ambling unemployed who look no one in the eyes, among peddlers and customers. She walked along the pedestrian mall without stopping anywhere. She passed the post office, was tempted to enter but had no one to write to. She took an avenue that led her toward Comayagüela, and before reaching the Mallol Bridge, which separates the twin cities of Tegucigalpa and Comayagüela, was frightened by the screech of a car braking suddenly in front of her. Two men got out and without a word shoved her into the car and covered her mouth. Her resistance was useless.

Once inside she discovered that all the men, including the driver, had their faces masked with ladies' stockings. They gagged her and navigated carefully through the city traffic, without rushing, obeying the stoplights, and it was as if she and the pedestrians were centuries apart, because absolutely no one knows what might be going on behind the tinted windows.

When they reached the Boulevard of the Forefathers in search of the road leading out of the city, one of the men pulled a black kerchief out of his pocket and blindfolded her with it. They stopped and guided her out of the car and toward a building.

She didn't know where she was, but her intuition told her she wouldn't come back. Unlike most of the country's houses, instead of climbing stairs she was walking down stairs, led by two of the men. Something like thorns brushed against one of her legs and tore her stocking, from which she deduced that she wasn't inside a house but had come down the stairs of a little hill of sorts. They stopped. One of the men took the blindfold off her, and then she was able to drink in the totally blue sky, the trees and the flowers. She realized where she was, looked upward and discovered the typical limestone houses and clay shingles of the little town called Santa Lucía. She and the men were too far out of anyone's earshot for her to scream. She guessed what they were up to. One of them took the gag out of her mouth and attempted to kiss her; she dodged him like a wild mare. He persisted. She pushed him away and screamed out an SOS that went nowhere. The place was so desolate she was sure the SOS was lost hopelessly in the underbrush, and her voice wasn't strong enough to yell out an SOS that would pierce through that blue sky and reach some god's ears. One of the men tore her dress in two; the others were spurred to help him, and made of the beautiful dress an infinity of tatters. She scratched, she screamed. The bra had gotten lost. She screamed even though she knew it did no good.

One of the men grabbed her panty strap and slowly, sadism glinting from his blade's edge, prepared to strip her of her last piece of clothing.

A yell rang out: "Stop right there!"

Was she dreaming? Was she awake? Had the nightmare come to an end? It was Agent 007 himself, pistol in hand, outfitted in a black suit with a dark tie and hair done in a shock that spilled onto his forehead. He held the gun just like in the movies, the barrel pointed upward, close to the face and showing his profile. The rapists didn't react for a moment. Then one of them leapt into the bushes and whipped out a pistol as he tumbled through the weeds; the others took advantage of the attention the agent gave the first fellow and hid behind some trees. At that point all of them had their revolvers in hand. The crossfire began suddenly. The agent twirled around shooting from all angles. One of the rapists' screams was heard, and Mirian watched as the agent pierced him with one lead slug and another, blood flooding his chest. The second rapist suffered the same fate. The third one came out with hands held high. 007 was aiming at his head. The man was trembling. The agent slipped back the safety latch, cocked the pistol, and placed it against the enemy's temple. Mirian could have sworn she heard the shot and saw the hood's head crack wide open like a pumpkin when you slice it down the middle with a machete. James Bond lowered the pistol. Mirian came to with a deep breath. The agent squared off in front of the *bandido*. Mirian was filled with pride for her 007 once again, because he was incapable of killing an unarmed man. He landed punch after punch on the goon's face, until he lost all motor abilities. It looked more like James Bond was sparring with a punching bag. The hoodlum crumpled to the ground. The agent reached for Mirian, who hadn't cried during the most critical moments but waited until it was all over. He hugged her. Both of them got into the car which had been the hoodlums' property. He lent her his suit jacket. Mirian put it on carelessly. The agent pulled away and drove uphill through Santa Lucía. Minutes later, at her request, 007 pulled the car off the highway and parked. Other cars drove by; some people saw the parked car from afar, but absolutely no one knew what was going on behind the tinted windows.

8

Nine and a half weeks and Eduardo still couldn't get used to his new living quarters. Valentine Avenue, in Kingsbridge, parallel to the main artery of the Bronx, the Grand Concourse, has little or nothing to envy the South Bronx. In the morning, when he headed to work, the danger was reduced to a minimum due to the great number of people who also ride the subway to work. It isn't dangerous in the daylight hours, but it's enough just for the sun to set and Valentine Avenue fills up with Jamaicans who sell drugs from building to building. The cars travel at a snail's pace and young men and women cop and hand the money over so no eyes will spot them. The police frequent the avenue but the Jamaicans, as if practicing their voodoo rituals, vanish and reappear when the patrol car is barely out of sight around a corner. When Eduardo would get home at night the terror would overcome him. The subway station at Kingsbridge where the D and C trains left him would be completely empty. The immense station, with its strong urine stench and its silence once the subway had pulled out, would strike terror in the bravest heart. Eduardo put his acting skills to use and dressed like just another train station junkie or mugger. He would walk as if he were spaced out or nuts. When nighttime caught him somewhere else, he'd buy a sixteen-ounce beer and wrap it in a brown paper bag and stagger about, zigzagging like a drunken bum, irredeemably lost. The hoodlums would pay him no mind, or at most approach him to bum a cigarette, which he never refused, because he too had learned to greet people in the mangled speech they used to greet each other: "Hey, bro'." He knew the tricks to greeting people without giving away the slightest fear. To the contrary, he would appear to be another one of them, down and out because he couldn't cop a thing that night. In summertime the Bronx just might be one of the most colorful and joyful places in the entire city of New York. People would come down from their buildings and meet in the parks and in the public squares, and the clamor of the children and the boys scampering and playing soccer gave it the air of any joyful corner of the Caribbean. This rhythm ran until nine or ten at night when the sun said good-bye to make way for war. If for Eduardo the South Bronx projects were a civil war after twelve midnight, it was also true that Valentine Avenue, while still not as plagued with machine guns, was certainly headed in the same direction.

One night out of many—when the fruitless search for something that was never to be found had turned him into an insomniac—Eduardo was reading in his apartment. Suddenly he heard gunshots and then some dogs. He peeked cautiously out the window and saw the police in full-blown chase after some Jamaicans who leapt with catlike skill over fences into the darkness, vanishing and blending into it. It was as if they were fragments of the night and the night paid them back in the only way possible, by making them invisible or becoming an immense multitude of Jamaicans stretching from sky to earth, so that the police would turn their flashlights on in vain as the night grew into a giant, and the flashlights grew smaller, or the night was transformed into a single giant Jamaican, impossible to cast light on using even the biggest, most hi-tech flashlights on the planet. Eduardo saw the police and heard them curse, and no one was anywhere to be seen. It seemed more like a cop comedy, with the policemen hurling insults at the void, yelling at the night, chasing after ghosts.

From that time on, Eduardo tried not to come back so late at night. He preferred to ask friends to give him a place to sleep, and they understood his fear, for they only had to hear the words *the Bronx* and the panic set in.

Casagrande advised him to cast off his fear and to anchor himself, not only in God, but in the mystical as well, in the unexplainable things that exist beyond human rationality. In fact, Casagrande would travel through any part of the city of New York at any hour he felt like and absolutely nothing ever happened to him. That could well be because of his mystical faith, which he never explained, or because of his style, his height, his unseemly Mexican poncho, the black one, which he never took off, not even in summer. It was part of him, like an extra layer of skin that nature had granted him. He strode like a weary giant, carrying a satchel and an old cap, and as he walked the poncho fluttered and he seemed like more than one person, a multitude enveloped in a tent. With that appearance there were two possibilities for him: either he wreaked terror in wrongdoers or inspired an unusual state of pity. Whatever the reason, Casagrande might have felt he was the owner of New York by night, and in fact he was.

Through his mysticism, Casagrande got Eduardo involved in readings of the Chinese horoscope. At first Eduardo sloughed it off, but it was enough for Casagrande to read a chapter on the personality of the *Fire Tiger* and Eduardo began to think that millenia-old culture was right about certain areas the West had left uncharted. Those days of unemployment for Eduardo and of Casagrande's ever-present pitcher of coffee at nine every morning brought them closer together.

Casagrande pointed out to him that their meeting wasn't fortuitous, but that they had been fated to come together, either to achieve great things in New York or just to survive in the big city by offering each other support. Eduardo, who had been completely incredulous before, now began to wonder as he recalled the great truths about his personality that he'd read in the chapter on the *Fire Tiger*.

"Casagrande, what's your take on death?"

He poured himself a second cup of coffee.

"Look, *huevón*, death is not to be feared. You believe you die. People believe you die, but no, you don't die. The truth is you fulfill a mission in one place, just like when you travel. For example, when you came from Banana Republic you probably never thought to live in the Big Apple. That's how it is with each one of us: we come here because somehow, even if it's in the smallest possible way, this city needs us and we need it. Except we're not authorized to be shown this in a clear and explainable way. That's how death is, you don't die, it's just a matter of a mission being fulfilled in one place and of being transported to another. You die here and reincarnate far away. Maybe when you die as

Eduardo and as the son of Banana Republic, you come back to life in China and your name is Chin Shan and you cook chop suey. Or maybe you're a black man and reappear over in Africa fighting against apartheid or, who knows, maybe you're a white separatist."

"You're unbelievable," Eduardo smiled.

"That's how it is, you don't die, you reincarnate. Most likely I'll reincarnate in the Banana . . ."

"Honduras," Eduardo interrupted.

"*Vaya*, your nationalism finally comes out. Let's do a test, let's conduct a survey and ask people if they know where Honduras is. I guarantee you no one knows, but mention Banana Republic, and anyone will answer you: Yeah, I remember."

"You're evil, Casa."

Casagrande leaned over the table and showed Eduardo the center of his head, the crown, the completely round part like a half grapefruit, where not a single hair was growing.

"I'm divine," he says. "Never, not even as a child, did I have hair there. That's a divine gift. That's how I am, divine. A little bit more than a simple foolish earthling."

9

James Bond was furious. He lit a fresh cigarette, scratched his head and uttered curses. As he held the smoke inside his body he said, "Fine, I'll take that. Sue me if you want to, but she's going to find out about everything, and I guarantee you she'll never forgive you for it. As parents you may as well forget about your daughter loving you, or ever loving you again."

The psychiatrist rejoined, "No, no, never that. There's no reason for her to find out about this."

Mirian's father addressed James Bond. "You didn't keep up your end of the deal. You're a con artist. You were supposed to defend her, rescue her and bring her home safe and sound."

Agent 007 violently belched a mouthful of smoke. "I did everything right. I rescued her, my costume was appropriate . . . I spent entire days studying Roger Moore. She believed the whole thing was real."

The other three actors who played the roles of kidnappers and rapists agreed. Mirian's mother didn't say a word. The father looked at James Bond.

"Look, Eduardo, it was all a matter of you passing yourself off as Agent 007 to cure my daughter, part of the therapy the doctor thought would bring results." He looked at the doctor, who nodded. "But I passed you, along with the other actors"—now he set his eye on the potential rapists—"in another car"—the rapists nodded, "and we saw you take a detour. You were parked and my daughter was inside that car with you and remember, she was almost completely naked, what else could you have been doing but having sex?"

"We were talking," James Bond lied.

"About what?" the father bore down.

"About my movies," the agent countered.

The father smiled sarcastically. "My movies . . . You took your role as James Bond too seriously. Take that costume off right now, you look ridiculous. Agent 007 is taller and better looking."

"No wonder your daughter's crazy about him."

"Don't bring my daughter into this."

"Fine," James Bond creased his brow, "all I want is for you to pay us and get it over with."

"Eduardo," the psychiatrist intervened, "did you tell her your name was James?"

"No, I told her my name was Eduardo."

"What was her reaction?"

"At that point my name no longer mattered . . ."

The father interrupted: "You mean it's true, inside the car . . . ?"

"No," the agent laughed, "I mean that no matter what name I gave her she wasn't going to hear it. For her it is, was and will be Agent 007."

"They must be paid," said the mother in a commanding tone of voice.

The psychiatrist addressed Mister Bond. "Did you agree to continue seeing each other?"

"She asked me to visit her. She wanted to introduce me to her parents."

The father was getting ready to sign a check and as he leaned over the desk he looked at James with criminal eyes peering over the eyeglass rims. "It doesn't sound like a good idea."

"He's the physician," the mother reminded him.

"Did she give you her telephone number? In that case call her tonight," said the psychiatrist.

Mister Bond had recovered his calm but had not forsaken irony. "It's part of the treatment. I imagine we'll negotiate this separately."

"Money's no object. The point is, don't you forget I'm paying you for the sake of my daughter's health. The third check I'm giving you is so you'll get lost."

Mirian and Eduardo continued seeing each other. She'd learned to stop calling him James. Once in a while "my agent" escaped from her lips, but both took it good-naturedly. The father crabbed about the romance. The mother not only approved of it but had sincerely begun to love her future son-in-law.

The psychiatrist called his work complete, although he didn't rule out new appointments. Mirian had matured. At times she encountered Roger Moore in other movies that weren't about James Bond but they didn't harm her in the least. The father considered the incident inside the tinted car forgotten. At times he joked with Eduardo, calling him "Mister Bond," and Mirian, evidently never caught on to why the men laughed at such foolishness.

10

The men were in suits and ties, the women in the latest fashions. They and the others were at work, creating a climate that would move business along. When circumstances allowed, Eduardo looked at the woman who worked in front of him at a computer. He was standing on a medium-sized ladder, stripping wallpaper. He was dressed in dirty, tattered jeans, with a T-shirt full of holes and his face covered with the fine dust that came off along with the wallpaper. He had a hammer in one hand and a screwdriver in the other. Charlie approached and gave him orders to remove part of the ceiling also. He told Eduardo to be careful, and reminded him that when he took off, he was to leave everything clean and put his tools away, to sweep the entire area worked in that day. Eduardo didn't want Charlie to say it in English, but to practice his Spanish so the girl would not understand, but Charlie was ashamed of his bad Spanish and would practice it only when they were alone in the office.

At that incident he remembered the previous week. He was working in a luxury restaurant. The building was old but well-preserved, decorated with modernist paintings and designs. He was hunched over, replacing some half-stained tiles with other, brand-new tiles. There he was with his dirty jeans and his T-shirt in a similar state, because he'd carried a load of materials from the first to the third floor, his hands full of cement, sweaty, taking no visible notice of the people who went from one place to another, close by but at the same time, far away. None of that would have mattered so much but for the fact that, as he looked for the service elevator, he passed a kitchenette and picked up a little pamphlet from among many on a small shelf and read "A Brief History of the Lotus Club." He learned that it was a club founded on March 15, 1870, by a group of writers, journalists and critics. The Lotus Club had lasted past the century mark. This lifted his spirits. He thought he was in the place that suited him, a club where arts and business people came to get their nourishment. One of the founding members of that club was Samuel L. Clemens (Mark Twain), who called the Lotus Club "The Ace of Clubs."

He returned somewhat excitedly to his workplace. He thought that some of the passersby would see him, and maybe intuition would tell them that this was not just another worker but a man with talent. He thought they'd be able to guess it, sense it, perhaps through one of the extrasensory perceptions Casagrande had told him about. Many well-dressed men and women walked right by him. He looked out to meet the gaze of anyone who might read in his eyes that he was a movie star playing the carpenter while he waited for opportunity to strike. It was useless. Absolutely no one deigned to throw him so much as a sideways glance. He imagined which might be a painter, an editor or a producer. They passed by him so close that he almost felt them walking over him, crushing him like a cartoon on a TV series. And in an instant he felt rancour, hatred, something unexplainable, but all the same, neither smiles nor hatred can be detected in invisible men. He told himself that no matter who passed by they wouldn't see him, even if he were to turn time back and Mark Twain or Saul Bellow were to walk right by him. Suddenly he saw himself in the future strolling through the Lotus Club in high spirits in the company of an elegant lady. Perhaps there would be another invisible man around, but the Big Banana wouldn't detect him either.

The young, comely woman pulled away from the computer. She disappeared into a small room and returned with a cup of coffee. He would have liked her to offer him a cup of coffee but they were at two opposite ends: he a shabbily dressed, dirty construction worker and she an elegant office lady surely aspiring to become a company executive. He hated himself. He did not envy the people who worked in that place and others, but he hated himself for being in a job that was not made for him. He was born for success, for celebrity, for a life of less sacrifice and more usefulness. He hated that hammer, hated his silence and anonymity, hated being the worker handling those tools while they all passed him by as if he didn't exist, as if that immigrant were far away, as if he'd never left his country. He looked at the beautiful woman and she caught him *in flagrante delicto.* He had to take advantage of that half-smile for his salvation, for her to know he was not just a worker; it was circumstantial, because soon he would be at another level, in the place of the consecrated. So he armed himself with courage in a matter of seconds and before the girl's half-smile disappeared altogether, he stopped being a workman, stripped himself of all prejudice, and smiled at her as if he'd been smiling at her forever. The woman smiled back. He seized the moment.

"Is there a cup of coffee somewhere for this here artist?"

She got up, disappeared into the little room and returned with the coffee and three small envelopes of sugar. He knew that consideration would not last unless he said something intelligent. And that's when he struck dead on target.

"The idea of asking you for coffee and of you seeing me here just as I am reminds me of *West Side Story.*"

"West Side Story? Of course!"—She seemed excited.

"With Natalie Wood, Rita Moreno and Bernstein's music."

In spite of the central heating, she was struck cold. He knew that was a good enough opening for the question that would save him.

She asked: "What's your real line of work? I'm sure you're not a construction worker."

With that, he had enough to drive a million nails, strip all the walls and be baptized in a whirlwind of fine dust. When that question reached his ears, he no longer cared if he was a worker, to be or not to be. And he smiled along with his answer: "I studied theater, a little bit of literature, too. But the truth is, I'm an unemployed actor in search of something. I did lots of theater in my country."

The woman returned to her computer, and from there asked him this question and that, whether he had seen *Othello,* which actor or actors were his favorites. He responded out of duty, because he did not really need to continue the conversation. The woman knew and that was what mattered: she knew he had not been born to hold the hammer, which he stopped hating, and in fact he hammered to the rhythm of the musical: "I like to live in America, everything's free in America . . ."

When Charlie and the others found them chatting, Eduardo was elated. They might think it was just a beautiful but compassionate woman talking to the immigrant so he wouldn't feel so lost. Eduardo ended the conversation and, as always, out of excessive happiness or sadness, he set out on an imaginary trip. This time it was to the future; he pictured it, sensed it as never before. The computer lady had guessed he wasn't a workman, or something less.

It wasn't that hard to come by success because he had the essential ingredient: talent. While it was true that it took some doing to meet with those people who could put him on the big screen, you wouldn't call it a huge sacrifice. He made contacts to audition for film actors and directors who had some affinity with Latin America. He sent a resumé and headshots to Robert Redford, Oliver Stone. He met Raúl Juliá and they liked each other. It was precisely to Juliá that he showed the letter in which Redford congratulated him on his willpower and promised to give him a shot, to give him an audition when he needed a Latino character of his type in one of his films. Oliver Stone, on the other hand, chided him for announcing himself so late; maybe if he'd told him earlier he'd have given him a break in that film he made about El Salvador, but all the same, he left it open for when he decided to venture again into some Central American scenario. The main ingredient for success was there. The hardest part, what promised to be impossible, was over. The hardest part of any career you can think of on the planet is not only for the big shots to notice the aspirant but for them to lend him a hand, throw him a lifeline so he doesn't get lost in the quicksand. And he'd made it.

Charlie stood dumbfounded, watching Eduardo work as he travelled in his thoughts. There wasn't a worker in the world who could outdo him: as he travelled to the future, the present rewarded him with unconscious craftsmanship. He hammered, ripped out wallpaper, sanded the walls, and gingerly handled the bunch of nails in his mouth. And the computer lady was overwhelmed: if this unemployed actor kept working that well he'd probably never again set foot on a stage. Charlie, mouth agape, thought to himself, *That boy has a future. In a few years he can start his own little construction company.*

11

Mirian's parents feared a relapse because of the madness that had invaded Eduardo's mind. Eduardo told himself that in Honduras he'd never be anyone, and no one could dissuade him from making the trip to the land of opportunity. Neither the entreaties of Mirian's mother, nor the economic advantages her father offered him, not even the sincere weeping of the woman he loved most, could stop him. From one day to the next he felt empty, he saw his life wasted in a void, and if he kept going without making a few drastic decisions, it would get worse. So New York seduced him. He'd always heard assurances that in the United States either your dreams came true or you came to the realization that you'd never been awake. It didn't matter, he'd risk it, he'd fight life's battles on the same field with the big shots. He'd read that in New York there was no middle ground: either you succeeded or you failed. For the latter there were many ways out; the least painful and most satisfying for everyone seemed to be suicide. He'd leave behind everything he had, which in truth was absolutely nothing of economic value, rather of human value: father, mother, brothers, kin, future mother-in-law and, above all, his bride-to-be, to whom he had promised he'd fight to the last. And should he fail to make it, he'd come back to his country to dedicate himself to something else, to grow old if nothing more. Once she'd resigned herself, she begged him not to commit suicide, for as a good student of journalism she was aware of the high incidence of suicide among artists who grow frustrated because they don't make it in their careers, who never felt satisfied, who demanded too much of themselves, far beyond what the capacity of body and spirit would allow.

Mirian didn't relapse. There was no need to return to the psychiatrist. Her love for James Bond was a thing of the past. Still, she wept heavily over Eduardo's departure and, once she was alone, suffered sudden crying spells, triggered by some memory of the man in her life whom she'd met thanks to Agent 007.

To avoid memories of Eduardo, she dug into her studies deeper than ever. She read books, preferring those that had something to do with New York. She would scan the crowds in films shot in New York, hope crossing her mind of suddenly seeing her Eduardo in one of those crowds, of recognizing him in the middle of some crush of people. But no, he was never on camera.

The letters and the telephone calls became Eduardo's only presence. How long would that last? Could he wait? She swore she could do it, but didn't feel so sure because in some of the novels she'd read and the movies she'd seen, women always made more promises than men and almost always kept fewer of them. From time to time she meekly published small articles in a few newspapers, which were reviewed beforehand by some of her teachers. This made her content, and she grew desperate for Eduardo to send his comments, for she was sure that with all the shortcomings he might have, with all his eccentricities, with all his madness, the smartest person and the one who made love better than anyone she'd met was named Eduardo. So an opinion of his, no matter how brief, was always like a revitalizing shot in the arm. And she wanted to keep on reading and writing so he would offer her his opinions, because she'd often said to herself: if he didn't read the things she wrote, what sense was there in continuing to write? A whole multitude could read them, but if Eduardo didn't read them, it was as if they were being read by blind people.

"Aló, Aló, hello, *cariño . . ."*

"Eduardo . . . I was thinking about you just this second. What a coincidence!"

"It's not a coincidence, it's astral communication, ultradimensional, telepathic, sort of."

"What's wrong, *amor*, are you becoming a Buddhist?"

"No, I don't think it has anything to do with Buddhism. Besides, I still haven't met Richard Gere . . . he knows about Buddhism."

"So then, what's it called?"

"What?"

"Whatever it is that's teaching you to take astral trips . . ."

"It's a friend, Casagrande. He believes in those things. I'll explain it to you in a letter."

"Yes, I hope you do. I wrote an article titled 'Bonfire of the Multitudes.' I hope you like it. I love it. I put it in the mail to you today."

"Good, *cariño*, I'll read it as soon as I receive it. This call's going to be brief; when it's over, I have to start cursing at the telephone company."

"Yes, *cariño*. Whenever you say."

"Where are you right now?"

"In my room, *cariño*."

"What are you wearing?"

"I'm in a bathrobe."

"And what else?"

"There you go . . . no."

"Yes, I want to imagine you."

"I'm braless."

"And what else?"

"I'm wearing teeny bikini panties like the ones you like."

"What color?"

"Sky blue."

"Will you take your bathrobe off?"

"No."

"Please . . ."

"No, *cosa*, what's going on?"

"It's love, *mi amor*."

"I'm embarrassed."

"Why?"

"What if the phones are bugged, and someone's listening in?"

"No problem, they can masturbate."

"Tonto . . ."

"Will you take it off?"

"Done, I'm in my bikini."

"I'm in my bed, completely naked. I'm hard."

"And now?"

"Now stroke your neck. Run your fingers lightly over your neck. Are you feeling me?"

"Yes, I'm feeling you, do you feel me?"

"Say things to me."

"Like what?"

"Like how we're going to do it when we see each other."

"I'm going to move down to your belly button, I'm going to bite that big thing of yours through your shorts. I'm going to scratch you slowly with my teeth, and when you can't take it any more, I'm going to pull it out and I'm going to eat it."

"What else? I can't take it."

"I have my fingers in between my legs. I'm wet. I'm getting wetter by the second."

"Close your eyes. I'm there beside you. Do you feel my tongue?"

"I feel it."

"Where's your clitoris? I can't find it."

"A little further up."

"Around here?"

"Yes, around there, over to the left."

"Am I doing all right?"

"You're on it. I feel your saliva. I feel your tongue."

"I cut my lower lip with a hair."

"What does it matter, keep going."

"I feel your mouth on my shorts."

"I'm there."

"I'm shorts-less."

"I know, *cariño*, I can feel that thing, it's hard as a tree, like an iron rod. That's how I like it, *cosa*."

"I can't take it."

"Come, *cariño*. On my breasts."

"No, inside."

"No, I might get pregnant. It's better if I turn over."

"Yes."

"I'll get like a kittycat."

"Yeah."

"You like it like this?"

"Yeah."

"Do you want to come? Pull it out and spread it all over my back, on my cheeks, careful not to get it on my hair, I'm too lazy to wash it."

"I love you."

"Me too."

"I want you."

"Me too."

"I'm going."

"Come, *amor*, come."

"I'm . . . oh no, oh Mirian, *mi amor*, I love you."

"Me too . . ."

". . . Thank you NYT."

". . . What? What did you say?"

". . . Thank you New York Telephone!"

She was in bed with the cordless phone, naked, like a kitten, as if she'd just finished making love. He was in his room, exhausted, gurgling into the phone, drawing circles on his belly and chest and writing Mirian on himself again and again with his index finger, like a pencil in the ink-like semen.

"*Amor*, you can get furious with the Telephone Company later."

He didn't hear it; the little silkworm had slid down his ear, through the spiral staircase canal, gently, slowly descending, and had finally nested in the last interstice of his heart, and he didn't want the little worm to abandon him. As for the rest, including the Telephone Company, some solution or other would come up. What mattered now was not to bid farewell to the little silkworm that played along the spiral: it rose and fell, caressed and ensnared, nestled and slept.

12

Eduardo imagined Javier was on the brink of death, because he'd heard the desperation in his voice when they spoke over the phone. Javier had been calling around for Eduardo and, once he'd found him he asked him to come down, it was urgent, he needed to talk to someone. Eduardo ran to the Kingsbridge Station. He was walking down the stairs when the silence reminded him it was Sunday. He turned around and decided to walk two blocks toward Fordham Station instead, where surely the number 4 train wouldn't take long. New York on Sundays: the trains are slow, the streets silent, and walking along Wall Street and the surrounding areas, the absence is so thick you'd swear the earthlings had decided to take a weekend excursion to the moon or to some other planet.

The 4 train was a long time in coming, but it took much less time than he would have spent waiting at the Kingsbridge Station for the D or the C. He spread open the subway map and looked for Grand Central Station. He followed the 4 line and checked for his transfer, then leaned against the side of the train. From up above, the Bronx now looked completely white: the houses in white, the trees in white, the streets upholstered in white, everything made of snow. The only thing not in white were the Latinos and the Blacks. The people in the train travelled the way New York City dwellers travel on Sundays: slothfully, not saying much amid the sprawling space, as if Sunday had become infected with lethargy. It seemed as if even the desire to pick a fight had packed up and left. Maybe if a survey were taken on delinquency in New York, Sunday would be less tragic, and not just because people were at home but because that atmosphere of doing nothing was contagious to the hoodlums, who might feel too lazy to mug anyone on a slow day.

Eduardo got off at Grand Central and took the S. In seconds he'd crossed from East to West, from Grand Central to Times Square, where he waited for the 1, 2, 3 or 9 that would take him all the way to 96th Street. He got off there and right by the token booth stood Javier, waiting for him.

"You're on time, eh? Rare in a Honduran."

"Yes," said Eduardo, "it's rare but we ought to start putting it into practice so we can get rid of that tradition."

"Let's go to my apartment, then figure out what to do."

"Agreed. I was worried coming over here: I thought you were dying."

They travelled five blocks downtown without exchanging a word. There were few people on the sidewalks, all of them dressed in warm coats. Javier protested over something that Eduardo didn't understand at first. It had to do with Javier's being stopped by the apartment owner, who hadn't hesitated to tell him he was two months behind and to ask him what his plans were.

"Take it easy, I'll pay you later."

The old woman flung a sea-rush of words at him, including, among other things, something about promising to confiscate his belongings unless he paid the following week.

"That's why they kill these old sluts," Javier said.

The old woman suspected he wasn't paying her a compliment or anything like that, and growing furious because she didn't understand Spanish, she hollered, "Speak English. This is America."

"Shit," said Javier in good English.

The old woman went her way on the winter walk she gave her mascot, a dog with big chops, a Pekingese which seemed to possess its owner's features.

Javier and Eduardo went in and up to the ninth-floor apartment. Javier asked Eduardo if he'd eaten already. Eduardo replied that he had and commented on how slow the elevator was.

"Sniffing makes you hungry," Javier said and laughed.

Eduardo didn't get it:

"What's that?"

"Flour, *pues,*" and he laughed again. He took out a piece of aluminum foil. Eduardo realized what it was. Javier unwrapped the cocaine. He pulled out a new dollar bill and patiently rolled it up into a little cylinder. Using a razor blade, he placed four small portions on the table, and with surprising precision turned them into parallel lines, as perfect as a tractor making rows in the snow. He stuck the bill up one of his nostrils, covered the other and inhaled until the line was done, and then immediately followed up with the other. He laughed and looked at Eduardo.

"It's your turn."

"No, I don't know anything about these things." Eduardo was dazed.

Javier's laughter grew louder.

"What's the matter, Eduar? You're in New York. Taste it, it'll fix you up nice."

"It's expensive. What if I become an addict?"

"No one becomes an addict from tasting it once."

He gave in. Javier gave him instructions because he was terribly bad at it. Javier protested whenever the most insignificant crumb fell to the floor. Eduardo immediately felt half of his face go numb, from the ears down. His entire nasal apparatus felt nonexistent.

"It's a matter of seconds," Javier said to him. "You'll see how good you're going to feel. And later on we'll smoke a little joint. The combination is perfect. It gives you a buzz . . ."

And he pulled out two sixteen-ounce beers.

"Drink up, sniffing makes you thirsty."

"Yeah, my throat feels parched."

"It's normal. Listen here. Do you think flour's bad? No, *viejo*, or it wouldn't be so expensive, nor would so many of us in the world use it. What's bad is the ban."

After the beer they went out. They walked toward Riverside Park. They sat down on a park bench overlooking the banks of the Hudson, alone in the midst of the snow and the frozen river.

The reddening of Javier's eyes betrayed the drug's effects. Eduardo figured his eyes must be the same. He felt good, or rather, he didn't feel himself: he was absent. Javier pulled out the piece of aluminum foil.

"One more snort and you'll feel totally all right."

Eduardo accepted, and they sniffed outside. Something made Javier laugh; Eduardo seconded him. Then he began to grow dim, like that Sunday: motionless. They no longer knew where the other was; they were navigating on different vessels. Javier began telling a story.

"Life is terrible here. I hate all this. I don't know how I ended up in this city. I don't know how but there was no choice left. This city . . . either you run off spooked with the desire never to return or it traps you, it starts winning you over. And you say you hate it but it isn't true. It's like a sadomasochistic relationship with New York . . ."

Eduardo was absolutely not hearing a word of it. He'd gone off on a trip to the future.

The movie he was making his acting debut in was about to premiere. He'd created a role that had left him feeling total satisfaction. He'd worked alongside the great stars, and his performance left nothing to be desired. It had taken work for them to give him the role. It only became possible when he met Woody Allen. The relationship with Allen was not an easy one, and he almost had to stoop to delinquency, to extorting the acclaimed director, actor and writer . . .

"And I've tried to go back to Honduras to live, but I can't. My own country's too small for me. I can't take it. I've tried. I don't like the people in Honduras, I really don't find them likable. They're very limited. They keep close track of your life. They find out about everything. Fact is, there's nothing else to do. Or more likely, there's a lot to be done but no one sets out to actually do it. I don't like that prying into your business. That's why I love New York . . ."

They'd told him that the best way to make it was to get in contact with one of the big shots. No matter how much talent you have, if there's no big shot with you, it can't be done. And where were the big shots to be found? The big shots had houses in private, restricted areas. They had offices which they didn't run; other people ran them. So to write a letter to a big shot meant that first it would be read by one person who'd pass it along to another, and this one in turn to others, and then others, and maybe it makes it to the one who's closest to the big shot, and maybe this one will tell the big shot about it, and the big shot may be curious to read this letter sent to him . . .

"Honduras and Hondurans let me down. I don't get along with Hondurans here. At most with three Hondurans. Aside from that, I get along with Puerto Ricans, Colombians, and even with gringos, but not with Hondurans. They don't do anything. They have nothing to say. If you want to get caught up in gossip, get involved with Hondurans. That's why I'm not going back. I'm not going back to stay, maybe I'll go there just to visit family but never to stay. They say more than one hundred thousand Hondurans live here in New York, and where are they? What do they do? Why doesn't anyone see them?"

But the big shots could also be found on the streets, that is, in disguises. From the time he found out about the big shots' disguises, he roamed the streets with an analyst's eye. He'd see a somewhat unusual get-up, which are plentiful in New York, and start checking to remember which big shot's face it resembled. They'd told him the best way to get a big shot to notice him was like that, in a public place, to uncover his identity and insist that the big shot hear him out. The big shot would feel flattered that one of his fans had caught on to his disguise. And the day he surprised Woody Allen was special, special because it was summer.

"It's terrible to reach forty-one and not have made up your mind. Nothing concrete. I have no wife, I don't have a son, I don't know whether to stay and die in New York or go back to my country. But I'd go back married to a woman from here: I don't marry Honduran women. I'm not making that mistake again. I was married once. What a horror! I married a Honduran woman out of sheer loneliness. And I thought she'd be different because she'd spent her whole life living in the southern United States. That made me think she'd be different."

Eduardo was walking through Central Park. Minutes earlier he'd come out of the subway, the 2 train, and had gotten off on West 72nd. That Saturday he couldn't find anything to do and decided to go to West 72nd and sit in front of the Dakota, John Lennon's house. And he was on one of the benches in Central Park following Casagrande's advice, who assured him that visiting the homes of the big shots who'd passed on was very good because it gave off positive energy. He was there to take in John Lennon's house and think about Lennon, but didn't neglect the faces of the passersby. Maybe he could nab one in disguise . . .

"I married that Honduran woman from the southern United States, who I met in Mississippi. We got married in Houston, and everything was going well. The problems started when we had the notion to take off to Honduras for a season. We were both homesick, that's why we went. She had to go back to Alabama to continue her studies. I stayed in Honduras for some time to see what kind of business might work for me. And I met a professor from Massachusetts who was doing literary research in Central America. She asked me for help, and I gave it to her. We went out as friends. I was appealing to her because of my good English and because I knew something about her culture. We were friends and that's all. She told me about her husband, a fisherman. And I'd tell her about my wife, a Honduran woman from the southern United States . . ."

Eduardo had a hunch, like when you stumble across treasure. He looked at the man dressed in a wide T-shirt and knee-length pants, brimming with yellow and blue flowers in the background. He wore a Panama hat, a small one. He walked slowly, enjoying the afternoon. The man was walking toward lower Manhattan. For some reason he was sure his thoughts weren't betraying him. There's no doubt, that's Woody Allen. *And he followed him.*

"That was enough for my wife to get a hateful fax confirming that I was having an affair with the *gringa*. While all this was happening, I wasn't aware of anything. When I went back to the South, to the State of Mississippi, where we lived, she'd just returned from Alabama and didn't go to the airport but sent her father, a man from a humble background but very intelligent and a good person, and maybe that's why I didn't notice anything unusual about him. When I got home I tried to kiss her and she avoided me. I thought maybe she was being unfaithful to me sooner than I'd expected. The mother didn't return my greeting, which didn't strike me as odd, because many years earlier she'd been committed to a psychiatric ward in Guatemala . . ."

Woody Allen sensed that the man who had been sitting in front of the Dakota was following him. Terrified, but attempting not to provide him with a motive, in case it was some wacko—to keep him from shooting—he discreetly picked up his pace. Eduardo followed him from a prudent distance and only began speeding up when he saw Woody turning out the longest strides of his life. Many blocks ahead, inside Central Park, a crowd could be seen. Woody was heading in that direction. Eduardo picked up his pace. Woody started running. Eduardo set off in hot pursuit.

"And that's where my problems in the South started. I was tempted to dive into the Mississippi River more than once. My mother-in-law was a fanatic of an extinct sect which believed that Satan possessed cockroaches and whose followers were dedicated to the capture, torture and assassination of the plentiful insect. She terrorized all of us. When we didn't go with her to the Saturday cockroach-hunter sermons, she'd stop speaking to us for three days and wouldn't cook either. As an enemy she was one of a kind, and she'd allied herself with her daughter to attack me. I asked my wife what the reason was. She never told me about the damned fax. We had sex once in a while, only when I had twenty dollars to pay her for her services as the cheapest whore in the South . . ."

Eduardo caught up with Woody. They were running like two athletes in the middle of training season.

"Listen to me, Mr. Woody."

"You're making a mistake. My name isn't Woody."

"Don't kid around with me. You're Woody Allen."

"I'm telling you I'm not. If I were him, I'd have a bodyguard with me and maybe you'd be in jail by now."

"That's not true, you like eccentricities. And going out alone and in disguise is one of them."

"I begged that woman. I asked her for explanations. I asked her if there was another man. Things kept getting worse from then on. She kept on charging me every time we had sex. First she'd provoke me, she'd give me an erection and then say to me, 'You have to pay me. Seeing as you like whores. I'm your whore.' And I'd look for money in the smallest of my pants pockets, or I'd pawn off my watch or any of my personal objects because I couldn't take the lust. And my mother-in-law didn't speak to me. She'd throw the food issue in my face. One time she told me to drink water from the Mississippi, because you had to pay for bottled water. A gallon costs twenty-five cents . . ."

The men ran, huffing and puffing, and kept the conversation going.

"My name isn't Woody, do you get it?"

"I just want you to give me a chance. I want to prove I'm a good actor. You won't regret it."

Woody stopped near the group of people; he felt protected. Eduardo sensed that he hadn't run in vain.

"I wanted to flee the South, abandon my Honduran woman from the southern United States forever. I wanted to flee but never to Honduras. That's when I started losing the love for my country . . ."

Eduardo had a feeling if he didn't take advantage of that opportunity, he wouldn't get another. He noticed that a hefty woman, dressed in a T-shirt and shorts, was sweating by the bucketful; she'd run after a child and a ball.

"So no one can make me love Honduras. I'm never leaving New York. Not until a year later did I find out about the damned fax . . ."

"You're Woody," Eduardo said in a serious tone. "And if you keep on denying it," he fixed his eyes on the hefty woman drenched in sweat, with the appearance of a sponge just taken out of water, "I'm telling that woman you're Woody Allen, and I'm sure she admires you, because fat people have this great sense of humor."

"And now what? Honduras divorced me. It ruined my life. I've come to distrust women so much I'm convinced they're only good for overcoming stress with an orgasm . . ."

Woody looked at the fat woman. His eyes bulged with horror. He imagined that sweaty woman hugging his neck, totally closing in on his body, and showing her adoration with kisses of sweat and saliva.

"Yes, I'm Woody," said Woody and he placed his index finger over his lips. Eduardo understood the call to silence.

"Well, who knows. I shouldn't generalize. Maybe I'll find myself a good woman . . . even if she's not from the South . . ."

Now Eduardo was waiting for the premiere of the movie in which he made his acting debut, and was sitting with his favorite director, his friend, Woody.

"I'm thirsty," said Javier.

"I'm thirsty," he said again when he got no answer.

"Me too," Eduardo reacted.

And they both laughed as they left the bench. They turned their backs on the Hudson River and went to the small apartment on West 91st Street to get some beer.

13

How could she escape Tegucigalpa? She wanted to go far away but not just anywhere. She wanted to be reunited with Eduardo. A year without seeing him seemed like a century, and the telephone and letters were less and less effective. If she asked her parents to send her abroad to study, they wouldn't do it, because even though she wasn't seeing the psychiatrist, they were, and he'd advised them that at the moment Mirian wasn't fit to live in any country but Honduras. The psychiatrist assured them that in larger countries it was possible that James Bond, in this case Roger Moore, could make a sudden appearance, either while shooting a new film or on some campaign or just taking a vacation. And if she saw him as real, in flesh and blood as he was, the quickest prognosis you'd come to was that she would suffer an irreversible relapse. The psychiatrist smiled, flooded with happiness in the parents' presence.

"And what could Agent 007, Roger Moore I mean, possibly come to Honduras to do?" asked the psychiatrist.

Don Jonás and Doña Rosaura limited themselves to smiling and to following the doctor's recommendations to the letter.

Though Mirian was aware of the psychiatrist's ban, one morning as they ate breakfast, she said, "I need to speak with you very seriously this afternoon."

Doña Rosaura's appetite for breakfast vanished. Don Jonás was less severe with himself and begged God for it not to be news of a relapse.

That day Mirian was happy at the university, she had a hunch her parents wouldn't say no to her. She strolled down one hallway and another, attended her classes with uncommon interest, and, to lengthen her parents' wait, and sat under some trees to write an article no newspaper would publish.

"Mirian's taking a long time," said Don Jonás.

"It must be public transportation, that's why she insisted you give her a car for her personal use."

Don Jonás folded the newspaper and placed it on a little table. "The psychiatrist says it's not advisable for her to drive."

Doña Rosaura grabbed the remote. "The thing with the psychiatrist is fine, but don't you think he exaggerates sometimes?"

"No, doctors are doctors, that's what they studied for."

Doña Rosaura channel-surfed without paying any attention to the screen.

"You and I studied too, and if we were to be sincere, we'd both agree that we really didn't learn so much about our professions."

Don Jonás smiled. "But we studied management, it's different."

"Who knows," Doña Rosaura smiled. "I think ours is more rigorous because it's about finances. Math is an exact science. Is psychiatry exact?"

Don Jonás let loose a guffaw. "What do you think, should we ask the doctor?"

They heard the jingle of keys at the vestibule door.

"Mirian's home now," Doña Rosaura said, and sent a call out to the void. "You can serve dinner, Marianela."

Mirian came in as always: leaving the umbrella in the vestibule, the notebooks in the first place that seemed timely and the bag in one of the big chairs in the living room. She blew a little kiss to *mamá* and another one to *papá.*

"I took a long time," she said as if she hadn't taken a long time.

"A little," said the father.

Mirian looked into the void through which Doña Rosaura's call had crossed moments before. "I'm hungry."

The mother stood up. "Let's get going, they're serving."

The parents had agreed not to say or insinuate the least thing to her about the request she'd made in the early morning hours to speak seriously with them that afternoon. She seemed more interested in appeasing the famine that had overtaken her than in starting some conversation.

At dinner's end, when she detected the hidden question in her father's eyes, she said, "Well, it's nothing to be alarmed about."

"What's it about?" the mother asked.

"It's simple." When Mirian said it the way she did, it seemed like the least interesting thing on the planet.

Doña Rosaura, from whom Mirian had inherited that knack for understatement, said, "Are you pregnant?"

Mirian laughed: "You can't do that over the phone, *mamá.*"

"So much the better," the father blurted out.

"Don't you want to be a grandfather again?"

Doña Rosaura's face puckered. She caught herself and smoothed it over with a prefabricated smile. Don Jonás was already a grandfather, but by a son he had had before this marriage.

"I took longer because I was with Fernando," Mirian said.

Fernando was Don Jonás's son, who for some time had been the seed of discord between the couple, for upon Fernando's mother's death, when he was an adolescent, Don Jonás had taken him to live at his house. With Doña Rosaura as his one and only opponent, Fernando had been compelled to abandon the house and had found himself completely alone, with no money with which to wage those battles life places in one's path.

"And how is he?" Doña Rosaura asked.

Mirian smiled. "We all know he couldn't be better. He's always so gracious. I would have liked for him to have lived with us forever. With him I feel like both of us were your children: I feel closer to Fernando than to Ricardo."

Ricardo had sailed off on a ship. He'd never stood out in his studies or in any trade, art or sport. He was the couple's son and up until a few months earlier he'd never lived without his parents' protection.

"So what was it you had to say to us?" Doña Rosaura steered the conversation off the scabrous path it was taking.

"Simple. I want you to give me permission and financing for a little trip to New York."

Don Jonás coughed, not a natural cough but one of protest. "That's impossible."

The mother seconded him: "New York, *hija mía,* that city's a monster."

Mirian tried to shrug it off. "It's only my vacation, *mamá*, and that's where Eduardo is."

"You're not married," the father interrupted.

"And what does that matter? We can get married over there."

"No, never," the mother said, "if you marry, you marry in your own country."

"I want to see New York, *papá*, and to see Eduardo, more than anything else."

"You're not married," Don Jonás insisted.

"Papá, I'm twenty-five years old."

The father was puzzled: "You told the psychiatrist you were twenty."

"He's not family, *papá*, and it's well-known the world over that we women lie about our age. If I tell you twenty-five and you see me five years later, you won't forget it, and you'll say, this woman is old."

Don Jonás smiled. "You're very intelligent."

"Whose daughter is she?" asked the mother.

Don Jonás replied with irony. "Mine, one would think."

"Don't start," Mirian interrupted. "If you don't want me to, I won't go to New York, but at least let me know why."

"The psychiatrist . . ."

"The psychiatrist," Mirian interrupted her father, "that piddly doctor's like a ghost in my life."

"He says that if you go to big cities you might run into him."

"Into who, *mamá*? Come on."

The mother hid her eyes. "Into James Bond."

Mirian burst into gales of laughter. "So you still remember that?"

"I argue with some of the things the psychiatrist says, but your father . . ."

"He's the doctor," Don Jonás defended himself.

"So, *mamá*, as far as you're concerned, I could travel without a hitch?"

"That's right," said Doña Rosaura softly.

"But I'm against it," said Don Jonás.

Mirian knew that by that method her aspirations would go nowhere. She switched her tactic.

"The thing about James Bond is no problem. It's never easy to see a famous artist anywhere. According to a psychology class I'm taking, this thing that happens to a woman after adolescence, falling in love with heroes or movie stars, has its roots in infancy. Some shock one had in one's childhood related to love and sex. Which is just what I had, remember, *papá* . . .?"

"Enough," Don Jonás interrupted, "I'm fed up with psychiatry and psychology . . . Let me think about it a bit. I'll see if it's a good move or not." He addressed Doña Rosaura. "Ask them to make coffee, *cariño*, and let's move into the living room."

In the living room Mirian and Doña Rosaura were talking about New York. Mirian knew for a fact that there would be no further opposition. Don Jonás sat there with an arm over the arm of the chair and the index finger of that same arm resting on his temple. He was mulling it over, but he wasn't thinking about the inconveniences of his daughter going to New York. He was wondering whether in fact all the blame for certain disorders evident in Mirian could be attributed to him.

It had started many years earlier, yet the sin dragged the predators of the past along with it as if yesterday had never ended. The beginnings could be traced to that handsome maid Doña Rosaura had hired for household matters.

"Don Jonás and Doña Rosaura had gone out shopping and left Jimena, the maid, alone in the house with Mirian, who at that age was the kind of girl who—according to the tenants of the house—you couldn't get out of her room in the morning hours until the afternoon and evening, which she'd spend in front of the television set watching spy movies. The reality was something else: the girl was exploiting her catatonic act as a way to spy from the least suspect places. This she'd

learned in movies about the United States and the ex-Soviet Union. She loved espionage and put it into practice.

The doorbell rang, and Jimena looked through the peephole to see two uniformed men. They're the men from ENEE (Empresa Nacional de Energía Eléctrica), she thought.

"Good morning," said one of the two uniforms. The other just said 'buenas.'"

Jimena opened the door for them and looked at their uniforms—she'd always liked uniforms. She could read Empresa Nacional de Energía Eléctrica on one of them—no doubt about it, they were the men from ENEE.

"May we come in?" said one of the men.

At first she didn't resist, but then she remembered she was alone—she wasn't counting Mirian.

"The thing is the gentleman and the lady aren't at home."

One of the men bent over, opened a metal box, and said, "We're here on the lady's behalf. She wants us to check the lights. Seems they're failing, sometimes like they go down and like other times they go up. Have you noticed?"

Jimena thought for a few seconds.

"Yes, yes, I have noticed. Yes, yesterday in the middle of the eight o'clock show, when Mauro was going to kiss Laura, and they didn't know that Laura's husband was spying on them, the light went off for a bit and I didn't catch what happened, because when it came back on they were selling Maravilla Soap."

"We've come to fix that," the man said. "You'll see from now on you won't have a problem."

Jimena cleared the way for them, and they entered. She shut the door because the lady had told her over and over, "You have to keep the door locked."

One of the men got busy inspecting the house. "Everything has to be checked," he said.

The other one stayed in the living room, with Jimena, searching for his tools in an old satchel.

"What's your name?" he asked her.

"Jimena."

"Pretty name, very few people have that name."

"Yes, in my town I'm the only one named Jimena. Once when I was queen of the fair they put a sash on me from here to here: JIMENA THE FIRST."

The man laughed as he pulled out a pair of pliers. "I bet you're the prettiest queen your town ever had."

She blushed. "Well, that's what some say."

The man pulled out pieces of cable, staples, screwdrivers, a pencil, electrical tape. "So, do you have a boyfriend?"

"Boyfriend? I'm not one for boyfriends any more. I did have a husband up until a little while ago."

This amused the man, who tinkered with some screws. "How's everything going?" he yelled to his companion.

The other one answered from some corner of the house. "Everything's going well, I'll let you know in a minute."

Jimena was surprised. "He's in the gentleman and the lady's bedroom. How did he manage to get it open?"

The man took her by the shoulders, smiled at her, and said, "Don't be scared, the lady lent us the keys. She wants everything left in good shape."

*Jimena sighed, "*Ay Dios*, I was pretty afraid for a second there."*

The man let her shoulders go and gently ran a hand over her chin.

"Won't you treat me to a little cup of coffee?"

She took a few baby steps. "Yes, I just made some."

She came back, coffee in hand. The man had seated himself completely at ease in an overstuffed chair. After she served him the coffee, he asked her to hit the switch, which she did. The light didn't turn on.

The man yelled, "It's not on yet. You've got to hurry up because we still have three houses to go."

Jimena felt relieved. She sat down beside her guest. "Are you the boss or are you a great big loafer?"

The man laughed. "No, we're just workers and nothing more. Thing is, see, we take turns. I get to work here in the living room, but only after he's found whatever's wrong in the interior of the house."

Jimena nodded. "It makes me mad a lot of times when it's at the best part of the eight o'clock show, trás! *the television set goes off or starts shaking all over and there's no picture."*

The man sipped his coffee. "That won't happen anymore. You're going to be able to see the eight o'clock show just fine."

Jimena was content, clearly happy that her eight o'clock TV show would not be interrupted.

The man continued drinking his coffee, at ease, as if he'd been a longtime resident of that house.

Jimena stood up. "I'm going to go see your partner."

He stopped her by gently holding on to her wrist. "No, it's better if you don't go. He's alone in that room and you're a very beautiful woman. I imagine there's beds in there, so if something happens it won't be his fault, you'll tempt him so."

"Uy, *what a scoundrel, you wouldn't think it to look at you."*

He stood up. "I have a better idea: let's do a little something."

She gave him a startled look. "With you? Here in the living room?"

Once more he ran his hand over her chin. "You're the one thinking naughty thoughts. No, get yourself a chair and table so you can give us a little help."

She showed him a small table they could use. He placed it in the middle of the living room, right under the light fixture. He put the chair on top and asked her to climb up on it, remove the bulb from the fixture and put in another one, which he would hand her.

She shook her head in refusal. "Can't you see how I'm dressed?" She lowered her eyes to the plaid short skirt, cut above the knees and wide as an umbrella.

He shrugged it off. "And what of it? I won't be looking at you. All I want is for you to climb up, put this other bulb in and twist it around, loosen it up or screw it in, until it lights up. When it lights up, you let me know because that means everything's done."

She climbed up with his help. At first she tucked her skirt in between her legs with one hand, but she couldn't hold it that way for very long. The risk of falling forced her to spread the umbrella. As he stood under the tent, he ordered another twist.

"Is it lighting up?" He stood dazed under the tent, which was like a cinnamon sky over Jimena's exposed thighs.

"I thought you used those big ones like all the ones who come from the interior use."

"What are you talking about?" Jimena asked, her eyes on the light-bulb.

He held his silence a few seconds. "Your panties."

She let out a half giggle. "Didn't you say you weren't going to look? You see, the lady once gave me three of these bikinis, and I've liked them ever since and that's all I wear. But stop staring at me or I'll climb down."

The man took a step out from under the tent. "It's fine, don't worry, I'm bored of all this: different houses every day, it gets old very fast. Thing is, until today I've never seen anyone like you, someone who doesn't use those oversized ones, and with such gorgeous legs."

She laughed. "That's what you tell them all."

He stepped all the way out from under the tent. "No, really, it's not like that. Stay there, I'm going to go see what that guy's doing. Yell to me when it lights up."

Jimena looked down at him: "And you tell me if the other fellow comes, so I can climb down, because I don't want him staring at me."

Ten minutes went by. The man finally called, "Jimena, did it light up?"

"No, not yet."

"Not even a little spark?"

"Not even a little spark."

"Hold it like that until it lights up."

Jimena thought about what a pretty boy the electrician was, and a few naughty thoughts even crossed her mind, like what a shame he'd come with company because it wasn't possible for a man to be so used to it he could see her cinnamon legs, nice and shaved like the lady had taught her, and not want to do something. She even told herself if he offered to come back she'd say yes, but he should come back alone. She dreamed of herself awake and lying with him in a room, the one at the other end, her room, which the lady'd given her for anything she liked except for bringing men there.

After thinking about so many things between her and the electrician, she yelled, "I'm tired already, my neck hurts, when are you going to turn the light on?"

No one answered. She justified the silence by imagining her electrician driving screws into the wall, a length of cable held between his teeth, a cascade of sweat erupting on his forehead and pouring over his chest, his brow creased from her screams and impatience.

The front door opened. Don Jonás suffered a huge scare as his eyes set fast on the umbrella's epicenter. Dumbstruck. Eyes nailed to that bikini which he knew, but on other grounds. Elbow jab from Doña Rosaura in the very hollow of the rib that woman stole from man.

"Move it, what are you standing there looking at?" Doña Rosaura scolded. "And you, what are you doing up there, Jimena?"

Issuing a little yelp from the neck pain, Jimena answered, "I'm helping the fellows."

Doña Rosaura, a fanatic of fainting spells, leaned against the wall.

"What fellows?"

"The ones you sent to fix the lights."

Don Jonás, after another peek at the umbrella, headed inside, followed by the lady, who was yelling at Jimena, "Get down from there, and take off that dress."

The bedroom door was unlocked, sawdust was on the floor, papers scattered, the closet ransacked, shoes strewn about, little jewel boxes empty, the place where the money was kept empty, piggy bank butchered, travelers' cheques traveling, mattress rifled. Doña Rosaura collapsed on the bedroom floor. Don Jonás stood at the bedroom door, his head shaking back and forth.

"Oh my lady, God help her," Jimena screamed.

"Don't worry, she'll come to in forty-five minutes, but it would be better for you if she never came to. As for me there's no problem, except you have to pay me for the damages. I don't know what sort of an arrangement you're going to make with her."

Jimena wiped her now profuse tears. "And how am I going to pay you, Don Jonás?"

Don Jonás was silent, his eyes staring at the umbrella.

"But sir!"

"I'm a man. I'd never really noticed you. I can't deny I always liked your face, but I'd never seen you so, so . . . alluring." Don Jonás drew closer to Jimena, lowered one hand and slowly drew the curtain open.

"Right here, Don Jonás, today?"

"Right here, today and other days. And don't call me don *when we're alone. Call me by my name."*

"And what if the lady wakes up?"

With all the signs of someone familiar with the little snaps on the bikini, Don Jonás unfastened it, tossed it aside, and gave the cord on the blouse a small tug as if he were unlacing a shoe.

"Concentrate on what we're doing. Her fainting spells never last less than forty-five minutes, and she's only been out for five, so we have forty left."

He climbed on top of her completely naked body, squeezed her with all his might. Suddenly the faintee's hand landed on his bare cheeks like a felled tree, causing Don Jonás to grumble, "You wouldn't stop being a pain in the ass if you were dead."

As he finished with Jimena, he felt as if someone were watching him. He persuaded himself his fear was making him imagine things. He rolled off Jimena with a half turn on to the rug and saw the childish shadow crossing away from the bedroom area.

At supper time the girl acted as if she hadn't seen a thing. She was born to be a spy, and the Cold War films had helped her hone her skills; she knew how to keep secrets.

The doubt about whether the childlike shadow had been real or a product of his imagination, aggravated by his nervousness over the misdeed he'd committed, stuck with him forever.

Mirian and her mother continued talking about New York. Don Jonás snapped out of his reverie. He felt exhausted. He got up.

"Mirian, I think you can go to New York. We'll talk about the details tomorrow. I'm going to get some rest now. We may have to visit the doctor. Good night."

14

After three months of living on Valentine Avenue, Eduardo hadn't gotten used to his new place yet. He was always terrified when he came back after nine in the evening. He didn't go walking around his building. The only thing that entertained him was named Casagrande, with all manner of talk. In times of insomnia they stayed up until the wee hours of the morning, drinking wine or coffee in the kitchen.

By day the apartment was uninhabited. The renters, José and Rosa, were out at their jobs. Eduardo could not get used to those people, much less to Mauro and Alfredo, the other two tenants, who were born to be not just blue-collar workers but immigrant blue-collar workers who had come to lend their services illegally to the United States, as if they were doing time. José, the subletter, was young but had the personality of a veteran of a lost war. He never went out anywhere. He never spent more than was necessary. All the money he earned had to go strictly into savings. He liked to drink, but only when one of the tenants or a neighbor treated him. No one would drink a beer at his expense, not even he himself, for he counted everything in *sucres*, the Ecuadorean national currency. This way a dollar became many *sucres* and ten became thousands. Never—even though he'd been living in New York for many years—had any of his expenses not been counted in *sucres*.

At times he had screaming arguments with his wife.

He wasn't even capable of taking her or his seven-year-old daughter for a Sunday stroll in Central Park, because the subway trip cost was equivalent to the cost of travel from one city to another in his country,

Ecuador. His poor daughter spent most of her days cooped up in the apartment with an Ecuadorean babysitter who worked for a wage that everybody agreed was laughable. Everybody, that is, except José, who pointed out how much it was in *sucres*, and the babysitter herself, who didn't have a sharp grasp on the city where she lived.

That outlook on life in terms of *sucres* annoyed not only Eduardo and Casagrande but also the other tenants, Mauro and Alfredo, and other neighbors. As for Casagrande, not only was money of little significance, he didn't even have an idea, nor did he care to, about the rate of the *peso*, the Chilean currency, against the dollar. In that sense, Eduardo was a carbon copy of Casagrande; he was only interested in making enough to pay off, in order of priority, his phone, rent, food, transportation and drinks. No one ever heard him talking about the Honduran national currency, the *lempira*, until the question was posed one day by José, for whom living was impossible unless he kept current on Latin American exchange rates against the dollar.

"What's the name of your national currency?"

"Lempira."

"How is it against the dollar?"

"Honestly, I don't know. I have no idea."

Such a reply was inconceivable to José, not because of patriotism or any nationalist sentiment, but simply because to him the language of Latin Americans was based on *sucres, soles, pesos, nuevos soles, australes, quetzales, lempiras, córdovas, guaraníes, balboas* . . . and no one was to be allowed to spend one cent on anything if they didn't know how much that cent amounted to in their respective countries.

José would not rest when he came home from work. He'd look for a rag and fluids instead, to clean his television set, over and over, his sound system, his camera, his VCR, and the other electronic objects he'd acquired. Absolutely no one aside from him, not even Rosa, his wife, was allowed to turn on any of those devices. If she wanted to watch television or listen to music, she would have to plead: "You ought to put on some music. I have such a craving to watch television." Depending on his mood, which was mostly foul every day, he might turn on one of the appliances.

Casagrande, whom José respected not only for his size but also for his age, advised him to diminish his love of things and pay more attention to his wife and daughter. José could hear him out for a full afternoon without contradicting him. To the contrary, José would agree many times over, but his love of objects above all gods proved to be not the least bit affected.

On Fridays, about a dozen Ecuadoreans would meet in José's apartment. On one particular Friday, Eduardo and Casagrande joined them for beers, courtesy of the guests. They sat around the living room, as always. Mauro got things going with, "When I return to Guayaquil I won't come running back here."

"I'm going to go to Quito. I'll set up my little business, and I won't want to hear about this country anymore," José said, half-drunk on his guests' beers.

Casagrande, evidently, had a lot in common with one of the recent arrivals, for they moved from the kitchen to Casagrande's room and were clearly not inclined to allow anyone to come between them. The other recent arrivals got hungry so he collected money for take-out Chinese food. Everyone, with the shameful exception of José, pitched in ten bucks for the food and beer. José, whining about monthly expenses, protesting the high cost of living, unabashedly reminded the guests that he was providing the house. Then he pulled out hundreds of *sucres*, which barely amounted to five dollars.

Hours later, the crowd that had assembled—of ten or so men and four women—was drunk. Casagrande had disappeared into the kitchen to help Rosa. José was in charge of the music, not because he had an exquisite taste for music that coincided with the taste of the masses, but because not even at parties could hands other than his own touch any of his electronic possessions.

After the meal, Casagrande appeared with a bowl in hand and several types of burning leaves in it, which sent up an aromatic cloud of smoke. He explained that what they were doing was called *limpia* and it was to scare evil spirits away and reinforce cosmic communication. He locked up those who so desired, among them Eduardo, in the kitchen, and ran the bowl close to them, from head to foot and back again, which enveloped them in the smoke.

The Ecuadoreans insisted on requesting Julio Jaramillo's music from José. The Jaramillo cassette had been misplaced and the group's annoyance was growing. José smiled, baring a gold crown on one tooth and the hollow space of a cavity in half of the other.

"Here's the man," he said.

The Ecuadoreans hushed as if the National Anthem of Ecuador were being played on a solemn occasion. Julio Jaramillo filled the silence. *No quiero verte triste porque me mata tu carita de pena mí dulce amor* . . . One of the Ecuadoreans started sobbing. Julio Jaramillo didn't stop. *Si yo muero primero es tu promesa sobre mi cadáver dejar caer todo el llanto que brote* . . . the sobs of the Ecuadoreans didn't stop . . . *y si los muertos aman después de muertos amarnos más* . . . Their sobs grew to a fevered pitch and the song moved other Ecuadoreans, even José, who Casagrande and Eduardo considered incapable of crying . . . barring the loss of a considerable sum of *sucres.*

15

Casagrande invited Eduardo to a party, and assured him that his life would change there. He'd meet people from the world of Latino arts and literature as well as a few statesiders with a yen for Latino culture.

"Banana, are you ready, *huevón*?"

Eduardo came out of his room. He and Casagrande in one house were a crowd for a single mirror.

"Check out Casagrande, he's vain, that Casagrande," José said.

Casagrande flashed a smile, as if to say *Who, me?*

"Don't be stingy, don't be such a *huevón*, José, take your woman out for a walk or some other guy will."

José gritted his teeth. "Look here, Casagrande, don't kid around like that."

"It's no joke, *huevón*, it's a fact. Today's Friday, *chingado*, take the old lady out for a spin somewhere. That poor woman goes nowhere beyond the factory or the house. Keep it up and a few years down the road, all you're going to hear from her is howling, *chingado*."

José disappeared from the living room as always. He'd get mad but never went beyond an oral protest. It was as if his subconscious betrayed him and gave the others credence. No matter how often he got miffed, he'd never take it further. First, because he really wasn't a bad man, just a stingy one. Second, because he'd never take the risk of throwing a tenant out without having another one sleeping in some corner of the same apartment, waiting for a vacancy.

It happened for the third time: they went out together and to Eduardo's puzzlement, instead of taking the street to the Kingsbridge

Road subway station, which is much closer, Casagrande chose to walk above Valentine Avenue, as if he were heading to Bedford Park Boulevard or the New York Botanical Gardens. He always entered the same station in search of the same D or C train. Eduardo didn't think that Casagrande, in his flights of mysticism, wanted to get close to the Botanical Gardens as a way of staying in contact with nature in the great concrete city. He wasn't about to believe that because never, in the hundreds of hours of conversation they'd had, did he hear a passion for ecology or a longing for some rural region of the planet from Casagrande. No. Evidently, Casagrande was, beyond any doubt, a man of cement.

They got on the D. The subway train on Friday lives up to that very stateside phrase "Thank God it's Friday." People are noticeably happy. They dress differently, laugh differently and even Friday noise seems different from Monday through Thursday's noise, or Sunday's silence. The noises on those days are off the beat; Friday noise is right on the beat: the sound of the train, someone's guffaw, the yelled-out greeting or some protest or other, for whatever reason, take on a different tone than they would any other day. Everything seems to complement the great Friday melody.

At 47-50th Streets in Rockefeller Plaza, they changed to the F, which took them all the way to Delancey Street. They got out and walked along half-darkened streets. It was freezing. It was no longer snowing but the snowdrifts on the streets and sidewalks had grown several inches deep.

"They say this area is dangerous," Casagrande warned.

"I've heard that so much, I can't tell where it isn't dangerous anymore, from Manhattan to Queens, from Brooklyn to the Bronx, Staten Island, in short . . ."

"You're right. I think it's something supernatural. To some people even heavenly paradise is dangerous. They get there and sure enough they fall or someone pushes them."

"It's like the whole planet were dangerous and not dangerous at the same time."

"So it is," Casagrande played at losing his balance, "something so simple can kill someone. The issue is not whether such and such a place is dangerous, but what did you come to the planet for: to be mugged or to do the mugging? So, then, no matter how much you flee, your destiny catches up to you. It's the same with everything, with success: some were born for it, others weren't."

"Sometimes I think one's tragedy is fuel for another's success. A plane accident, for example, is tragic for those who perish in it, and also for some of their family members on land. But there will always be others who win, because if it weren't for the plane crash some of them would never collect that hefty insurance settlement, and if it weren't for that, they'd have a miserable life. There's another issue, too: someone writes a novel about the tragedy and it may be a smashing success, or they make a film. In short, if a photographer accidentally takes a photograph at the right moment, that photograph can represent the triumph of his life. And all of it, you see, is an offshoot of the tragedy of those people travelling on the plane."

"Incredible, Banana Republic, you do know how to think. Seriously, I can't completely come to grips with having found someone who thinks, and in fact does it well, coming from a little country like yours. I'll have to eat more bananas." Casagrande laughed, which was probably his peculiar way of scaring away evil spirits, especially mugger spirits.

They went up to the second floor of a fairly large apartment building. A lot of people were there. Casagrande stood out, as much for his height as for his Mexican poncho which, in his own words, he'd never remove for the rest of his days. His friends immediately caught sight of him and approached to say hello. Casagrande had magnetism: the permanent smile, the fact that no one could make him lose his poise no matter what they said, and his always having something new to tell them. As they greeted him, he introduced Eduardo:

"Hey, I want to introduce this *bananero* to you. He's good people and.very intelligent. You can call him TBB: that's The Big Banana."

People laughed because of the *bananero* thing and asked for an explanation.

"This *huevón* is from Central America, from the Banana Republics."

It amused Eduardo, and that made him instantly likeable to those he'd just met.

After the introductions and a few beers, Casagrande said to him, "Well, Banana, look for an old lady out there. It's early, see if one comes your way."

Eduardo had no experience with New York parties. He'd only been to two, which Javier had taken him to, but they seemed boring. He wasn't able to unwind. This time, though, his view of parties was changing. He couldn't take his eyes off a woman with shoulder-length black hair, light skin, and a body that left no room for doubt that it was a model's body.

"You like the *peláa*?"

Eduardo was surprised. He saw a young man next to him, beer in hand and a smile on his lips. "What's that?" Eduardo asked näively.

"I said do you like her? The one you're looking at, the girl. You're not Colombian."

"No, I'm Honduran."

"No wonder, we call the girls *peláas*, and the guys *pelaos*. It's pretty standard among Colombians."

"Of course I like her," Eduardo hurried to reply.

"Don't rush it, *pelao*. I'll introduce her to you. It's a matter of being patient."

"I'm patient."

"So what's your bag?" the Colombian asked him, immediately realizing that Eduardo couldn't fully understand him. "Fine, *pelao*, I have to speak standard Spanish with you. I asked you about your calling."

Eduardo rattled off his brief resumé of the unemployed actor in search of . . . The Colombian was a painter who'd been living for many years in New York, in Queens, in Little Colombia. He promised to introduce him to Colombians and to people from other Spanish-speaking countries working in the theater, and reminded him that was the starting point. It would be hard to get to big things without taking small steps. When the woman who'd stolen Eduardo's attention grew weary and was less solicited, they went up to her. The Colombian had told Eduardo beforehand that he wasn't alone, many others were after that *peláa*, too. It seemed that getting her to bed was a forbidden dream. She wouldn't make love with anyone unless they could prove to her that they really were intellectuals, genuine intellectuals. Several of the Colombian's friends had invited her to their apartments to unrequited ends, because she would check out their books, review the aspirant-to-coitus's lifestyle and grow disenchanted if she mentioned a certain subject and they faltered, lost as a louse in a wig. That was reason enough for her not to consent to getting horizontal.

"Hey, Andrea, I'd like to introduce you to Eduardo. He's from Honduras. He studied acting and literature at the academy and on his own."

Andrea smiled, extended her hand, and asked if he danced.

Could dancing in Tegucigalpa be the same as dancing in New York? Eduardo took a brief trip to the past.

He was in high school and hadn't been trained to dance by anyone. Two of his classmates, also among the untrained, had invited him to the disco, but he refused, until one day they persuaded him. First, they gave him beer to drink. He finally found himself crossing through a disco doorway, lost in the dark with the change of lighting, walking the length of a hallway covered with phosphorescent photos of semi-naked and half-dressed women. As they listened to the sound of the music making the walls vibrate, they walked the length of the hallway, which seemed endless. The dance floor was jam-packed with dancers who looked like shoeless beings on an enormous anthill.

Once inside, they had a few more beers, which sent their courage up to the surface. With all the daring in the world they got up from their seats to seek out the women who would accompany them to dance, talk and drink. They would never again hesitate before any woman, no matter how beautiful she was. They were the champion high school dropouts, drunk on beer, and all they were missing was female company. Though they didn't know how to dance, they were willing to learn along the way. No one would be able to resist them, they were the unbeatable trio in school, the only ones, the greatest. The greatest had to be begged to dance, the women inviting the powerful ones, the women willing to give up everything for them. With an effort, by mak-

ing things up or pretending to be drunker than they seemed, everything was allowed: stepping on your partner's toes, a false move, bumping into the couple next to you, slow dancing when the music was fast, losing and re-losing the rhythm, all on account of the drunkenness, which made even the best dancers make mistakes.

When he came back from that brief trip, Eduardo didn't hesitate to reassure himself he could also dance in New York. He was brimming with confidence. The problem was something else, a problem without a solution. In the half-light, dancing with him, was Andrea, a woman who inspired all sorts of desires—to be a cannibal, to squeeze her as she placed her arms around his neck, and he had thought the neck was only good for making the head turn, but the neck as a sexual vehicle had been unthinkable before. She was choking him. She rested her neck a quarter of a millimeter away from his mouth, and he started thinking he was Dracula. Their dance became eternal, and his mind began to wander: he was a failed actor, one of his family members had died, he hadn't paid his phone bill . . . He thought of the most horrible thing that could happen to him in life just to stop the erection. He thought about being struck by a lightning-bolt in midtown Manhattan in front of the Public Library and everybody surrounding him, watching him give up the ghost. He saw the legs from the ground and knew they were Andrea's legs stuck in a skirt, which brought him back to the party. Somewhere, little by little, the image of the girl dancing with him, Andrea's image, was returning, but the slowness of the image made it worse, worse because it became more erotic.

He knew he had to trick himself, but there was no hope of escaping the reality of dancing with a woman temptress. Their dancing in the almost total darkness and that damned aroma wafting up from her hair; her sweat, what was it?—the scent of sex, perhaps; that was it: he was discovering the aroma of desire. And Andrea appeared to become aware, to be torturing him, tempting him on purpose. She squeezed his neck harder with each turn, and she seemed to want to kiss him, but he wasn't sure, could it be fear? And the music kept playing and the light spinning slowly, and the couples, like automatons, almost motionless, danced on a single tile without stepping off it. He had to choose his destiny: either tell her he didn't want to dance anymore or let his body act totally natural, without repressing it a second longer. He opted for the latter and embraced her tightly, latching onto her waist. Andrea did not protest. Eduardo squeezed, and the unavoidable came like a rocket launching in slow motion, like a submarine in deep water, like a train in no rush to leave its tunnel. He was hard like he'd been only rarely before in his life.

When the song was over, Andrea lingered with him a few seconds and laughed as she pulled her arms from around his neck. He also laughed sheepishly. Fortunately the light favored him.

"*Pelao*, you almost made love to her right on the dance floor," the Colombian said to him.

Eduardo tried to shrug it off. "I really like that *peláa*, I like her."

"Did you ask for her phone number? If you didn't, don't leave without asking her for it, because in New York it's hard to run into someone by chance."

At two in the morning Eduardo and Casagrande met again. Casagrande was half drunk and smiling more than usual. He told Eduardo they were going to a friend's house in Queens to continue the party. They left with two women and got into a taxi. As they drove off, they discussed whether to take Queensborough Bridge or the Queens Tunnel. The Tunnel won.

Maribel lived near 82nd and Jackson Heights, and the four of them got off there. Elizabeth, a New Yorker who lived at Union Square, laughed at anything Casagrande said, and hugged him as one hugs a family member.

When they arrived at Maribel's apartment, she asked for everyone's coats and took them to a bedroom. She put a bottle of whiskey and a bottle of wine on the living room table and said that whoever wanted beer could get it in the refrigerator.

The women wanted to find out about Eduardo. Casagrande kept interrupting to paint a broad portrait of Banana Republic, the future famous Big Banana, and what brought him to the Big Apple. They laughed every time he said Banana Republic or The Big Banana. Maribel vanished into the interior of her apartment and reappeared with several joints. Elizabeth and Casagrande celebrated the gesture.

Eduardo realized he had to smoke one of the joints, and a kind of guilt invaded him deep inside: it was the second time he was doing drugs. Maribel, a Puerto Rican who had lived in New York for many years, passed Eduardo one of the lit joints. Not only did he not have the chance to turn it down, but he felt mechanized by the woman. By smoking with her he was allowing her an intimacy that in a matter of minutes could lead them to bed. Maribel had dressed down in just a T-shirt, and her bulging breasts pressed aggressively through the sheer fabric.

Elizabeth spoke in English and sometimes stuck in a Spanish word or two that Maribel had taught her. She'd tucked her legs under her facing Casagrande, who shared the sofa with her. They laughed about a sixties story that Casagrande told with dazzling historical faithfulness.

Maribel talked about the theater and movies with Eduardo. She took him by the hand and gestured to the others for their permission. She told him to come with her to see some photos and books about her career that might interest him. He followed her, even though Elizabeth was the one that interested him, for she, according to Casagrande, had some important contacts in the film world.

Eduardo looked at one of the books from above her clavicle, and then lingered to navigate the brimming breasts, which were partially visible from where he was. He embraced her from behind. She let the book fall to the floor. He hitched up her T-shirt and reached for her breasts, and they tumbled onto an enormous water bed that hammocked them back and forth.

Later that same evening, Casagrande was telling them how he'd been arrested once in San Francisco. He had kept the photo he appeared in with other handcuffed hippies as they entered a police precinct. Elizabeth watched him in a daze. Eduardo and Maribel returned to the living room.

"How were the books?" Casagrande asked slyly.

"I'd like to read for a while, too," said Elizabeth.

Eduardo crossed a look Casagrande's way to ask him why he didn't take action.

"I'm retired," Casagrande laughed.

They drank, and smoked the last joints, passing them around. Elizabeth said she was hungry. From her seat, Maribel suggested she prepare something and pointed to the kitchen.

When Casagrande fell asleep on the sofa, Maribel covered him.

"You're going to sleep with me," said Maribel to Eduardo.

"What about me?" Elizabeth said in a tone of protest.

Eduardo smiled.

"Sleep with Casagrande, the old man's not bad."

From the last car of the dream, from the unconsciousness of a cosmic trip, from a faraway planet in a faraway galaxy, from the most solitary astral dimension, from time's limit, from the place where dead and living can't be told apart, Casagrande said, "I'm homosexual."

Eduardo was stunned. The women paid no mind. Eduardo sensed his bad performance and to cover it, he said, "So am I to blame?"

From the place where all oceans meet, Casagrande mustered one last gram of energy and smiled.

Maribel smiled, too.

"The bed's big enough," she said. "And three of us don't make a crowd. Besides, we're civilized. We won't turn you into the Banana of Discord."

16

Eduardo had told Mirian over the phone how excited he was that she would visit him in New York. He also told her it was better to wait for summer, but it seemed too far away for them and they agreed on winter. From that day on Mirian felt revived. She studied, she read, she compulsively wrote articles about the national police, ecology, culture. Days earlier she'd had a session with the psychiatrist, in whose hands the decision about her trip rested. Persuading him wasn't easy. The psychiatrist was more obsessed with Agent 007 than she was.

"Why are you thinking of going to New York?"

"To see Eduardo and get to know that beautiful city."

"How do you know it's beautiful if you've never been there?"

"I've seen it on television, in magazines. Anyway, who doesn't know New York is beautiful? Tell me, do you think I am sexually delicious?"

"Yes."

"Why?"

"Because I saw you naked here in the office."

"You see, it's the same. New York gets naked for me in magazines and films. Now it's a matter of trying it. Would you like to try me?"

"No."

"I know the answer's yes."

"I'm telling you the answer's no."

"You say that because they're looking at you. If we were truly alone, you'd say something else."

"Why do you say that?"

"Because I'm neither mad nor foolish. What about that little hidden window? Don't you think my parents are watching and listening in on me right now?"

Behind the little hidden window her parents embraced each other. They couldn't figure out how they'd been detected.

"That's not a little window."

"Then if what you say is true, let's make love here, right this moment."

"No, I'm a professional."

"I have no proof, we've never done it before."

"No, I mean a medical professional."

"Can I go to New York?"

"I don't think you're in any condition to do so."

"What you've done having my parents spy on me is unethical. I could expose you and sue you."

"Your parents wouldn't allow it."

"I'm of legal age."

"Legal in years, which isn't the same thing."

"So I can't go to New York?"

"I don't know yet, we'll know by the end of this appointment."

"How should I act in order to persuade you?"

"Most likely by not acting."

"How?"

"I mean, by being natural."

"I swear I've been natural."

"What about James Bond?"

"I don't know whether he's natural."

"I mean, what about your relationship with James Bond?"

"It's over."

"Read me the last thing you've written, did you bring it? It may depend on that."

BONFIRE OF THE MULTITUDES

It's just four knuckleheads, the President had said. It's just a dozen bums, the General had said. It's just a couple of useful idiots who scare no one, someone else had said. And none had been on target, because it was neither four nor twelve but a couple of hundred protesters carrying signs, traveling the length of the city in a heat, singing the national anthem first as it is, then to a coastal beat, then to a rock beat, then to the beat of a Honduran folk song and, finally, to a blues beat in which the national anthem sounded so different and so much better, as many would comment for days afterward. The multitude spewed fiery speeches under the eyes, patience and tolerance of the highest government officials, who, between jokes and cups of export coffee, said it was better to allow the agents of disorder to vent in speeches rather than resort to other measures, because with one speechlet and another they exhausted themselves and went back home without the energy to climb on top of their despairing mate. They were speaking, or rather yelling, about social injustices, violations and everything that was said every time there was a demonstration. Weary or maybe bored of always having the demonstration take place in Parque Central and nothing come of it, of going back home and waiting for a new reason for a demonstration, a new venting, as the presidential spokesperson would say, the now highly heated, furious and indignant carriers of signs, bullhorns and placards took up the march outside Central Park, leaderless and guideless, all of them guiding themselves, moved as if by common telepathy or common fury, and what might have been a brief, inspiring walk of fifty yards started step by little step turning into more yards, and amid claims and remembrances of all the things that had been done to them before, the multitude grew agitated, and some of the unagitated who watched from the curb were infected and joined the raging sea.

The good fortune of the uprisen and the bad luck of the uninsured store owners met when the former ran up against the construction site for a new hotel. The bricks came to two per demonstrator. The multitude continued boiling over like a seaquake and as it passed a bank, it hailed bricks and stones, and the plate glass windows came crashing down. This made the heated-up literates pick up glass shards, which they used as pencils to deface the walls, damning the Nicaraguan counterrevolutionaries to hell, demanding more education, demanding fewer weapons or at least that they be split half and half between the army and the demonstrators. Some of the wounded used blood as they wrote váyanse *to the Yankee troops and* viva *to the self-determination of nations, and other demonstrator-creators drew the Constitution of the Republic with knives, lances, penises or encrusted bayonets. The human mass kept moving along the main avenue, slogans, songs, and later—with nightfall—torches that came out of nowhere. Now they had one per thousand, and in an almost diabolical or divine state, the torches burned so strongly the feverish human ralliers began to boil, which made their shouts of* muerte a los invasores *grow louder, to such a degree that, because of Tegucigalpa's topography which is jailed amid mountains, the slogans were heard throughout the capital, either directly or like the bounce of a first echo when the voice collides with the mountain ahead, or on its third or fourth rebound. Tegucigalpa was like a pool table and the voices were balls ricocheting from side to side and infecting the whole atmosphere. Meanwhile, at the seat of government, the politicians were frightened when they first heard the defiant buzz cut through the air; a loose-lipped minister had already said it was the Sandino-Communists who came in the form of bats. But the inordinate intelligence of the Assistant Press Secretary, the wasted genius of the Casa Rosada, the natural talent coveted by Yale University, claimed by La Sorbonne, and dreamed of by Lomonosov craned his neck, shook his head and rolled his eyes to signal that it was the Sodom and Gomorrah of the subversives, last-minute news which the president and those around him received with a flutter of sighs, which caused several paintings hanging on the wall, among which was the portrait of the president himself with a sash in the national colors crossing his chest, to fall. A minister brimming with initiative, the ace target-shooter of his town fairs, finished pacifying the situation with a right-on-target "let them yell their heads off, that's it, after this one there will be no more throats, therefore, there will be no more demonstrations and to your health," washed down with export coffee.*

The march, like an enormous centipede in shape, followed its route toward the U.S. Embassy and once there stopped, this time not asking but demanding that the Yankees leave the country. Some time later, and no one knew how—neither the demonstrators nor the police nor the government nor the U.S. diplomats—a torch shot out from the center of the multitude. For some it was science fiction, for others the Star of Bethlehem or from one of any number of Biblical passages, and for the few who'd traveled a bit, it was the Statue of Liberty's, and it fell squarely on the embassy building and, as if that very spot had been marked and drenched in kerosene, before the torch landed, an enormous flame shot up.

The rest of the torches no longer arose mysteriously. They, in fact, were launched, and not only with the intention of hitting the target with all the passion, all the desire, all the suffering accumulated over the course of years, but with the full conviction that a bonfire of such magnitude, at the rambling five-story building, was just and necessary to counteract the cold front, otherwise they would freeze to death in that ice, in the North Pole that furnace called Tegucigalpa was becoming. But it wasn't enough, it wasn't about to be enough for the building alone to burn, but everything that had something to do with it, inside it, had to burn, too. They scaled the fence and bounded over the gate, coming close to the objective and proving to themselves that the wall could one day come crashing down, that the glass panes were not bulletproof, much less fireproof, and even if they were, mañas quiere la guerra (all's fair in love and war). They stepped over the fallen doors and others leapt and some scaled the walls and the torches yellowed everything in their path: they yellowed some thirty cars, they yellowed the building, they yellowed a flag, several flags but all the same, they yellowed the last of the fifty little stars, they yellowed the dark hollow into which Tegucigalpa sinks, and it seemed as if the sun had set on Honduran soil. It was as if the sun had decided to rest, rest for a while, lay down in Tegucigalpa soil for a few hours; they had the sun at their feet, the sun casting light up from below onto the wall of mountains that hold Tegucigalpa prisoner, the sun casting light on the faces that had built it, happy faces that looked as if they had discovered or invented light, faces that were no longer furious but proud, contented faces of *adult-children who learned there's one thing fire was good for. Into the center of the flaming building came the army trucks, the pistol-packers disguised as civilians. They were all impotent, dumbstruck, nervous in the fire's presence. They'd look at the fire and retreat, crabs in uniform, and the heat and the devastating crackle brought to their pyromaniacal minds the memory of what they were, and the non-scattering shots found their marks in the heart of one, two, three, no one ever found out how many sun-builders.*

The multitude was terrified, the human shadows collided with one another on the lit-up ground, the stones fell on the crabs, they shot into the sky, spat into the wind. Finally the firemen appeared, this time not with alarm sirens but festive sirens, as on the Day of Independence from the Spanish Conquerors, September 15th, and no one could explain why the firemen were so slow, slower than anyone had ever seen them. Some looked at the bonfire and shook off their sloth, yawning, turning the valves in the wrong direction, that is, closing them. Others hooked the hoses up as if they were unanimated drawings. Those firemen whose job it was to run, ran not like they usually do, but like the man on television, the Six Million Dollar Man, the nuclear man, the man who, because he was out of shape, always ran in slow motion. The torrents of water, perhaps unintentionally on the firemen's behalf, shot up in arcs, doodling on the night sky like the scrawls of a three-year-old, and fell sometimes close, sometimes far from the flames but almost never on them, and it wasn't because the thousands of demonstrators had posted themselves behind a mountain and started blowing in unison. No, it was Nature itself which, for reasons no one knows, had become rarefied: it had brought along with it a wind that stoked the fire.

"Mirian, you wrote that?"

"Of course."

"Are you sure you didn't copy it from somewhere else?"

"Yes, I copied it. I copied it from reality."

The psychiatrist smiled. He'd supported the burning of the U.S. embassy by a multitude on a date not so long ago because a Honduran accused of narcotics trafficking had been kidnapped by national and foreign authorities and extradited to the United States. He supported the fire not because he harbored any passionate sense of nationalism or anti-Yankee sentiment, but because all his life he'd dreamed of being a moneyed man and in case he didn't achieve it in his profession, he'd do it by resorting to delinquency, and if he got caught he was resigned to serve his sentence in his country but never to be extradited.

"That article's very good. It should be published. Do you agree with the embassy's having been set on fire?"

"It doesn't sway me one way or the other. The only thing I liked about it was the party feeling it had. It was quite amusing to see Tegucigalpa completely militarized the next few days."

"But do you agree?"

"Why should I agree or disagree? Remember I'm majoring in journalism and I've seen a lot of films. I don't see events flatly like most people do. Haven't you wondered whether it might have been the intention of the United States to let them set the embassy on fire?"

"For what purpose?"

"Ay, doctorcito, think about it. They probably wanted to justify a bigger building, construct a fortress without inflicting any damage on Honduran sensibilities, build an impenetrable embassy."

Behind the little hidden window the parents were feeling proud. The psychiatrist was mortified.

"Why do you believe that?"

"Because had they wanted to kill him, they would have, or they would have kidnapped him secretly or anything. Do you get me? The fact that it's become a scandal isn't gratuitous. It has its reasons."

"What reasons might there be?"

"Let's say, to set an example. Yes, an example so that whoever dares defy them can see what will happen to them, in spite of our national opposition."

The psychiatrist was sweating. He removed his glasses and cleaned them again and again, as if to see whether once they were clean he could make out the dark hallway into which his future had transformed itself.

"You can indeed go to New York."

"Really, and why so suddenly?"

"That article is very good, it's very well written. It contains truth and fiction. You aren't ill. The problem is simply that we don't understand you because you're an authentic artist."

"Thank you, doctor."

The psychiatrist addressed the little hidden window.

"Come out, turn around. She knows you're there anyway."

17

December found Eduardo and Casagrande cruelly alone. None of those in the apartment, except José, his wife and daughter, had any family. The dozen Ecuadoreans showed up on Christmas Eve. Eduardo tried to escape his loneliness. He called Andrea. She had family engagements. He called Maribel, in vain; the telephone screeched a few times and then a recording blared like a dying echo: *You have reached the telephone of . . . I'll call you when I come back from Puerto Rico . . .* And the tone wheedled that it was time to leave a message. He wanted to call Elizabeth but didn't; she was a New Yorker, she wouldn't be lacking for family. Giving up, he resolved not to leave the apartment, to stay and drink with the Ecuadoreans, to weep with Julio Jaramillo's music in solidarity or sincerity as midnight approached and the first effects of the booze set in.

Thirty years without a family turn any heart to metal; nostalgia into an eternal smile: They make any human being enjoy the everyday routine as if it were a routine only recently put in practice. For Casagrande, Christmas was just another date made up by partymongers, another excuse for drunkenness, sleeplessness and lovemaking. On holidays, on celebration days, on anniversaries, most people are infected by memories that help them achieve coituses that are different from the routine year-round ones. It's as if humanity feels it has license for eccentricities, for inventiveness in love. For Casagrande, it was the same whether he spent the Christmas holidays in the apartment with the Ecuadoreans or with strangers in Brooklyn, or in Mexico City, where he'd lived for several years, or in South America or any

European country. Perhaps the only place he'd feel any longing for, to the point of making him lose his smile and flood him with tears, would be San Francisco.

The party started early. As if a collective order had sprung from their insides, the Ecuadoreans wanted to get drunk as fast as possible to escape thoughts of the supposed things their families would be doing from one end of Ecuador to the other. They drank implacably, they challenged liquor knowing they'd end up defeated, sunken in a pool of hazy dreams, adrift in the bitter tides of beer, rum and whiskey. They couldn't figure out any other way to speed up time, to push the Christmas holidays into an abyss before Christmas pushed them first into the abyss of depression. They wanted to addle their brains just like you erase a tape by pushing a button.

By ten in the evening, three Ecuadoreans were down for the count on the canvas. Another two were facing the sentence of excess: vomiting and dizziness. The phone rang, and the hearts of the survivors of the alcoholic flood choked up with the ringing. Eduardo was the lucky one. Before reaching the telephone, he imagined the little silkworm brushing his ear and nesting in its favorite place. It was all a miscalculation, a wrong hunch. It was a call from Javier, whom Christmas loneliness had crept up on in Riverside Park, making him conspire with his body to see whether, OD'd on alcohol and cocaine, he could, with his forty years, defy the Hudson River either underwater or doing a breaststroke. When he heard about how aimless Javier's life was, Eduardo invited him to come to the apartment. Javier accepted and said he was bringing a friend.

Christmas Eve spun round like a disciplined soldier's heels carrying out an order to about-face. It turned for Eduardo when the doorbell to the apartment rang and he opened the door. Javier was laughing because he was the surprise-maker. Eduardo froze just like when you rehearse a freeze in the theater. Leo laughed and hugged him. They hugged under Javier's approving gaze.

Leo was an aspiring Honduran inventor who'd abandoned Honduras because of the lack of opportunities. He had won a scholarship to study in the former Soviet Union, and a comrade who was in charge of delivering some papers to another comrade in charge of scholarships got drunk the day he was supposed to present the documents and lost them. Leo had been waiting to be notified of his date of departure to Moscow. Time passed and no news arrived. When he found out about the tragic fate of his papers, he became so disenchanted he not only abandoned his communist stance, which up to that day had been staunch, he also decided to travel to the United States.

Julio Jaramillo went for the heart of the Ecuadoreans: *No quiero verte triste porque me mata tu carita de pena mi dulce* . . . José knew Jaramillo's songs would squeeze the tears out of him, so he hid his heart behind his liver. But Jaramillo invaded the entire body: ankles, nails, hairs, ears—*si tú mueres primero, yo te prometo escribiré la historia de nuestro amor* . . . The Ecuadoreans wept with Jaramillo. José wept abundantly as well, as if he were doing it in *sucres.*

"Take it easy, *huevón,*" Casagrande said to him. "You pansies can't have a single drink because you start crying right away."

"Who knows what the hell he's remembering," protested Rosa.

"No," another Ecuadorean said gravely. "You see, Jaramillo reaches into the heart. You remember your country."

"What do you say we walk a bit?" Casagrande suggested.

"We're in the Bronx," said Javier.

"So?" Casagrande smiled. "It's Christmas Eve. Christmas touches even criminals."

Eduardo tried to walk to Kingsbridge. Casagrande pulled him away and took the New York Botanical Gardens route. Eduardo wondered again why Casagrande always avoided Kingsbridge Avenue and the Grand Concourse. He didn't think that mysticism could ban him from going by certain places, or maybe it could. He didn't ask at that moment, but vowed to do so later on. The question might make Casagrande uncomfortable, especially in front of other people.

They walked along Valentine Avenue. You could feel the happiness in building after building. People were talking in English and Spanish along the avenue. Sound systems had been set out on the streets. The drug dealers moved speedily from one place to another, because demand increased on holidays. When they took a street that led them to Grand Concourse, it occurred to Casagrande to search for a friend of his who lived near Jerome avenue. They got to Aqueduct

Avenue. It turned out that Casagrande's friend had moved. But the group of four friends stayed there on Aqueduct Avenue taking advantage of the line of benches and trees, a long narrow park, like a miniature Chile. There, warmly dressed and stocked with a gallon of wine, a bottle of whiskey and a dozen beers, the four of them challenged the night. Casagrande took the bottles out of his satchel and, as if the outside temperature weren't cold enough, dug holes in the snow and buried the bottles. A light dusting of snow fell on Aqueduct Avenue, where the Christmas spirit invaded all, as did the music and the boys having snowball fights on the streets.

Leo told the story of his life in New York. An aunt had brought him over and put him up for an indefinite time at her apartment in Astoria, Queens. Things didn't turn out so well, because the aunt was excessively conservative, and Leo, at thirty-two years of age, had to hide to have a beer, had to genuflect before every meal, and could never come home after a certain hour. Having no other choice, he complied with his aunt's requirements, but to not waste any time, he registered at Queens College. Despite knowing his aunt like he knew her, one day he brought a classmate home from Queens College and didn't lock the door. His aunt, as always, came in stealthily, without a peep, and finding Leo's door unlocked, she opened it with a single yank and found Leo making love to his classmate. That same night Leo was thrown out into the cold. His aunt reminded him pointedly that the problem wasn't his lovemaking; it was the obscene position in which he did it.

They laughed. Casagrande tried to tease out an explanation for the thing about the position, but Leo flatly refused.

"So what are you doing now?" Eduardo asked him.

"Well, I'm still studying at Queens College. And I teach part-time at Hostos Community College."

"What subject?" Casagrande asked.

"Math."

"Do you plan on going back to Honduras?" Eduardo inquired.

"Honduras," Javier interrupted, "Honduras, you mustn't go back to that country. It would be better to deport all the people who live there, distribute them throughout the world and give that territory to the Palestinians, who would surely get more out of it."

"What's with you, *huevón*?" Casagrande smiled. "What they say may be true, but let others be the ones to say it."

"The thing is," Eduardo said, "in some way or another, we resent our country, but that doesn't mean we don't love it."

"That whore's the thing," Javier lamented.

"What happened?" Leo grew interested.

"The Honduran woman from the southern U.S. . . ."

"That's it, leave it at that," Eduardo interrupted. "Wind him up and you'll never hear the end. It's better not to talk about old ladies who've betrayed us, because you get all bitter, while she might be enjoying her Christmas with a penis about as long as the distance from here to Tegucigalpa."

They laughed. The frost thickened slowly.

For the first time, Casagrande talked about Chile, his infancy, his father and his mother, about his only sister, whom he hadn't seen in thirty years. He talked about Mexico, his friendships, his only love left behind in Cuernavaca. He also talked about San Francisco, then corrected the thing about his only love and said my only two loves. When he talked about his loves, he never gave names and always used the neutral article, avoiding mention of the masculine or feminine adjective in Spanish.

Leo held forth on his great passion: neither Marxism nor any other political doctrine could compare with the ideal of his most important countryman, Francisco Morazán. Morazán was a mid-nineteenth-century revolutionary who attempted to unite Central America into one nation, to make it large and powerful. He combated dictatorships, fought honorably in several Central American countries. Just as Leo had said, there was nothing to keep you from transporting yourself instantly from Aqueduct Avenue in the Bronx to some mountainous region of Central America to echo Francisco Morazán and fight by his side, to win battles on horseback and by the sword.

Amid conversations about Chilean wine being the greatest thing on Planet Earth, about the southern United States, about the future Honduran star on the big screen, and about the Morazanist revolution reconstructed in the Bronx, morning crept up on them. They'd survived Christmas Eve.

18

New York Telephone and Eduardo extended their sadomasochistic idyll. While it was true that only some two days earlier he had cursed New York Telephone, now, just forty-eight hours later, he was declaring his love for the phone company. He dialed the number and in some cranny of the planet Earth his little worm awaited to be transported by satellite magic. He dialed again and the call didn't register; the satellite, because of year-end festivities, was as crowded as the Ark, carrying voices from one place to another. Eduardo treated the telephone, New York Telephone and Hondutel (Honduras Telefónica) tenderly. He believed that if he treated them that way, his calls would get through to the other end where his little worm was surely watching and waiting.

Finally the call went through. Doña Rosaura, his mother-in-law-to-be, picked up the phone. She said that Mirian would be there right away, because at that moment she was heading for the phone in her room. For a few impatient seconds he imagined his little worm caressing his ear, coming down slowly by way of the snail-shaped ladder, a spi—

"It wasn't worth your while to call until now?" Mirian interrupted his dream of the little silkworm.

"No, Mirian, look . . ."

"Where were you on the twenty-fourth? I called you at midnight, I called you several times, I called you in the early morning. Who were you with?"

"Look, *cariño*, let me explain. I was with Casagrande . . ."

"With Casagrande. Or could it be *Culo*grande?"

"But Mirian . . ."

"Why don't you tell me the truth."

He tried to win over his ex-little worm cum serpent, the anaconda that threatened his eardrums, flicking its tongue at him. He explained it so sincerely and in such wealth of detail that Mirian was persuaded that on the twenty-fourth there had been no women, just a bunch of single guys on Aqueduct Avenue.

"Forgive me, *cariño*, I get restless, jealous."

"I know, Mirian, me too. I think about you, I imagine you with another man."

"No, *cariño*, put your doubts to rest. This is insane. You have to come back as soon as possible. You don't need to be over there. My dad will give us a house."

"I'll try a little longer. I promise you if it doesn't go well for me, I'll take off. If it does go well, I'll bring you here to live with me."

"I miss you."

"Me too, I hurt so much."

"Come back, Eduardo, come back as soon as possible."

"Be patient, *amor*, you're coming here soon. April's around the corner. I guarantee you we'll have a great time."

"Yes, for a few days, and then . . ."

"That won't last long. I promise."

"Don't aspire to too much, Eduardo. What's the fame and that sort of thing worth if we're not together?"

"You're right, Mirian. Maybe I'll go with you."

"It would be fantastic. I cried a lot on the twenty-fourth, I was so frustrated because you were never in your apartment."

"Sí, amor. I went out to keep from torturing myself by remembering you. I love you, I want you."

"I want you too. When I see you, I'm going to grab you like a madwoman . . ."

Eduardo had won over the little worm, which now inched round slowly circling his neck, flirting with his eardrum . . .

19

In mid-January, Andrea, the Colombian, called Eduardo. He invited her to lunch at a Mexican restaurant on Eighth Avenue. Afterwards they walked along the nearby streets. They went in to *Macondo* bookstore. Eduardo wasn't about to be dazzled by her knowledge of books. He knew the owner of the bookstore; he'd met him there. Don Jorge was a Colombian, a good friend of Gabriel García Márquez, such a good friend that once when García Márquez was teaching a course at Columbia University he transferred his classes to the bookstore. This event was well-known in New York: the most outstanding intellectuals were seated on the floor in *Macondo,* taking classes with the patriarch.

Don Jorge had the look and attitude of someone not interested in making new friends. Maybe because of his status as a prestigious bookseller, one too many writers and aspiring writers had sought him out in their zeal to get to other personalities of the literary world. At first Eduardo was taken back by Don Jorge's cutting responses. But when Eduardo became interested in Fernando Alegría's *Novela hispanoamericana,* which cost twenty-four dollars and Eduardo barely had eight, Don Jorge agreed to let him owe the rest. He took advantage of that exchange of words to come back, not only to pay off his debt, but also to talk about the prestigious Baranquilla Writers Group. From then on he considered himself Don Jorge's friend, and apparently began stirring a fondness in the owner of *Macondo* for that reader fellow who dreamed of being a movie star.

Eduardo told Andrea the anecdote of García Márquez' classes that were transferred to *Macondo* and also introduced her to Don Jorge.

Andrea was in awe of Eduardo's literary knowledge and his friends in high places. Eduardo gave her a novel published recently in New York, titled *La importancia de llamarse Daniel Santos,* by a Puerto Rican writer, Luis Rafael Sánchez. They decided to walk as they talked, until they were exhausted.

"Where does your literary passion come from?" Andrea asked him.

"From my childhood, my mother, my father, you know? But I also believe that if I want to excel as an actor, I have to know many things, literature above all. Besides, when I read I act, because I start getting into each character, and while I'm reading I cease to be me so I can be others."

"*¡Pero hombre, qué vacano!*"

"How's that?"

"Pablo was right, we have to speak to you in standard Spanish."

"Which Pablo?"

"Which Pablo? The one who introduced us at the party."

"Sorry, of course, Pablo."

They were walking along Second Avenue. They walked up from Union Square towards Grand Central Station. The city was completely carpeted with snow. Walking with Andrea in a New York swathed in white seemed romantic. He would have wished not for Andrea but for Mirian to be with him. He remembered his little worm. He wanted to go back to his apartment and call her, which wasn't possible. He had to rein in his impulses, talk less and write more. What little he made he put toward the New York Telephone bill. Could he be the only foreigner who had these phone problems? Could there be others who cursed the phone company at month's end, cursed themselves and inevitably returned before the end of the following month and fell into the soft web of the satellite again? What would happen when they installed the new telephones with a screen so you could see the person you were talking to? Would suicide rates go up?

"What are you thinking about?" Andrea asked.

"About New York. About how I'd like to be the owner of New York Telephone."

She laughed.

"That's how much you miss someone you left behind in your country?"

He didn't even try to lie, he never lied about those things. "Yes. A lot. It's cold. Should we go for a hot chocolate or something? I know a nice place, an Irish restaurant on Park Avenue."

"Okay."

They looked at the city through the window a while. The restaurant was empty because of the late hour and the weather.

"Beer?" he said. "They sell good draft here."

"That's fine with me." Andrea didn't know what was coming over her: whether boredom or maybe the nostalgia she'd detected in Eduardo was catching up to her.

"Something worries me," he commented to her. "I'm drinking too frequently. I've never drank as much as I do now."

"That's what happens in New York."

"Why do people who live here always say that: *New York? This is New York; get used to it because New York is like that.* It's like a complaint, don't you think? But an unfair complaint."

Andrea was touched.

"Why unfair? You come to New York looking for something and find nothing, so you have a right to complain, to protest."

A blonde waitress set a pitcher of beer on the table. She asked if they wanted to eat. A no and a thank you sent her away from the couple.

"You come to New York," he said, "but who put you up to it? Who forced you to do it?"

"Thirst," she sipped the beer.

"Poetic," he smiled, "but I think differently. I agree with people who complain about New York, though I know it's not because of New York. It's because of other particular circumstances that go beyond that. Maybe New York isn't that innocent, but neither is it fair to set it up as the big culprit."

"I don't get it."

"I mean, from my point of view, when you, someone else or I myself, when anyone rails against the city or puts it down, they're not talking about New York, but about the world, about themselves. It seems to me New York is a synthesis of the world, it's Planet Earth on a small scale, so that we human beings who are so much smaller, may have if not the total opportunity, at least something, through the window called New York, with which to see ourselves, to see the world in which we live, or to half-see it and get the rest by intuition, which explains the railing and the nausea."

"In other words it's not to blame?"

"No place is to blame, no city's to blame. We're the culprits. We humans are the culprits, and you wait and see, it will get worse. If New York is called the Big Apple, not too much longer from now it will be known as *The Great Wall of Lamentations, The Great Fount of the Disconsolate.* I don't know, human beings probably created New York so they'd have someone to blame."

"You're like a philosopher."

"I'm like an observer who is beginning to experience fear."

She poured beer up to the rim of his glass, then hers. "Why do you think it will get worse?"

"Because there's no longer a Soviet Union; those countries we saw as remote and living another lifestyle no longer exist. Maybe neither you nor I nor many of us agreed with the theories they lived by over there. Still, consciously or not, somehow inexplicably they nourished us. Most likely we'd never want to live over there under their political system, but the simple fact that we believed there were other human beings in other parts of the world who did enjoy living that way, that simple fact in some way gave us relief."

"It's true, maybe because when a woman approaches thirty she feels old. Especially when you haven't done what you wanted to do. I want to return to Colombia, stay over there and devote myself to teaching."

He wanted more beer. The blonde approached and he ordered another pitcher. Through the window you could see fine granules of snow wrenching themselves loose from someplace in the Universe and falling over the Great City.

"It must be sad to be a teacher," he said.

"No, not at all."

"You're right. I mean, you shouldn't be a teacher without having a vocation for it. Teachers by vocation are happy: they give classes, they read so they can be better every day; they fight among themselves and bad-mouth each other, they have long vacations and the luxury of feeling sorry for themselves for being teachers. In reality they wouldn't want to be anything else in the world. Now, when you're a teacher without the vocation, because it was the last resort, when you have failed at everything else and teaching's your sustenance and refuge, then it must be sad to be a teacher."

"You're scaring me. You've left me without a Soviet Union and you also want to leave me with no vocation for teaching. Who destroyed socialism?"

"I'm sorry. It's not to make you feel bad. It's just a conversation. Interesting, the question you pose to yourself. I believe all of us destroyed socialism. Right now, half the world is asking itself that question. Scholars, political analysts, intellectuals—they all get bogged down when they have to answer it. And I believe it's simple: under socialism the government got its citizens used to having the basics within reach. So then, why would they worry about producing if everything was put in their mouths without any effort? They got lazy, production dropped, and a crisis was born. They neglected something that seems like a puny detail but in fact is not; it's something fundamental: vanity. They neglected to please human vanity, something inherent in us. There are the seemingly minor details: a bottle of perfume, lipstick, a pair of tennis shoes, a sweater, etc. They manufactured the same things for everyone. That's called the Soviet dream, the great Impossible, the great Utopia. They should have remembered that they were human beings, far from perfection. The apparent racial and economic equality, the apparent conformism, had to be unmasked one day. Here they say that the United States won the Cold War. I don't agree. I think the U.S. contributed but wasn't the determining factor. Humanity won the Cold War, or defeated itself. It all depends on what corner you're watching from."

"You might be right. If you don't have a vocation for that, how can you get it?"

"There's a very New York saying, something to the effect that if you can't find it in New York, don't look for it anywhere else in the world. We'd have to visit some shops and ask, can you sell me two kilos of teaching vocation?"

"So vocation comes in liquid form?"

"I hadn't thought about that. It'd depend on the price, or on the dose you need. Can you sell me a liter of teaching vocation? What's that, you only sell it by the gallon . . . ?"

Andrea had left Colombia when she was eighteen years old. Because of her beauty and intelligence she thought she'd find her future in New York. She studied Dramatic Arts. In the beginning she dreamed of being a model, which didn't turn out to be quite so easy. In Colombia she'd acquired some brief experience in directing plays. In New York, Andrea returned to the stage and dreamed of making films some day. But that dream was also far from coming true. She was now tired of her decade-long quest. She, nevertheless, had learned to love New York in spite of all she had suffered there. For that reason alone she didn't leave New York, she wasn't sure she could readjust to Colombia. Andrea did not use drugs to defeat the constant depression she found herself mired in in New York, but she began reading compulsively, looking for second-hand books in Spanish and in English in the Village street stands.

Thus her great passion for books: a depressive decade channeled into books was no mean feat, anywhere you were. Finally Andrea got used to New York and resigned herself to teaching at a Harlem school and buying second-hand books.

"Well, there are worse things than teaching. At least they haven't mugged or raped me."

Eduardo smiled.

"Share the joke?"

"What if you don't like it?"

"I'll laugh anyway." She laughed.

"No, the fact that they haven't mugged you is fine. Now, although they haven't raped you, if you insist on remaining single, the one who'll end up doing the raping is you."

"Raping who, you?"

"Possibly."

"Yes," she shifted to a worried expression. "The problem is it's been a long time since I've gotten excited. Every time I've tried has been a failure."

The frost thickened on the other side of the window.

"A difficult task," he said.

When they finished the second pitcher they decided to leave. Eduardo suggested they take the subway; the number 6 was good for both because it would take them to Grand Central Station, where she could transfer to the 7, which would take her all the way to 61st Street in Woodside, Queens. He could take the D all the way to Kingsbridge.

They said good-bye to each other at Grand Central. He asked to see her again soon. She told him she'd call and asked him what he was doing the following Friday. He declared himself available. She invited him to a meeting of Colombians near her house. He accepted but warned her that a friend was going to come with him. She laughed and told him that Casagrande was always welcome. He laughed and asked, *Who doesn't know Casagrande?* He tried to give her a good-bye kiss on the mouth. She gave in.

20

The house felt larger for Casagrande in Eduardo's absence. They hadn't seen each other for close to a week, even though they lived in the same apartment. Eduardo was working for Charlie. Casagrande had cooked up a two-month photography course at Hostos Community College, which he taught for two hours a day, from Monday to Thursday, earning enough to cover his limited living expenses for six months. When either Casagrande or Eduardo came back to the apartment, there was no knowing whether the other would be there; even if so, one might be sleeping off a drinking binge. The only form of communication they had those days was by leaving notes on each other's doors. They both agreed to get together because they missed each other. Their friendship had strengthened, maybe because of the few demands they made on each other. The apartment was quiet without one of the two. Casagrande had found in Eduardo the person he'd wished for in that terrible apartment, where he'd only learned to add and subtract in *sucres*, to multiply—never divide—in *sucres*. With Eduardo, that routine changed; other conversations came into play, whether it was about art or life, or the political and economic situation of Latin America. Eduardo's life transformation also had to do with his meeting Casagrande. He had met people, had slept with a few women, and always had somewhere to go. Casagrande's joking, almost palpable flippancy about everything was infectious, a great stress reliever.

That Thursday Casagrande promised himself not to go out. He had called off his class and stayed in the apartment to wait for Eduardo. He started drinking coffee at first, only to trade it in after the third cup for the never-absent gallon of wine nestled in a corner of his room. When he heard the keys jangling in search of the front door lock, he was overcome with joy. It could only be Eduardo coming home. The Ecuadorean workers came home later, and without the spirit to make the keys jangle like that.

Eduardo came in, ducked into his room for a few seconds and came out yelling, "Anyone here, anyone home? Otherwise, I'll dive from this twelfth floor and say good-bye to this bitching life!"

Casagrande's voice reached all the way down the hall to Eduardo.

"Dive, *huevón*, but do it through the front windows so you don't give the neighbors or the ambulance men too much work."

"Casagrande, *jodido*, long time no see. You still live here?"

In the living room, Casagrande had stood up so they could greet each other with a hug. *"No jodás, huevón,* you've been lost. I thought you'd gone from carpenter to Hollywood star: Banana Jones."

"Work, Casagrande, is the key to success."

"Don't be so sure. The thing about work being the key to success was invented by the rich so that you settle for eight-hour shifts and never aspire to be like them: plenty rich without lifting a finger. In fact, others work to make them richer."

Casagrande disappeared into the kitchen and returned with a glass of wine filled almost to the brim.

"You're going to make a drunk out of me, Casa. I just guzzled about two pitchers of beer. To our health and New York's."

"What's with the euphoria, *huevón*?"

It was because he'd thought a good deal on the train ride. Maybe with the beers, he'd seen the future clearly. He checked out all the people traveling in his car and wondered how many of those wretches thought about and struggled for artistic, literary, political or economic success. He was convinced that they were very few. The majority of those unfortunates thought about trivialities: settling for a third-hand car, a television set, returning to their countries with a couple thousand bills of their respective national currency in their pockets. He was sure that few among the human mass thought about life, about where they were headed. No, they just got on the train, confident they'd get somewhere, but very few, maybe none, mistrusted the subway. Why did they always trust the train to take them to their respective destinations? Didn't they wonder whether something unexpected could take place, and the New York trains, suddenly and apparently without anyone's knowing, might abandon their everyday routes and take that bunch of semi-sleeping, smug people to a concentration camp like the Nazi ones? But these would go deeper because the trains were no longer conducted by humans, but had turned into huge worms burrowing into the earth like a fish into the center of the ocean. Why were they so trustful? Maybe Europe didn't exist, or man hadn't really reached the moon yet. Who had any evidence? Only those who'd gone there, barely anyone else.

He thought about all that as a way of telling himself that what was wrong with the human mass on the train, the streets, everywhere, across the spectrum, was the unquestioning attitude, the failure to learn to say no to everything, even though you're saying yes. If all people thought that way, or, even better, didn't think, then it was laughably easy to stand out in a world of standardized brains.

"You're right as can be, *huevón.* Nevertheless, I believe that for success you need not only that but a little magic, too. If by chance you don't have it, you must acquire something of mystery, something like ritual. I don't know, at some moment in your life you'll realize it on your own. It comes unannounced."

"Casagrande, I have two questions to ask you."

Casagrande had rarely looked so serious.

"The first, the one that most interests me, is: Why, whether you're coming or going, you won't get off at Kingsbridge, which would be the shortest way, but you take the street above, which is much longer and out of the way? The second one is about that day at Maribel's house, when you left me with her and ignored Elizabeth, and you said you were homosexual. Since we were drunk and you were half asleep, I wasn't clear about it. And, well, it didn't occur to me to ask until today."

Casagrande wore a picture-perfect smile, like a mischievous child. "I'll answer the second one for you; the first one I don't want to talk about. Yes, it's true, I am homosexual, but I no longer practice, I'm retired."

Eduardo filled the glasses with wine. "Why the retirement?"

"Seniority. Besides, when I left my love, I promised not to have anyone else. And now I've found a method for getting by without needing sex. It's enough for me to see a boy I like, talk with him, stroke his hands. I don't talk about it here because you know it can get me in trouble; these Ecuadoreans are incapable of understanding it."

Judging from Eduardo's reaction, he knew that he understood him. Now he could be heard as he had yearned to for so long. He got excited and, assured that Eduardo lent him an ear, as Milan Kundera would say, he set in motion a whole river of love stories he had inside which was ready to flood over its banks, rush up through his pores, fill up his life. He had a secret ocean inside with waves at hightide. Had he not found Eduardo, it would have drowned him, swept him into a secret whirlpool and plunged him into his own depths.

He talked about his love in San Francisco, the man of his dreams. At times he was nostalgic, sadness pouring from his eyes which were like two black, brilliant suns. Then he got excited and laughed with Eduardo and the memories. He brought the story of that old love with whom he'd shared an apartment in San Francisco all the way to the twelfth floor on Valentine Avenue in the Bronx, in the city of New York. He didn't spare a single detail of his and his mate's haphazard but lovely life. He talked about the ongoing squabbling the couple's jealousy provoked. With picture-perfect smiles, fragments of his yesteryears came to him in which he saw himself, with the singular clarity of all good storytellers, insulting his mate and dumping his belongings out the window. He repeated the charges he yelled at him as if he were experiencing it the same day it had happened. The neighborhood was scandalized to see the two men in the middle of an exchange of oral fire. His mate tried to climb up to the second floor through a window that led to the fire escape. Casagrande, enraged, hurled shoes, underwear, socks, curtains, living room objects and kitchen utensils at him, to the bewilderment of the neighborhood. Finally, the mate returned to the apartment, and they managed to quiet down. Afterward, they had to face the neighbors, who would most likely ask for them to be evicted.

Thirty minutes later, Casagrande, who was given to fantasizing and persuading and speaking in public without a hint of modesty, stood on the second floor of the fire escape and called to all the neighbors who wanted to hear him. A group of neighbors gathered in the patio. Casagrande was a complete gentleman during his introduction. He spoke for a few minutes about theories of art, street theater, and the theater of audience-participation, which was exactly what he and his mate had just finished rehearsing. They were actors rehearsing; they couldn't let on about it beforehand because advance warning would make people lose the spontaneity and naturalness they needed, not only to test the piece's effectiveness, but also to write a sociological-artistic essay about the neighbors' reaction to their representation of a love scene between two men who insult each other and fight about one of the partner's jealousy.

Casagrande's words were so penetrating that the neighbors applauded the artists frenetically, not without warning them afterwards that the rehearsal thing was fine as long as it didn't disturb anyone's sleep. They also asked for opening night comps.

Casagrande rocked with full belly laughs.

"And afterwards, we locked ourselves in to make love. Reconciliations are so beautiful!"

21

Tegucigalpa is unrivaled from a distance and at nighttime. Neither the White House Christmas tree in Washington nor the Golden Gate in San Francisco with all its lights can compare to it from a road a few miles outside the city, from some nearby mountain. Depending on where you look from, at those times and from a distance it might well have the shape of several enormous Christmas trees, or of a gigantic transatlantic cruiser on a holiday, or an illuminated pyramid set on its head. From that distance Tegucigalpa dons its uniform and, with the lights, the poor go unseen, which, of course, makes it more beautiful. The same thing can happen anywhere on the planet from a jet or even, why not, from a car.

Mirian accelerated. The drivers she passed were frightened by her speed and driving skill. Despite the smallness of Tegucigalpa's downtown, it could be elected the car-horn capital. The streets are narrow, a legacy of the Spanish colonial era, and the sidewalks much more so. Pedestrians have to walk in single file and, when in a hurry, have to pass one another by stepping into the street while avoiding being hit by swerving cars.

Mirian knew she'd given the police the slip, as James Bond would have. Where had she learned to drive like that? Could anyone compete with her? Don Jonás had bought her that car, thanks to the therapy she'd given the psychiatrist, who'd gone helplessly from being a physician to being a patient. She liked to speed; a passage in a book talked about the importance of speed in human beings for a longer life, for success, for defeating depression. She also learned about speeding in her romance with Agent 007. A speedless film, a slow novel, anything that did not fulfill the requisite of constant movement wasn't just boring to her, it was useless and unnecessary. Her theory, a pragmatic one, was not lacking in logic: if the Earth moves, water moves, fire moves, air moves, and the finest things possess movement, like reaching an orgasm, then the reproduction of the human and animal species was therefore, beyond a doubt, founded on movement.

She continued writing articles that none of the people she knew with access to the media wanted to publish. She didn't care. She needed them for her own peace of mind. It was enough for Eduardo to like them. She wished he'd come back for good. She daydreamed about the day both of them would give the police the slip in her red car. They would laugh and thank James Bond together for being such an excellent teacher.

To write and drive well had become a sedative so that calendar dates would not matter to her. She was in a hurry for March to arrive and, with it, spring, and with spring, her trip to New York and a romance worthy of a film or a novel in search of a happy ending. She was afraid something might happen to Eduardo in the great urb, from which all manner of news came: undocumented workers found floating in the Hudson River, foreigners jumping off high skyscrapers, desperate immigrants throwing themselves under a subway train. Eduardo would persuade her in letters and over the phone that people tended to exaggerate. She calmed down for some time, but the least bit of bad news from New York alarmed her, as if no one else but Eduardo lived in the Capital of the World.

She reduced her speed and slipped smoothly into the labyrinthine traffic. She saw Parque Central from her car. How many times had she walked that way even if she didn't need to, just to forget some obsession? On countless occasions she had walked the length of that plaza which was always overrun. Today it featured a preacher with a voice so loud he didn't need a megaphone, a band blasting out a *merengue*, a snake charmer surrounded by a crowd who counted the bites the insubordinate reptile gave him. Students, loiterers, and vendors all joined in the racket.

Something made Mirian anxious and she retraced her path home. She dialed Eduardo's number in New York. No one answered.

22

When Andrea greeted Eduardo and Casagrande at her door, she looked more beautiful than ever. A group of Colombians, between beers and whiskeys, was already discussing who was to blame for the crash of an AVIANCA plane near John F. Kennedy Airport. The Colombians' version was that the traffic controllers' racism had caused the accident, because there were reports that the plane had flown over New York City for over an hour, waiting for its turn to land. The control tower's version was that the pilots never pronounced the magical word *emergency*, which would have immediately allowed the craft to land. The accident had taken place several months earlier, but it still weighed heavily on the hearts of the Colombians, who were furious because, according to them, the people of the United States see only the negative things about Colombia, never the countless aspects of the cultural and economic life of other nations.

Eduardo limited himself to listening as he sat next to Andrea. Casagrande offered his opinion; he always offered his opinion on any subject, whether he knew anything about it or not. He believed that his fifty-two years, with thirty-two divided between Mexico, San Francisco and New York, and his circumstances of leading a double life, gave him license.

Eduardo was introduced by Andrea to the Colombians who immediately joked about Honduras being bought lock, stock and barrel by the U.S. Eduardo held a grudge against his country's politicians, who, more than the people of the U.S. themselves, were to be held accountable for Honduras's being held in such disregard. The ambition and ignorance of most Honduran politicians in signing off or conceding everything for a few dollars had the country in such low esteem that there were more than a few Hondurans abroad who denied their nationality, preferring to state merely that they were Central American, or even Salvadoran, Guatemalan or Nicaraguan. Eduardo, on the other hand, took advantage of the propitious circumstances these get-togethers provided to talk beyond the little that was known about his country, beyond the military bases and war games. He did not contradict what's clear to see, but allowed for the other side of a country that dreams, sings, laughs, and cries to be seen, too. He took pride in telling about contemporary Honduran poetry, about painters, musicians, theater.

The Colombians listened attentively. Clearly, this wasn't some fool standing up for ridiculous nationalism, but a man who had lived in one of the hardest-hit regions of the planet. He didn't play it up with helpless whimpering or appeals for sympathy. What was clear above all was that he was a worthy representative of his culture, with a strong yearning to somehow create a better country.

Eduardo felt good because he sensed that they understood him. A Colombian writer who had lived in New York since childhood wanted to know more about Honduras, and asked him for his number for future conversations. Andrea was all over him, which surprised everyone. "The Honduran turned out the winner," someone commented.

"How far is it from here to Honduras?"

Casagrande smiled and, before Eduardo could respond, chimed in, "It's close, two centuries away. Right, Big Banana?"

"Well," Eduardo smiled, "one century, that is to say, much closer than from here to the Amish."

The reply produced the expected reaction. "You're something else," the writer said.

"And I'm the laughingstock of the family."

"So are you thinking of staying here a long time?" asked a woman theater critic.

"Depends on how it goes."

"It's rough for dreamers in New York," said Casagrande.

"Who knows? We probably don't dream enough," the painter offered in support.

"Yes, that could be," added a woman passing by, who joined the group. "Maybe we know how to sleep but haven't learned how to dream."

"Laura," the writer yelled, "if you keep those thoughts up, we're going to have to repatriate you to Colombia to make up for brain drain."

A voice from the small crowd changed the subject. "Is the war in Central America over?"

"The war goes on," answered Eduardo. "They say that in the not too distant future El Salvador's guerilla fighters and the government will negotiate. But the truth is, a lasting peace in Central America is difficult. There may be peace for a while, but if social injustice persists, war will return to Central America sooner rather than later . . . If it isn't a Marxist rebellion then it might simply be a rebellion because people can no longer take the misery of injustice. Besides, we mustn't forget that historically Central America has always been a war zone." Eduardo thought that was enough.

"Guerillas, at least the Marxist ones, have no future anywhere. Like it or not, the fall of the Soviet bloc affects all these struggles directly. It would be pointless to insist," said Laura.

Casagrande moved the glass of whiskey away from his mouth. "Who cares about the reason for wars? The world has gotten used to war. There will always be reasons for them to continue. If it isn't the Marxists, it will be the oil people . . ."

"That is favoring war. I mean, saying it like that, with such resignation."

"What can we do?" Casagrande defended himself. "A book, a song, a poem won't keep wars away. I'm playing the pessimist, I know, but you see, I don't believe the world can reach that degree of evolution, when we could really call ourselves civilized. Right now we're the most damaging bacteria on the planet. Maybe even animals and plants, in their own language, which may be superior to ours, bad-mouth us, criticize us, and clamor for our extinction. Without us they might be happy. We mustn't forget that we, not they, are the ones who are finishing off the oceans, the ozone layer . . . We make up wars, and they must not think well of it at all, because the Earth belongs to them just as much as to us. Maybe they're conspiring against us, waiting for the right moment to attack us . . ."

Andrea lit a cigarette and said, "True. Maybe in the future, wars will start because one country wants to take a forest away from another, or some species of animal becoming extinct in one country is stolen from another. It's not for nothing they say we've entered the age of ecological warfare."

"Excellent," the writer laughed. "Can you imagine soldiers standing guard over a tree, a rosebush, or a carnation, in full combat gear? A commando watching over a garden, armed frogmen protecting undersea life, men with cannons defending the last existing lions, and planes flying side by side with birds to protect them . . ."

"You're crazy," Andrea gibed.

"It's not bad as a hypothesis. You ought to write it down and develop it, get one step ahead of history," Eduardo advised.

Casagrande could not survive another hour without turning the cassette of his memory back to the sixties: "In 'The White Negro,' Norman Mailer says something really nice about the hypothesis of future wars. He says, something like, one may very well wonder whether the last of all wars will be between blacks and whites, or between men and women, or between the beautiful and the ugly, *pelados* and managers, or rebels and legalists. Which, clearly, is to carry speculation beyond the point at which speculation is still serious."

"Listen to Casagrande," Laura cut in excitedly. "He knows Mailer by heart. If Mailer found out, he'd be very proud."

"But Mailer," the writer intervened, "as far as what you say, Casagrande, may be ignoring us Hispanics, which is to say, he doesn't take us into account in the final war. That's racism. Or maybe by then we'll have become extinct due to famine or the next-to-last war, or maybe by that time in Latin America we will already have developed a superior world where wars have gone out of style."

"Hosts," Laura yelled, "what did you put in this whiskey?"

"Well, to sum it up," said Casagrande, "whether wars are impossible to eliminate or not, the important thing is to do something against them. Maybe the antiwar things we do now are the first grains of sand so that in a million years we can have a worthy planet Earth. Even if we never see it. We helped it come about."

"So what are you writing?" the writer asked Eduardo, who was hugging Andrea.

"A bestseller," the writer laughed. "If I could live off what I write, I'd write thousands of things."

"The same story with all writers: they're lazy is what they are," Laura poked fun at him.

"You're getting even," the writer said to her. "I wrote two books of stories about this city because it's the city I live in and know best. Now I'm attempting a novel, but it isn't easy for a foreign writer, and above all a Latino, to write novels here that deal with this reality. The *gringos* like books that question them and make jokes about them, but only if they're written by their own. They don't let us do that."

"How true is that?" said a poet who'd just joined the group. "Maybe it isn't as you say it is, but, plain and simple, our sense of humor is probably different from theirs. You know what's happened here with Latin American literature? It's very strong, questioning events both here and over there."

"I give up," said the writer. "I don't have the least interest in getting anyone on my side. My position is that they try to use you as a court fool, but if the court fool laughs at them, they cut you off."

"Don't give up so easily," the poet said. "This is the world and that's how the world is. Is it any different in Colombia when you put a book out and you're helpless? In short, it's the world; join the Mafia that suits you and accepts you, and things will work out. That's not the situation just in this country, much less only in New York."

"Mexico's difficult," said Casagrande. "It's true, getting in isn't easy."

"It's the world," the poet insisted. "That's just the way the world is."

"If you've noticed," the writer defended himself, "the Latin American novels that are most successful here make Latinos out to be drunks and sexual terrorists."

They all laughed.

"You're unbearable today," the writer said to him. "You must have had a bad orgasm."

Andrea was a step ahead. "But not with a Latino. You yourself said it: sexual terrorists. That's why we love you and don't allow other women to steal you from us."

"Anyway," the writer continued, "I won't play anyone's court fool. I'm going to keep writing about this reality, and I'll poke fun at whatever I please."

"You can poke fun at whatever and whomever you please. If it's done with high literary standards, it will be accepted here and everywhere," said the poet.

"Well, I'm a great novel reader," Laura interjected. "For me, a novel can be about anything it chooses, wars, sex, politics, whatever, if it stirs up my sense of humor, I consider it good. I don't read novels to make myself bitter, but to entertain myself. I'm not a masochist, and books are expensive."

Amid the laughs Pablo, the Colombian who'd introduced Eduardo and Andrea, came in. He greeted everyone warmly, especially the couple. He winked in complicity at Eduardo. Andrea took advantage of the interruption for the kidnapping. She took Eduardo to a balcony with a view toward Manhattan. The subway went by almost at the same level they were on.

"I really like this city," Eduardo said to her.

"Me too. Especially when it snows."

"I also like the people at this party: they're smart and friendly."

"We're Colombians."

"And that's your greatest virtue: modesty."

"Casagrande's more modest."

"Yes, he often says, 'I used to be immodest, now I'm perfect.'"

They laughed in the semidarkness of the balcony. He kissed her.

"Aren't you afraid?" she asked.

"Yes."

"Me too."

"Could the solution be not to see each other any more?"

"No, don't even say that. I want you to show me the thing about the sexual terrorist."

"I will."

"How?"

"You can't talk about it. If you put it in words, you break the spell, the secret's out. It's a cosmic thing. But trust me, I'll show it to you."

"I told you my problem, I don't get excited."

"This time will be different."

He kissed her again.

On their way back from the party, Eduardo and Casagrande rode the subway together silently. Maybe the booze had opened up their private worlds, or they kept quiet unconsciously so as not to attract the attention of the supposed evildoers who might be traveling on the train. Casagrande napped with his head tilted backward onto a window. Eduardo found it impossible to sleep outside his house, and much less at that hour on the Bronx-bound D train. He watched the other passengers inconspicuously, keeping them in his sights in case he detected any threatening behavior. He was a bit afraid and preferred to take a trip to the past when he lived in the South Bronx:

He had two dollars and an infinite loneliness. Mairena, his childhood friend, the black man from the Atlantic Coast of Honduras who'd offered him lodgings in his apartment, had gone out to a family party with his wife. Eduardo was sinking into depression, thinking of Mirian, his parents, his brothers. When he'd lived in Tegucigalpa, he hadn't been much inclined to visit his kin or even think much about them. Distance had given him a different point of view on his own family. He watched his father turning sixty, and while he'd only actually lived a few years with him, he'd always possessed a sort of precocious astral communication that would carry him on the wings of a thought to wherever his father might be. He lived with his mother for a few years, but his childhood made a traveler out of him: he never stayed put in any one house, never came to feel any house was his own, he was in them all and none belonged to him. He lived with uncles and aunts, grandfathers and grandmothers, a few years with Dad and some with Mom, which was maybe why he still shied away from conversations about his family. No one could recall him mentioning his mother, quoting his father or seeking out his brothers.

With two dollars in your pocket you couldn't aspire to much. The depression grew and he shrunk. It reduced him, like an adult returning, unstoppably, to beyond his mother's womb, splitting into two meaningless things, an egg and a spermatozoa. He looked for a drink in the apartment and found nothing, nor would he ever, because Mairena took religion quite seriously, seriously enough to be a deacon in a nearby church.

Not the television, nor pornography, nor music, nor reading could mend the split between the egg and the spermatozoa, which the depression had brought on. None could turn him into a human being, or even into a defenseless baby on the twentieth floor of a South Bronx project building. He thought about diving into the void and cursed his lack of courage.

At midnight, as the nightly civil war began on the streets of the South Bronx and he couldn't bear it a second longer, he decided to go out for a walk. He combed his hair and dressed up in the only suit he owned. He went downstairs, walked several blocks. He deliberately approached some of the gangs prowling on street corners. He went right up to them so they'd finish him off, which greatly confused the boys in the gangs. They weren't used to this. They cleared the way for him, looked at each other dumbstruck, and mumbled among themselves that the man in the suit must be crazy. He walked far from his building. He walked fearlessly. Still, what he was searching for—death—never stopped him in his tracks. It was as if death were amusing itself at the expense of the living, and when someone came looking for it, it would hide on purpose. On the last rung of desperation, he stopped in front of a gang that was banging chains and flashing knives. A Nuyorican asked him what his story was. Eduardo answered him recklessly. For some unexplainable reason the gang member didn't pay attention to him. Eduardo asked him to tell the others to kill him. The gang member laughed and passed on the request, and they all laughed. The Nuyorican told him they weren't murderers, it wasn't like that at all, they might attack and fight with other gangs, but wouldn't kill anyone just because they asked for it. "We ain't murderers, bro', when we kill it's accidental."

Eduardo went back to the apartment. He called Mirian and told her how sad he was. The weeping infected the little worm which, on that occasion, slid down the snail-shaped spiral staircase, like a teeny river, like ear drops.

The D reached the Kingsbridge station. Eduardo woke up Casagrande. They got off. Inside the station they walked one block uptown, which Casagrande suggested to avoid walking by that place, so mysterious and unknown to Eduardo.

23

Javier and Eduardo were snorting up in the small apartment on West 91st Street. They did up the drugs and quenched their thirst with beer. Javier suggested they walk along Riverside Park.

"It's pretty cold," Eduardo replied as he looked out from the ninth floor window.

"Blow is divine, and even better combined. It's got all four seasons of the year. All you have to do is choose which one you want to be in. Do another toot and a little joint, and fast-forward to summer. It's like a time machine." Javier unwrapped the tinfoil, cut two lines on the table, snorted and let Eduardo have his turn.

"Welcome summer," Javier yelled. "It's midsummer, who cares if history says it's been sixty years since we lived through this cold a winter. Cold doesn't exist, it's just an illusion."

Eduardo laughed and looked out the window: "It's true, it doesn't exist. That white layer you see everywhere, I thought it was snow but it's not, it's lava, burning lava."

They left the apartment, went walking in the snow and came to the grove of trees on the banks of the Hudson River. They were the sole owners of the river; there wasn't a shadow of a human being to be seen. On Sundays in winter, and especially winters as harsh as the one they were experiencing, most city dwellers in New York stayed at home. A few cars crawled by on the nearby streets. A few panhandlers were freezing to death on park benches. The New York authorities usually patrolled the places where the homeless stayed, picked them up and gathered them in heated places strategically located throughout Grand Central Station.

Eduardo and Javier swept the snow off a bench with their gloved hands and sat down facing the sleeping river. The drugs had made them silent. They were together and not together at the same time. With his eyes fastened on some undetermined point in the river, Javier began, as usual, to talk aloud as if someone were listening. It seemed as if the only thing that mattered to him was satisfying that imperious need to say something, even when he couldn't hear himself, or maybe even when he couldn't understand himself, which could be for better or worse.

He spoke in a tongue apparently foreign to his own ears, after which he heard an ongoing buzz like the white noise from a radio left on after the station's gone off the air. It was as if he were traveling in a spaceship, full of white noise, that would vanish among the far-away stars.

"I loved the Honduran woman from the southern United States. Little old me put my life on the line for her. I picked her up, rid her of her vices. The only vice I couldn't rid her of was her nymphomania. I was more a good guy than a bad guy, had more virtues than shortcomings. She betrayed me. I was running fast at the peak of my career, I knew my business and worked harder at it for her future happiness. My life in the South became like a Golgotha when she and her mother joined forces to conspire against me. Because of her I landed in that damned city where I knew no one; there were no trains, no buses, you had to have a damned car to go out, or a lot of money for cabs, and I had nothing. That whore of a Honduran woman from the southern United States went out alone or with her family and came back any time she felt like it just because her parents were on her side and I didn't have a penny with which to run away."

Eduardo wasn't listening either. Javier's words would not go anywhere, not even into the river because it was frozen, or into the air because it was still. His words could only fall on his own ears, but they were distorted like an echoing cry for help, the original cry indistinguishable and therefore confusing to anyone running to the rescue.

While Javier traveled to the past to squeeze it dry, to destroy it with the power of memory, Eduardo traveled to the future to destroy his present, a hopeless one, depressing and weighted down by financial distress.

His performance in the film had been extraordinary. Some critics were comparing him to Dustin Hoffman, others called him the new Robert De Niro. The paparazzi followed him diligently: they wanted to know about his childhood, his life in Honduras, his life in New York, his loves, his intimacies, but he eluded them, his bodyguards protecting him, forming a human barricade so he could pass untouched all the way to his white stretch limousine. He'd decided it would be white because of his love of snow. His personal secretaries kept him updated on his success, and several famous film directors were interested in having him work in more than one new production, but he gave his colleagues' invitations higher priority than business matters. That afternoon the most important thing he had to do was honor the invitation his friend and colleague Robin Williams had sent him, to celebrate his birthday over dinner . . .

"I detest jazz and blues and everything that even remotely reminds me of the Honduran woman from the southern United States. When I picked her up I knew nothing about drugs of any kind, and thanks to her I came to discover marijuana and more. I got her off drugs and turned her into another woman—beautiful, well-mannered. My mother-in-law was a hateful, evil old woman, a fanatic of the anti-cockroach sect, a woman who never followed the sect's doctrines. Because she had a neighbor who was adding a second story on to his house, and she was dying of envy, she clamored for the cockroaches to destroy the house, and told people he was paying for it with money from drug sales. The old lady didn't even suspect that her daughter was smoking marijuana and doing cocaine and sleeping with several men at once in her own house, until stupid me allowed her into my life. And I was so näive I thought she'd change, she'd appreciate my grappling with Honduran society. They all knew I'd married a drug addict, an ex-dancer in five cabarets in the fuckin' South . . ."

He was an Oscar nominee for Best Actor, and the Central American presidents had all gathered to honor him on behalf of their countries. In his country, in Honduras, there was national coverage so that no one there would miss that historic moment in the country's arts when he, Eduardo Lin, was to be awarded the Seventh Art's most coveted statuette. The broadcasts carried a lead-in by the president of the republic, who extolled the glory his countryman had bestowed on their land from Hollywood. He got telegrams from everywhere, from personalities in film, literary and political circles. There were so many telegrams it took fifteen days to read them all to him. Many women sought him out to win him over and marry this most famous and coveted bachelor, but he could always escape. Besides, he was preparing a sumptuous marriage in his native country, with his beloved Mirian . . .

"Fortunately I never had a child with her. My life would be sadder if I'd had a child by someone who didn't deserve my son. I'm lucky she had an abortion. The damned bitch stole my savings, my assets, my businesses, manipulated my family and turned them against me. I'm lucky there were no children, because I'd be the most wretched man on earth.

"My mother-in-law stopped speaking to me after she woke up one time and jarred all of us who were sleeping senseless because she'd dreamt about the Almighty. He'd forbidden her to speak to me because I was with the Armageddon crew, whose presence could already be detected with the rise of the great empire of the North (the ex-Soviet Union in this case), and it wasn't a dream, but a revelation the Almighty had given her, to alert her that Satan the Devil was lodged in her very house . . ."

After several entreaties and a million-dollar offer, he allowed himself to be interviewed by Playboy. *He didn't consent to the interview for the money but because he wanted to fulfill a childhood dream of someday being interviewed by that magazine. His agents took charge of the session with* Playboy, *and so it was that he came to pose for the magazine's photographer and answer questions.*

PLAYBOY: *When did your interest in film first bud? When did you discover you were an actor?*

EDUARDO LIN: *Well, it's been since forever, I think. Do you know the first thing I did when I was born, after the doctor slapped me on the ass to make me cry? I stuck my tongue out at him. An ingenious beginning, don't you think?*

"The trauma was getting to me so much that one night I dreamed that I was Satan running full speed through an endless desert. I was terrified, escaping my mother-in-law who was chasing me in a biplane. I was running exhausted on the sand and the terror my mother-in-law struck in me was so bad that none of my Satanic powers worked. I ran and ran looking for some end to the desert or some oasis where I could commit suicide. The desert kept spreading out before me and my mother-in-law was yelling the crudest things at me from the biplane, things which even I, being the Devil and all, had never heard. It was unbelievable to hear my mother-in-law utter so many filthy expressions and use language to inflict torture. Plus she was threatening me with a giant can of bug repellant. I ran through the desert and my mother-in-law in the biplane was about to catch up with me when, away in the distance, I saw a human soul, which made me happy because I figured I, the Devil, had somebody running over to save me . . ."

PB: *Do you believe this country has opportunities for people with talent?*

EL: *I think that from the moment you say someone is talented you shouldn't ask yourself whether such and such a country has opportunities. If you are truly talented, you don't wait for a place to have opportunities, you make them up. That's part of having talent. Look at me!*

PB: *Have you fallen in love with any of your co-stars? Would you marry an actress?*

EL: *I can't fall in love because I'm already in love with a woman from my country. Her name is Mirian, and please don't put her name in this interview because if you do she'll kill me: you don't know our women. I have nothing against actresses—there are many very beauti-*

ful ones. For me, if I didn't have a girlfriend I still wouldn't marry an actress, because we Latinos are very jealous, and I am very jealous and wouldn't allow my actress to kiss anyone. She'd have to work in films with no kissing.

"I had the biggest scare you can imagine: the human being coming toward me was the woman from the southern United States. Even though I was the Devil, she and her mother had me between a rock and a hard place, between the hard place and their claws. I swear, even being the Devil, I couldn't have suffered greater damage if I'd run into a cross or taken a shower in holy water, than bucking up against my mother-in-law from the South and the daughter from the South. Maybe inspired by the terror itself, one of my devilish tricks worked just as the biplane grazed my head and the other one threatened me with these terrifying prefab nails. Right there in the desert I split into two devils, and escaped by becoming one and the other, both running in opposite directions. We two devils ran in terror listening to the cackles of the Honduran women from the southern United States, which stuck in our ears until they bled . . ."

PB: *Do you mean you're against kissing?*

EL: *No, not at all. The kiss is the symbol of love and I'm not against love. I am against anyone who isn't me kissing the woman I love. That's very different.*

PB: *So if you got married, you'd stop working in films in which you had to kiss an actress?*

EL: *No. I don't think so. It's my job, you know. And I'm passionate about my work.*

PB: *Isn't this stance of yours like* machismo?

EL: *Marxism? That's out of fashion, and if it isn't, it's been at a standstill for at least a couple of centuries.*

PB: *Machismo, not Marxismo.*

EL: *No, I don't think it is. Don't forget, I'm Latino. And we aren't* machistas, *we're passionate. And the concept of passion is pretty broad—you know what I mean?*

"I don't ever want to go back to Honduras. I won't go back. I don't want to know anything about that country. I want to devote myself to working and getting off that damn drug. I can't take the damn blow any more. What am I doing? *Mamá, Papá,* what do you think I'm doing at the age of forty-one in the Capital of the World and the Land of Opportunity? They think I'm making progress. My poor folks. What do you think I'm doing if I have a good job and don't even send you a single dollar because I spend it all on the damn blow? Who can help me out of this hell? Who put me here? It wasn't me alone with that Honduran whore from the Southern United States! *Papá,* what's your favorite son's name? Answer, old man: his name is Javieeeeeer!"

PB: *What do you hate the most?*

EL: *War. I hate war. It's not that I'm afraid of death, of my own death. No. That's different. Someone else's death is one thing, your own is another. If something in my life as an artist could be of any good, if as an actor I could leave something behind for humanity, it would be a huge NO to war. Any war, you know. An atomic bomb hurts me the same whether it's dropped on Tegucigalpa or Havana, Tokyo or New York, Bangladesh (well, they don't need a bomb, the cruel bomb of famine is enough), or London. You get me? A bomb dropped on any part of the planet, any place inhabited by human beings, animals or nature, hurts me. It hurts me when any part of the planet is destroyed, and most of all when it's not from natural causes but because humankind itself has done it.*

"IS SOMEONE GOING TO GET ME OUT OF THIS?"

Javier's scream brought Eduardo back from his trip to the future. Javier ran through the snow on the banks of the Hudson River. He ran off screaming words that were barely intelligible. Eduardo watched him running. He saw himself reflected in that mirror. He felt guilty for doing nothing to keep Javier from going down that road, from which there was practically no turning back. He blamed himself, too, for taking the first steps toward the infinite. He felt himself getting small, every passing second turning him into something microscopic, invisible, like the Hudson River might become if a weak match were thrown into it at that moment.

Javier came running back. “Let’s go back to the apartment. I’m freezing.”

From the ninth floor window of the West 91st Street apartment, Eduardo looked sadly at the snow falling once again on another winter’s day. Javier invited him to do a bit more coke and reactivate himself; Eduardo refused and thought about telling Javier that he shouldn’t either, but Javier’s eyes told him it was a waste of energy to try to put a lightning bolt that had already broken loose back into the sky.

24

Doña Rosaura turned halfway around in bed and said No, no, and no, not until she saw that that bum was out of the house. His eyes were open in the half-light; he was excited but couldn't guarantee her anything. He attempted again: he touched her knee, she let him climb on top, she got comfortable for him so he could feel the triangle of her underwear. He thought everything would turn out okay; she took his hand and submerged it in the triangle of the jersey, led it through the jungle region. "But you promise me that bum will be out of my house as soon as possible."

Don Jonás yanked his hand away. "Don't forget he's my son. Besides, as far as I know he's no bum."

Doña Rosaura walled herself in with the blanket, turned over on her side with her back to him. "Figure out what you're going to do: you can either masturbate or do something else."

Don Jonás switched on the little lamp on the night table, reached with his foot for his pants, which were lying on the floor, shook them in search of cigarettes, opened the little drawer in the night table, touched the full pack, pulled one out and put the lighter close to it, giving it a long pull. By the dim reddish light of the little lamp, it looked like a frozen firefly.

Doña Rosaura pretended to talk in her sleep. "It's so hot," but she didn't disrobe completely, only the part of her body that was pointed at Don Jonás. He looked at the white skin peeking out from the bikini panties; he wanted to grope it, touch it, feel it, but he didn't dare. The idea of taking her up on her suggestion crossed his mind more than once: to masturbate. The moment was right: he knew that just looking at that pair of buttocks peeking out from the panties could bring about the end. He was ashamed of his thoughts; he was too old for those things. In times past, years ago when he and his classmates had cut a peephole in the roof of the ladies' bathroom in his house, it was different; everything was allowed at that age.

He stubbed the cigarette out; Doña Rosaura was breathing as if she were asleep. He was trapped in sleeplessness. He stuck his hand under her panties and stroked. She acted as if nothing were happening. He unsnapped her; she turned halfway around with her short hairs pointing skyward. Don Jonás climbed on top. At the precise moment when he was about to invade her, she clapped a hand over the triangle like a mousetrap. "But you promise me that bum will leave my house?"

Don Jonás got off her, clasped his hands across his forehead. "You spoiled the whole thing."

She turned halfway around again. "I've got nothing to lose. You're the one who doesn't know what to do."

He switched off the little lamp. "This scene's been playing for fifteen days."

She covered herself from head to toe. "And it will continue to play until I see that bum's out of my house."

Don Jonás spat at the bedside. "This is the last time I'm telling you; Fernando isn't a bum and he's not in anyone's way except yours. He gets along well with Mirian and Ricardo. I don't see any problem with it."

She gritted her teeth, moving as far away from him as possible. "It's up to you. You're going to rot with your lust if you don't do what I tell you to."

Don Jonás smiled along with the semi-darkness. Three weeks had gone by since the thieves had visited the house. He was pleased with them, he'd even gone so far as to give them an award. If it weren't for them, he'd have never discovered what he had in his own house; he'd have never found something better to shelter him from the storm. He got cozy with the blanket up against his chest; he was happy. The following day he would ask Jimena, the maid, to wear the one she'd worn the first time: the short, plaid one, wide as an umbrella.

Mirian, the child spy trained and inspired by the Cold War, walked slowly, moving away from the door to her parent's bedroom, which she'd kept ajar to watch and eavesdrop on the sexual battle between the makers of her days.

The psychiatrist agreed: "At that age, when this thing you're telling me about took place, did you have any notion of what sex is?"

Mirian smiled. "Know? If what you mean is did I know, no, but I did know it wasn't something bad; the bad part I attributed to my mother's rejection. I learned that from the movies. Have you noticed that spies in films always end up in bed with someone?"

Behind the little hidden window, there was no one.

"Do you think they ever suspected you were spying on them?"

"My dad: I think he believes he caught me a few times."

"And whose side did you take?"

"My dad's side, because I didn't think he was doing anything wrong, and if my mother didn't want to, then it made sense for him to do it with the maid. Besides, my mother called Fernando, my half-brother on my Dad's side, a bum, and Fernando and I have always loved each other no matter who our parents are."

"I'll speak to your parents."

"Don't tell them about the maid. They still fight about it."

"I promise. Have you continued writing?"

"Yes. What do you think of Michael Jackson?"

"What? Look, for our next session, bring me something you've written recently. I think that will be our last session before your trip to New York."

The psychiatrist had the air of a professional who was happy with his work. Mirian got to her feet, opened the door, and said, "Don't you think we're making progress? Did you notice that we didn't even mention James Bond in this session?"

25

Eduardo and his friend Leo were walking along Grand Concourse looking for porno video stores. They went into several and couldn't make up their minds, mostly because the thought of being seen by someone scandalized Eduardo, even if they were people he'd never seen before and might never see again. He had come at the insistence of Leo, a man who described himself as highly sexual.

"I have an idea," said Eduardo. "I don't know 42nd Street, but I've heard a lot about it. Why don't we wait for nighttime and pay a visit to some place down there?"

"Nothing could be better. I've always said you're a thinker."

"What about in the meantime?"

"We'll drink a couple of Buds in brown paper bags so the police don't use us for entertainment."

"Done."

They left the supermarket with two sixpacks of beer. They looked to one side of the Grand Concourse and to the other, searching for the right place to drink and talk at no risk.

"I've got it," said Leo. "There's a park near your house. It's perfect."

When they got to the corner of the park, Leo set his sights on a small white house with huge trees and a few pigeons pecking at the grass; the house was surrounded by high black bars, even though it was part of the same park.

"I admire that guy. He was marvelous," Leo said as if he were talking to himself.

Eduardo looked at the house and couldn't see anything special about it.

"It's a white house, so what's new?"

Leo looked him squarely in the eye, completely surprised.

"Don't tell me you don't know who lived here!"

"I'm sorry to let you down, but I don't."

"Eduardo, this was the home of a genius. This is Edgar Allan Poe's house."

"I can't believe it. Let's go in," said Eduardo, jaw gaping, half-smiling, dumbstruck.

"Of course. Poe lived here. This is Poe Park, in his honor."

Inside, the house seemed cramped but clean. After crossing a small porch, they entered the first bedroom, with a small bed where the young Virginia, Poe's great love, slept and passed away. In front of the bed stood a bust of Poe, with his eyes on the bed as if watching over his loved one's slumber. There were clothes and small objects that had belonged to the couple. Eduardo and Leo climbed up a narrow, spiral staircase to the second floor, where the genius wrote. Here a slide presentation told the story of Poe's life, of his trips from Baltimore to Philadelphia, from Philadelphia to New York, of the misery in which one of the greatest men on the planet had found himself.

As they were about to leave the house, a seemingly magnetic force kept them from doing so.

"Well," said Leo, paying homage to the *maestro,* "let's sit down here in front of his house and drink in his honor."

And they stayed there, next to the iron fence bars, silent and thirsty.

Leo's life was extremely routine: in the mornings he ran to Queens College to take classes, and from Queens College he flew to Hostos Community College at 149th and Grand Concourse. Then he'd come back late at night to his small apartment in Queens to study. On weekends he taught private classes for a few extra dollars. His life had to be that routine, not only because of the scarcity of time, but because of his meager assets. In times past he'd had the good life in New York. He'd met a New Yorker at a theater that was hosting a Nicaraguan film festival. He'd been wearing a T-shirt that said *NICARAGUA LIBRE*, with a drawing of Sandino holding his fists high. When she saw him walking down the hall, Sandy approached him and asked, "Are you from Nicaragua?"

For some reason he couldn't figure out, he said yes, maybe to have a little conversation with her, maybe because he didn't know anyone in the theater and she, it seemed, was by herself. She got excited and asked him if he'd been a soldier. One lie led to another. They went in together to see *Azul,* a film about social injustices and revolutionary struggles sung and narrated by Nicaragua's poets. There was a cocktail party afterward and Sandy stuck close by Leo who, fortunately, had read a good amount about Nicaragua. Sandy invited Leo to a restaurant and then to her apartment on 28th and Park Avenue. He kept spinning tall tales of combat, in which he was almost always on the front line. It might have seemed hard to believe if he hadn't had the required bona fides: an operation scar across his arm, the other arm in similar shape, a crater near his navel, an uneven clavicle and a pronounced scar on his right foot, which left no room for doubt.

Leo amused himself with every lie. Sandy got more excited. And so they made love for a few days until she made him an offer to move into her apartment, because she knew the poverty he lived in, somewhere far away in Brooklyn. He accepted. The first days it seemed marvelous to live in Manhattan with everything at hand. But soon, he was swept over by a feeling of responsibility that plunged him in to sadness. He wasn't in love with Sandy and he knew he never would be. At first he'd lied as a lark, then the game started getting serious, and he didn't dare shatter his heroic image. How could he tell her that the scar on his arm was from a car accident, the other one was from falling off a roof he was repairing, that he'd unhinged his clavicle diving into a river in his village, that the crater near his navel was from a bat bite, the scar on the right foot from running around in the fields, running shoeless until his little foot stepped on a Coca Cola bottle shard?

His dignity as a revolutionary, as Francisco Morazán's fervent follower, with principles based on mutual respect between human beings, was crumbling, and he wasn't willing to let his insides fall apart over an apartment in Manhattan, or all the comforts in it, or over Sandy's salary, which she was already learning to share with him. So one day he went back to Brooklyn, but his little apartment was no longer there.

One of his *compañeros* set him up in Queens, and he said good-bye to Sandy with a final lie: the war was over in his country, and it was very important for him to go back and continue struggling for his people in a civilized way, the way of dialogue, the way of peaceful coexistence. She believed him, even though he didn't let her come with him to the airport, using the reputation Latin men have for being sentimental as his excuse: he didn't want to cry or see her cry. That way, he let himself off the hook for her suffering and saved himself from having to undo the myth she had created in her mind. It turned out best for both of them. Some day when she went to Nicaragua she could just ask about *Comandante Leo*, one of the heroes of the Sandinista revolution, a veteran of that war.

Poe Park was filling up with bums, drunkards, junkies, nearby neighbors and newspaper readers. Poe's house was a minute away from where Eduardo lived, and he couldn't figure out why he hadn't discovered it earlier. They each popped open their fourth beer, and with each beer they drank, their passion opened up, too.

Leo talked about history: he recalled how Francisco Morazán had been deeply concerned about Central America's becoming a single nation. The isthmus would have acquired great strength if Morazanist ideals had come to be.

Eduardo traveled to the past without listening to what Leo was saying. He went back to his childhood, when the first flashes of his acting genius had sparked. He had always walked around with his forehead wrinkled; he imitated John Wayne's forehead in films where Indians were murdered wholesale. Another time, he shaved in a widow's peak in an attempt to imitate Jack Nicholson. His classmates asked him what had happened to him and he pretended not to know what they meant. He showed his large forehead proudly and haughtily, its shape pointing crownward, and, as if that weren't enough, he shaved his eyebrows like Nicholson, too, or like Dracula.

Meanwhile, Leo was still saying that the Morazanist ideal fell through because of the Costa Ricans, and Costa Rica would be such a beautiful country if Costa Ricans didn't exist, because they thought of themselves as Europeans and were always opposed to uniting their forces with the other Central American countries' forces.

Eduardo jumped from the past to the future, to a gathering of stars he was attending in the company of a beautiful woman who, naturally, was not an actress.

They were elegantly dressed, and Nick Nolte cracked a couple of jokes and pulled his date as far away as he could from Warren Beatty, who'd already laid eyes on her. All his fellow stars hailed Eduardo for his performance in a newly opened film directed by his friend and favorite director, Woody Allen. He stopped to chat with William Hurt and congratulate him for his brilliant work in Kiss of the Spider Woman. *Hurt was courteous and returned the greetings by congratulating Eduardo and welcoming him to the club of the stars. He had a toast with Meryl Streep. He spoke Spanish, despite the mockery of those who didn't understand, with Edward James Olmos. He danced an oldie with Sonia Braga. Danny DeVito greeted him with a nod of the head and wiggling his eyebrows. He'd been rendered mute: a giant hamburger kept him from any form of oral communication.*

Leo and Francisco Morazán had won the war in Central America; a single President would be elected and after everything was in order, Panama and Belize would be invited to join the Republic of Greater Central America. If these countries didn't consent voluntarily, an invasion would be planned for the following months, all for the well-being of the people of both nations.

At the party Eduardo realized he'd made it; some people loved him and others were already beginning to envy him, because sooner or later he would be someone's rival when it came time to nominate actors for that marvelous statuette of the big screen, the Oscar.

Night fell and the beers ran out in Poe Park. Leo was finishing his exposé about how to re-ignite the Morazanist struggle for a united Central America. Eduardo answered, "Yes, of course, sure," but he was truly elsewhere; he was just coming back from a *wonderful* party.

They went into several establishments on 42nd Street, between Seventh and Eighth Avenues, flipping through porno magazines from the unimaginable to the most grotesque things to which a human being could stoop. They went into strip joints. They went into private rooms where the woman strips and strikes any pose the client requests as long as he puts a dollar down for every new pose; and if he wants to, he can masturbate, but can never touch her, unless he feels like risking a broken window and dealing with the police.

They went up to the second floor where someone announced that customers could fondle the dancers. It was a sort of rodeo, a big circle in which the naked women danced. There were small rooms around the circle like standing caskets with a little pane-less window, like a circular train with windows only facing the interior, through which customers could stick their hands and feel the cheeks and the vaginas because the little windows are right at that level of the body. The customers poke their hands through holding a dollar face upward. After paying most fondled with one hand while masturbating with the other. Eduardo peeped through his little window like someone peeking through a train window and saw the circle of hands calling to cheeks and vaginas. The hands were desperate, like a starving throng or like the hands of someone screaming for help to save from drowning. There it was, that circle of hands of all sizes and colors screaming desperately like crazed pantomimists. The number of cheeks and vaginas were not enough for so many hands, and the cheeks and the vaginas passed from hand to hand as if they were volleyballs being thrown over one side of the net to the other. The hands losing hold of the ball and not enjoying that brief moment were writhing there as if in a collective epileptic seizure from the anguish of losing what they'd had.

Eduardo recoiled in horror. He could not believe what he saw. He could not think, despite his penchant for philosophizing. He looked for Leo in the little window next to his, so they could leave, go somewhere else. A kind of shame for being human was overtaking him.

26

Javier had lent Eduardo his small but cozy apartment on West 91st Street. He would stay there for the two weeks that Javier would be in Boston, and the main objective in having it at his disposal was named Andrea. He knew she was willing. His problem was insecurity over whether he could manage to rekindle her lost excitement. A flash of inspiration crossed his mind. It occurred to him that Andrea's excitement might hinge on the décor.

On the seventh day of Javier's absence, he invited Andrea for a walk in Manhattan. They visited the Museum of Modern Art, an ice-skating show in Rockefeller Center, a few art galleries in the Village and stepped into a bookstore.

After the marathon tour of the city, Eduardo asked Andrea if she wanted to see the new apartment he'd moved into on West 91st Street. She accepted with a smile, knowing what she was getting into. They took the subway to West 96th Street.

As they ascended in the apartment elevator, Eduardo kissed her long and deep. He fondled her legs over her coat, managed to slip his hands onto her bare breasts, half-unbuttoned her coat and blouse and felt her hot skin. She fondled him as best she could. He didn't give her the chance to do much; he had her hands pinned down.

Before opening the apartment door, Eduardo asked the infinite universe to help him carry out his mission. He was afraid the same story as with the other men would repeat itself. They had gotten Andrea to their apartments, but it ended abruptly if her intellectual curiosity wasn't satisfied. He, whose seductive charms had never failed, did not want to disappoint her or himself.

When Andrea entered, she stumbled over something.

"What's this?"

"My rug," he replied.

She found it funny, but took her shoes off so as not to mess up the makeshift rug he had constructed, with a little duct tape, out of past issues of *The New York Times Book Review, The New Yorker,* and *The Village Voice.* She took a few steps in her stockinged feet, perplexed. Staring down at her from the wall were Walt Whitman, Marguerite Yourcenar and Jean-Paul Sartre. She advanced to the wall covered with lithographs, posters cut from magazines, and small pieces of folk art.

"Have a seat," he said to her. "Something to drink?"

She didn't reply. She was suddenly absorbed in the library on another wall. On one of the shelves, a silver statuette of Vladimir Nabokov greeted her.

"Have a seat," he said again, and when he saw that she didn't go for the chair, he pointed out a structure made entirely of books. "That's the chair. That's how I am—my friends think I'm nuts. Look at the bed."

There were books and more books stacked in the shape of a bed with some sticking out like pillows. She wasn't prepared for this much. She took off her coat, closed her eyes and began taking off her blouse as she softly beckoned to him. He didn't respond immediately, but watched her so she would grow even more excited. She slipped out of her skirt, and as she grew more desperate she moved to take her stockings off, and because they didn't slip right off, she began to rip them off. Eduardo, unable to proceed any further as an observer, stepped in to become an actor.

Hot and naked, they slammed into the wall under Pound's accomplice eyes, before Kafka's stupefaction, Borges' curiosity, Hemingway's envy and Neruda's excitement. They were all watching that divine inferno from their places on the wall, listening to the frenzied breathing, the search for the androgynous.

He took her in his arms to the bed of books. She was desperate to get there. Two yards seemed like a Sahara to cross on foot. They kissed and continued groping each other. Eduardo grabbed her hair, bit one of her breasts, pinched the other, passed the palm of his hand over her pubic hairs, hovering over the area, feeling for its heat. There was no time to lose, she couldn't wait for a single grain more of sand to fall in the hourglass before she was penetrated, and he sensed it and moved to fulfill her wishes. Asimov was desperately in need of an air conditioner with that meteoric rear end ensnaring him, covering him with fire and resurrection. Dostoyevsky, in masculine solidarity, held up Eduardo's knee, which was searching for support. There was the ineffable gaiety of Cabrera Infante's *Tres Tristes Tigres*. Mailer was there holding one ankle, Kosinski the other, Papini caring for the souls which by then must have left their bodies. Faulkner kept his pipe from coming into contact with the flaming bodies so as not to provoke a greater and more fearful hecatomb than the one already under way. Eduardo sunk one elbow into Dante, another into Shakespeare. Andrea's hair voluptuously blanketed Barthelme, Sábato and Flaubert. The bed was falling apart; Balzac tumbled down, followed by Vonnegut, along with the reproachful eye Tolstoy cast from beneath a feminine ankle. Torrents of sweat flowed like steaming lava from the couple's backs. Andrea's hands grew desperate as they announced the oncoming climax; she squeezed Cortázar in one hand, Chekhov in the other, sunk her teeth into Camus. The bed was falling apart like the Tower of Babel. Carlos Fuentes, Umberto Eco and Allen Ginsberg tumbled down. Eduardo wanted to come, too, but he was uncomfortable on the pile of books, and Andrea's buttocks slid around from Graves to Wilde, from Rilke to Martí, from Capote to Algren, so that he could not settle on an adequate position. Either luck was on his side that day, or the writers' cosmic ghosts were willing to help him come, for suddenly he felt himself get comfortable in mid-thrust; Andrea felt it too, when her buttocks landed on a gigantic, illustrated edition of *Don Quijote de la Mancha*.

Eduardo sensed the train approaching the city, the city wanting the train to approach, the sea opening to the submarine penetrating it, the submarine wanting to penetrate the sea, the rocket wanting to break through the cloud, the cloud wishing for the rocket to break through, the fruit dreaming of being pierced by the stinger, the stinger finding the fruit. They set off on a trip, away they went. Andrea had barely time enough to yell for the train to do it outside, she might get pregnant. The conductor in the distance barely heard the cry, he was already coming. Eduardo writhed, ejaculating as he'd rarely done before. And he stayed over Andrea, on his knees. He stayed there for a few seconds. When he recovered, he laughed heartily. He kept laughing and she couldn't understand why. Through unbridled laughter he pointed to the book on which his ejaculate had concentrated, and Andrea also laughed when she read, between the letters with no semen and those with less semen: *Anthology of Honduran Literature.*

Eduardo, still unable to contain his laughter, said, "I just impregnated my country's literature. Be fruitful and multiply!"

27

Mirian looked at the telephone. Her father had warned her to be careful with the long distance phone calls or she'd end up bankrupting him. She automatically picked up the phone and dialed. One ring was enough for Eduardo's voice to appear in her room. He couldn't sleep either. She asked him to come back, and had he been able to follow his own voice up through the satellite, he would have abandoned all his projects then and there. He'd bid the Big Apple good-bye; he wouldn't say good-bye to Casagrande or anyone. Eduardo was sure he would be happy. They talked about his return. He tried to change the subject and told her about Edgar Allan Poe's house, about the singular love between Poe and Virginia. She wanted him to return. He told her about his new friendships, about the smiling future that awaited her. She offered him a ticket for the following day, in case he had no money, and insisted it was important for him to return. He told her about the economic difficulties he would suffer in Honduras. Regardless, he'd be ashamed for her parents to support him. She hung up.

Eduardo pulled out a cigarette, sparked it up in the half-light, and sat down in front of the window to look at the darkness of Valentine Avenue. He imagined Mirian in her room, sleepless, her gaze on the darkness of the ceiling. He really wasn't so far removed from deciding to go back. He'd done absolutely nothing in New York, nothing that would make losing Mirian worthwhile, because nothing anywhere was worth as much as Mirian. Distance had taught him to love her as never before.

What would he do in Honduras? Mirian was probably right. He could end up working for her father, and money wouldn't be scarce. It wouldn't bother him to be a businessman, no, he could perfectly well do that, but first he had a challenge to meet, and if he was able to pull it off, then he could dedicate himself to anything and not be unhappy.

He was sure New York was getting the best of him. It was turning him into a construction worker: work with Charlie remodeling interiors, painting walls, tearing down ceilings . . . In the evening, he'd go back to his apartment and make phone calls or wait for people to call him. He'd drink at least six beers to fall asleep. On weekends, he'd go to parties and find nothing there but the same routine of listening to others' failures or triumphs. When would his triumph, or failure come? As he smoked his cigarette, he got up to find something to drink in the kitchen. Fortunately, Casagrande always had alcoholic beverages and a joint hidden somewhere; it was part of his esoterism, a way of keeping touch with other flights, other heights. He went back to his quarters with half a bottle of whiskey that Casagrande had zealously guarded for some special guest. He drank the whiskey straight from the bottle. Instead of liquor, it was as if he were drinking Mirian, as if she were going down his throat in liquid form, tying him in knots until it all unraveled in depressive sobs right there on the twelfth floor.

He drank down the half bottle. He dialed the number in Tegucigalpa and immediately the little worm started tickling his ear, descending until it found the nest and settled there like a boy lost in the storm who comes back to seek safe haven in his mother's arms. Once it settled in, the little worm pressed him to return, first just the voice, then the cracking voice and finally the liquid voice, tears drenching the nest, making it swell like a dry, compact sponge suddenly exposed to the rain.

The whiskey's results were positive; it gave him the courage to realize that his struggle was in New York, and until he broke through or lost altogether, he would not, could not go back. To freeze the liquid voice reaching his eardrum he uttered a lie, which was not entirely a lie, but which he knew would have a positive effect, so that his little worm could retire from its New York nest to its bed in Tegucigalpa to sleep happily.

"Mirian, *cariño*, I'll go back soon. Here's some news that should make you happy, or at least help you wait for me more patiently. Starting tomorrow, you can say I've taken one of the most important steps in my life. As of tomorrow, I'm working on Broadway, in one of the most famous theaters there."

28

"Where's my bottle of whiskey?"

The scream cut quickly through the living room and hallway and stopped right in front of Eduardo's room. He was awake and, up to that moment, had no great urge to get on his feet. He smiled. He got out of bed, yawned, grabbed a towel and walked down the hallway to the common bathrooms.

"Where's my bottle of whiskey?"

This time the scream stopped in the bathroom. He turned on the shower and began the combination game—which had irritated him so many times when he was in a rush—with the cold and hot water.

"You look good," Casagrande said as he placed the boiling coffee pot on the table. "Have a cup of coffee to scare away the cold and the hangover. You owe me a bottle of Jack Daniel's."

"Half a bottle," Eduardo replied as he filled his coffee cup.

"I had it in a single bottle. If I sue you, you'll lose the case."

"Well, I have the bottle in my room. I'm going to save it and buy a half bottle and pour it into your bottle."

"Now you're speaking Spanish, or perfect English," Casagrande laughed. "Who called you last night?"

"You're funny, Casa. I thought you were sleeping."

"No, I was up waiting for a call from San Francisco."

"I called Mirian."

"Did she dump you already?"

"No, not yet."

"Andrea's very beautiful."

"I love Mirian."

"Banana, Banana, when are you going to learn? Don't forget the pragmatism you need to get ahead in a city like this. Mirian is far off, Andrea a hop away on the train."

"You're right. I should probably go back."

Casagrande told Eduardo that his photography course at Hostos Community College was over, so he put together some private classes on the same subject, which he would teach either at his students' houses or in his apartment. He said that he also had landed an exhibition of his Mexico photographs in a small Village gallery. He was not one for lofty goals or great aspirations; it was enough for him to get money for board and wine. Casagrande went on to tell the story of how he'd become a millionaire in Mexico one day (which could have been true, taking into account the exchange rate for the Mexican *peso*), and how he'd squandered his millions on his lovers, most of all on that lover from San Francisco who he'd never forget. He spoke of San Francisco with great euphoria; he loved San Francisco, not because of the trolley cars or the Golden Gate or Sausalito or the gardens with thousand-year old trees and exotic flowers or the quaintness of the city, but because of that great love, the man of his life.

Casagrande's retirement from homosexuality—as he himself defined it—consisted of not making love. It was enough to get acquainted with a boy, talk to him, stroll with him, tell him he'd read his hand and take advantage of that to fondle him, drink with him and listen and be heard, all without having sex. At Hostos he'd met a Dominican fellow who was leading him down the path of hope.

"I think that rascal, if he doesn't already suspect it, knows by now about my hormonal preferences," he told Eduardo, laughing.

Eduardo remembered that Casagrande wouldn't tell him why he didn't go to Kingsbridge Station, and seizing on Casagrande's high spirits, asked him about it.

Casagrande grabbed a pencil and paper and began to scour the kitchen from corner to corner, writing down the things he needed. He was a one-of-a-kind shopper; he could stock the kitchen with fifty dollars. He'd go to the supermarket three blocks away from the apartment on Jerome Avenue and practice all the tricks he learned in *The Golden*

Age with the Hip Generation. He'd grab a cart and walk through the supermarket without making up his mind. On the second round he'd go to the fruit and vegetable stand, choose bruised, spotted or otherwise defective produce, or if there was none, he would make some, being careful not to get caught. He looked for dented cans, and if there weren't any, he'd masterfully dent them himself against a shelf. He'd talk to the store managers and ask them to reconsider their prices; a two-dollar can of meat ended up costing forty cents, a pound of grapes thirty cents and so on. Add to that the fact that as he shopped, he ate whatever he felt like, and his trips turned out very fruitful.

"Casagrande," Eduardo said to him, "you never walk by Kingsbridge, and you don't know what you're missing. Do you know who lives, well, lived, on that corner? No less than Edgar Allan Poe."

Casagrande would have preferred for an iceberg to melt inside him. He stopped cold. He opened his mouth but said nothing. Eduardo looked at the gray hairs hanging from his beard. Casagrande placed an elbow on the table and scratched the bald spot on his head. Eduardo didn't take his eyes off him. Casagrande figured the escape hatches were closed. He decided to face the situation.

He told the story of how years ago he'd rented a modest house outside San Francisco, where he lived with the lover he couldn't forget. One day they had a fight. His lover had gotten jealous because once, Casagrande had flirted with his lover's brother, who had come over to spend the night. The next day, early in the morning, his lover went to work. Casagrande and his lover's brother stayed in the house. Casagrande was friendly, and with all his attention and knowledge about good and evil, seduced him. They made love a thousand different ways. That afternoon, the brother came home with an enormous bouquet of yellow flowers as a sign of peace and remorse for his bad behavior the night before. A huge surprise was in store for him; all the doors, including the front door, were open, and he found his younger brother in his room sleeping like a baby in the arms of his beloved. He hurled the yellow flowers on the floor and stomped on them as he unleashed a furious monologue. A carpet of petals and pollen decorated the bedroom. He got into his car and sped off. The younger brother decided to leave to avoid his older brother's return, which would have only complicated his problems.

The third day came and Casagrande had no news of his lover. The younger brother had stopped mattering to him. Prey to infinite sadness, he started drinking, smoking opium and hashish and listening to revolutionary music that he'd brought back from Mexico.

On the fifth day of loneliness, unable to scare away the insomnia, Casagrande planted himself in the middle of the room. Suddenly all the lights went out. He checked the meter and the lightbulbs, and thought *how strange; something must have gone wrong with the electricity.* He lit a candle and sat awake in the middle of the living room. Suddenly he heard a strange noise. He looked around and shuddered as he made out the figure of a big black raven outside the window. It struck terror in him; it was the first time a raven had paid him a visit. He looked for a broom to scare him away.

The raven was unfazed: in fact, his beak moved and he said, "Casagrande, Casagrande, what are you doing, Casagrande?"

When he heard the raven, he dove into an easy chair in the living room, buried his head in a cushion, and covered his ears, but nothing kept the raven's voice from reaching him.

"Casagrande, Casagrande, you're misbehaving, Casagrande," quoth the raven.

He moved off the easy chair and cursed the raven. The raven looked him in the eyes and Casagrande tried to keep the curses rolling but only his lips moved; he'd lost his voice.

"Casagrande, Casagrande, unfaithful in love, Casagrande."

He grew desperate. He threw things at the raven. The windows didn't break. He made the sign of the cross with his fingers and arms, but the raven continued, "Casagrande, Casagrande, I've come to take you away, Casagrande."

At that moment he remembered Edgar Allan Poe's poem "The Raven." He knew he had it in a book with all of Poe's short stories. A voice from the fifth dimension, an inner voice, told him what to do to keep the raven from taking him away. He found the little book in his library. He lit the logs in the fireplace and placed a knife over them. When the raven saw that, he pecked at the window. Casagrande poured gasoline on the fire to stoke it. The raven broke the window pane and flew into the house. Casagrande ran from one place to another, the raven in furious pursuit. His Mexican poncho served him well. He used it to dodge the bird like a veteran bullfighter. Casagrande made it all the way to the fireplace. The knife was red hot. He placed the Edgar Allan Poe book on the table. The raven was preparing for another attack, like a dive-bomber. Casagrande took the knife from the flames, insulating his hands with the poncho. He stabbed the book with it, slitting it from side to side. The raven screamed in horror and vanished. Then there was light.

"You're nuts, Casagrande," Eduardo laughed.

"No, *huevón,* I swear. That's why I don't walk in front of that fellow's house."

Eduardo was sure he'd just made that story up, and that he would probably never tell him the truth about his anti-Poe behavior.

"Let's go one of these days. You were probably on drugs."

"No, *huevón,* I swear, I wasn't on drugs that day. Let's not talk about it any more. Let's go to the supermarket."

29

Javier came back from Boston. He was surprised to find his apartment crammed full of books. Eduardo told him about Andrea, explaining that the books were property of some of his and Casagrande's friends. Now he had to return them. Fortunately, he'd been lucid enough to keep detailed records of who owned what. Anxious and desperate, Javier barely heard the story about Andrea and the intellectual sexploit.

"Do you have any money?" he asked Eduardo.

"Not a lot."

"Thirty?"

"Yes," and Eduardo pulled it out of his wallet and handed it to him.

"Will you come with me?"

Eduardo agreed without hesitation; he was smart enough to know what was up. Javier put on a coat; Eduardo put on his. They got to the train station. They took the 1 to 59th Street and changed to the C, which they took all the way to 125th. Night was falling. The atmosphere felt strange to Eduardo. When they got out on the street they came face to face with the grime, with the car carcasses stripped of even the smallest parts.

"This is Harlem," Javier said to him, "watch out. It's dangerous."

They walked a few blocks. Javier looked from side to side, carefully checking out every passerby. They came to a corner and stopped.

"Wait for me here," Javier said to him. "This is a Dominican restaurant—it's very cheap. Give me fifteen minutes and I'll be back; if I'm not, take the train and head out."

Eduardo refused. Javier tried to set him at ease.

"The business I'm going to take care of is dangerous; it's better if you wait for me here. Don't leave, because you never know from what angle a knife may come at you."

Eduardo's arguments worked. He preferred to accompany Javier; he felt somehow safer with Javier than alone in Harlem, which he was visiting for the first time.

They came to an apparently uninhabited apartment building. The street was dimly lit. A few Dominican and Puerto Rican teenagers pretended to be playing outside. They yelled in code. Javier explained to him that when they yelled *"ta to'"* from a corner, and someone else in turn got the message and repeated it so it could be heard inside the building, it meant, in good Caribbean Spanish, "all's clear."

Javier lead the way into the building. After a few steps inside, a Caribbean mulatto pointed a pistol at them. Javier smiled and said, "Nothing's up, I'm a customer." Another one came out of the darkness to check them for weapons, then pointed the way out to them. They went up a stairway to the second floor. Two men with a small mill greeted them at a sort of desk; three were posted at the corners, armed with shotguns and machine guns. One of those who greeted them asked Javier how much he wanted. He turned a small crank on the mill and ground up some of the product. He gave Javier some to taste. Javier put some on his tongue and said, "It's cut too much." They ground up some more. Javier insisted it was still cut too much. Finally one of them gave him a taste from a hidden stash. Javier smiled and nodded. They weighed the grams on a miniature scale and gave Javier the stuff.

Back in the apartment, Eduardo was still shaking. Who would believe it? It was like he'd just come out of a rehearsal: the Harlem darkness, the men yelling in code on the streets, the half-light and the men with machine guns inside the building. "It's just like the movies," he said to himself.

Javier cut four lines and snorted two. He motioned to Eduardo.

"Today isn't Sunday." Eduardo gestured a push away from the lines of coke.

"You're right. What happens is you start on Sundays and after a while it doesn't matter what day, date or time it is."

Eduardo sensed the atmosphere was ripe for dispensing advice.

"You shouldn't keep this up. You're losing yourself."

Javier stopped himself from snorting the third line.

"You're right. I've tried, but it might be too late. One of these days I'll try again."

"Today might be a good day to start."

"No, it isn't possible today. If I don't snort, I'll die."

Eduardo noticed that Javier was shaking as he snorted the white line on the table. He covered his nostril, made the third line vanish, and took a deep snort with the other one until not a single white grain was left on the table. He brought two beers out from the kitchen and tossed one to Eduardo.

"I don't recommend you get into this. I'm a wreck, and I don't think I can do anything about it. I like blow."

"You make good money, you've been working for years in the same place, but all your money goes up your nose."

"I know, but I can't do anything about it. The Honduran woman from the southern United States left me like this."

"No," Eduardo contradicted, "it isn't her, it's you. None of us should depend on any woman or on anybody but ourselves."

Javier smiled sadly. "I no longer have an inside. She killed it. You know how you set goals for yourself in life and if you don't reach them, then what's the use of continuing to live?"

"You can start again," Eduardo said as he drained the can of beer.

"There's more in the refrigerator. Get me one too. No, at my age and with what happened to me in the South and here in New York, you can't start over again. I'm tired."

Eduardo came back from the kitchen.

"You're young."

Javier's laughter was self-deprecating. "At forty-one you can only be young if you've met at least fifty percent of the goals you set for yourself. I haven't even met ten percent."

Eduardo was disarmed. "I'm sorry."

"It's no use feeling sorry. I'm no fool, Eduar."

"I know."

"You know that damned addiction brings you to a place of unreality, but I want to be in that unreality. Nowadays it's different from when we drank a few beers out of curiosity or for fun, when you were starting high school and I was starting college. Remember? No, when men like me submit to alcohol or drugs, we submit consciously, out of our own free will, to avoid calling it cowardice. Don't you see, it's a cowardly way, maybe the saddest way, of removing yourself from life? That is, of committing suicide?"

Eduardo felt a shiver. "It makes me sad, you've always been so brilliant."

"If I was that brilliant I wouldn't be into this. The Honduran woman from the southern United States, who stripped me of all my things, is more brilliant, but those are material things. Not only did she abort my child, she aborted me as well. I hate that whore. I hate Honduras. Too bad it's such a miserable place that it doesn't even have any volcanoes, so at least five would erupt at once and wipe that little country off the face of the map."

Eduardo smiled. "A selfish way of looking at the world. My family, Mirian, my friends and the rest of the people who live in Honduras aren't to blame. There's no reason for them to suffer for other people's sins. It would be fairer if you wished disaster on the lady who sent the fax or on the Honduran woman from the South . . ." Eduardo could not go on because when he heard himself saying, "the Honduran woman from the South," he started laughing uncontrollably.

"Maybe you're right. Yes, I think you are, maybe Honduras isn't to blame."

They both laughed heartily. Eduardo vanished into the kitchen to get some fresh beers.

30

HONDURAN ACTOR MAKES IT ON BROADWAY

Eduardo Lin, the Honduran actor, touches heaven's edge with the opening in the next few weeks of a piece in which he plays the lead. Eduardo Lin plays a Southern millionaire who owns a lumber company that operates in several regions of Latin America and exploits the rain forests without the slightest consideration, until the trees in a virgin area of Central America, seeing that the area's inhabitants have done nothing to protect them, join together to form the Army of Trees. When the millionaire finds out about this army, he gathers his own, and they face off in bloody combat. After winning the war, the Army of Trees, resentful because the inhabitants of Central America had done nothing to protect them, calls a general assembly in which it is decided that the punishment for the Central Americans' indolence is that no tree will bear fruit for three years, including vegetables. Only thorns and poisonous plants will lend their functions. Eduardo Lin delivers an astonishing performance. ***(J.A.C. - El Heraldo)***

FROM TEGUCIGALPA TO BROADWAY

In the place where many of the leading stars of the seventh art (film) got their start, a play has opened which has U.S. and international critics retracting their claws. It's a performance by Honduran Eduardo Lin that has been hailed from the outset as awesome, marvelous, vital. Honduras is filled with glory for the triumph of its fellow countryman, a man who, by the way, went unnoticed while living in our country. This newspaper will report further on the matter in the coming days. ***(Diario Tiempo)***

FROM BROADWAY TO HOLLYWOOD

Eduardo Lin, a young and handsome Honduran actor, is about to open in a play in the theater of the stars on Broadway, in New York City. The play, directed by and featuring the young Honduran genius in the leading role, will move to the silver screen as soon as it ends its first season on Broadway, with the lead role reserved for our countryman. Based on a novel, the film is about a group of men without political ideals who want to live in isolation from the rest of the world. They long for a Caribbean island and at first try to buy it, but a tall, bearded man, who is supposedly in charge of the island, flatly refuses to sell. When he refuses, the group puts together a small but indestructible army with which they attempt to invade the island. They meet with stiff resistance and lose the battle. It is said that in part two, which will be filmed in a few years, they win the war. The film comes with the disclaimer that it is purely fiction, and any resemblance to reality is purely coincidental. It also emphasizes the fact that the island they refer to is not Cuba. ***(La Tribuna)***

A STAR IN HONDURAS

From the International News Service. Special to La Prensa. *Honduran actor Eduardo Lin has swept the box office at one of the main theaters on Broadway, in New York City. The play, which is to open shortly, has ignited the interest of the general public. Eduardo Lin has come far, and many other talented countrymen may very well follow in his footsteps. This daily promises to provide its readers an exclusive interview in the Sunday edition, straight from New York City, with this star who lights up the Honduran skies.* ***(La Prensa)***

Casagrande finished reading the newspaper clippings and returned them to Eduardo. He scratched the crown of his head, looked toward the floor, and smiled. The smile grew wider by the second, and he snickered and finally yelled, "You have problems, *huevón.*" Casagrande's laughter was a volcanic eruption.

Eduardo stood there, dazed, then joined in with Casagrande, filling the bedroom with guffaws like two madmen.

"And how did all that come about, *huevón*?"

"You remember a few days ago Mirian called me at midnight? The day I drank the half bottle of whiskey . . . ? She was desperate, crying, so I told her a white lie to cheer her up. I told her that I would be starting work on Broadway around this time."

"What's this thing about a white lie?"

"It's true. Casa, I managed to sneak on to Broadway, but it's not such a big deal. I told Mirian that only to comfort her. She, no doubt, spread the news around to her classmates, the journalists and reporters she knows. Now I'm like Javier, Casa; I can't go back to Honduras."

"But you hadn't told me about it . . ."

"I'm sorry. It was a surprise, Casa."

"But didn't you say you got something on Broadway, *huevón*?"

"Yes. That's part of the truth."

"Well, don't let the white lie bother you. Maybe those *bananero* newspapers exaggerated the story, but the important thing is you made it there, even if it isn't as successful as the newspapers say. Getting on Broadway is good, and it's good for it to be known in your country. Don't get bitter over that, *huevón.* That's what you get for abandoning me. Now let's get back to the living room and finish off that gallon of wine."

Casagrande raised his glass. "To your success, Mister Eduardo Lin. To you, to Broadway and to Banana."

31

The night before Eduardo had stayed in Andrea's apartment. He liked her, and he was sure she liked him. Dinner and the wine were fine; so was their lovemaking. He should have left it at that and not stayed over. What if Mirian called?

He was frank with Andrea in telling her about his love for Mirian. Andrea didn't pay much attention; on the contrary, she redoubled her conquering charms.

Eduardo worked to make a few bucks and forget his anguish. Noon came and he wasn't hungry. He was alone in the large living room. Charlie did everything possible to give him jobs he could do alone, first because he was a tourist with no U.S. work permit, and second, because he didn't get along with Robert, a young Texan who'd been working for Charlie for years. Eduardo and Robert couldn't even look at each other. It all started because Robert had slighted Eduardo when they met. He boasted about having studied history in Texas and about his search for fame, which was on its way, as a designer in New York. Eduardo didn't put up with Robert's impertinence for long. In front of Charlie and other employees, Robert started up a conversation to humiliate Eduardo. He made him feel inadequate not only about world history, but about U.S. history, too. Eduardo had studied U.S. history in Tegucigalpa so he could be prepared when he came to the country where he'd make it. Eduardo had decided that if he didn't know the history of the country he was living in, things would be even harder. From then on he and Robert, who almost came to blows, didn't speak to each other, and Robert asked Charlie not to give Eduardo any more work.

But Charlie, with all his standing up for Yankee superiority, his put-downs of Southerners, his belief that Third Worlders had no intelligence and that Europe had a lot to learn from New York, identified with Eduardo for no apparent reason. Maybe it was because during breaks or when there was no work, they talked a lot, and Eduardo, at the risk of losing his job, argued and debated some of his ideas with Charlie.

That day, Charlie told him that they would finish the job there and the next day would work near Chinatown. Eduardo was painting the wall, which he'd patched earlier with a layer of cement. While up on a ladder, and in order to somehow escape some of the thoughts that depressed him because he was getting involved in a love triangle more dangerous than the Bermuda Triangle, he decided to take a trip to the past.

Mairena, his black friend from the Atlantic Coast of Honduras who'd given him lodging for three months in the South Bronx, invited him to take a walk along the nearby streets to persuade him that the inhabitants of that place were human beings, too. Eduardo accepted, not without fear. They walked along Washington Avenue toward the Bronx Zoo. Mairena, who was deacon of a church close to his apartment, didn't drink, but on that occasion he decided to buy beer and drink it, wrapped in a brown paper bag, as they walked. That was to avoid problems with the police, because drinking beer on the streets and in public places is prohibited. The police know there's almost always liquor inside the paper bags, but they don't intervene because they have no proof. Mairena asked Eduardo if they could sit down in one of the little parks near the projects. The projects are a bunch of buildings where supposedly the poorest people live: the unemployed, those with low income and who survive on government food stamps. Three hundred or more families live in each building. Most of them are black, Dominican and Puerto Rican, and to a lesser degree Mexican and Central American. The buildings are bunched close together, and in the middle and on the paths leading to each one there are benches, in small parks.

"Mairena," Eduardo said to him, "the other day I felt pretty bad when you told me about that gringo *at the station."*

The day he was referring to was one afternoon when he and Mairena were waiting at the 81st Street Station at the Museum of Natural History. For some uncommon reason the train was taking longer than usual. They sat down on one of the benches. Other people were waiting too. A young, blonde American was standing at the edge of the platform, reading a newspaper as he waited.

Mairena looked at him once, twice, and finally couldn't keep his thoughts to himself. He said to Eduardo, "I've got this terrible urge to push that white boy onto the tracks when the train comes in."

Eduardo was horror-stricken. He couldn't believe the words he'd just heard. Mairena was a deacon, a religious man, a Honduran. How could such satanic thoughts be galloping through his head? Eduardo scolded him, pointing out to him that the American was reading his newspaper, not bothering anyone. He didn't know who that guy was, he might be a noble person.

Mairena bore down: "There are *no noble white people."*

Eduardo answered, "So don't complain when they say there are no intelligent black people."

Back at the park, Mairena said, "I made a terrible mistake that day. Afterwards I felt real bad. It seemed to me that I not only thought it, but that I actually pushed that white boy onto the tracks."

"We need to understand each other better."

"It's difficult," Mairena said as he chugged the beer. "Do you want to know why I came here? Because you mestizos *don't like us blacks. You think you're better than we are. In Honduras, we're more discriminated against than here in New York."*

Eduardo would have liked to contradict him if he'd had grounds on which to do so, but there were none. He was sure Mairena was right. In Honduras, the black population is a small ethnic group which at most comprises less than one percent of the population. This ethnic group lives along the Atlantic Coast of Honduras, in Belize and in Guatemala, and is often the object of discrimination by mestizos. *This ethnic group is known as the* Garífuna. *They take refuge in the rites of their African ancestors; they speak with the dead, they perform dances tied to their past with the object of diminishing the anxiety discrimination causes them. Their rites bring* Garífuna *families together from far away. They spend up to three months in preparation, which culminate with all members reuniting with the spirit of their ancestors.*

"I know it's hard, Mairena," Eduardo said as he contemplated the beer can "but some day things will change. I don't believe in the supremacy of all whites or in the submissiveness of all blacks. I believe we all have the solution, but neither whites nor blacks nor mestizos *want to give in."*

"You remember," Mairena's eyes searched for Eduardo's, "when we were classmates in school? What did the mestizos *say to us? Black man, color of the night, black* cabrones, *and, the least offensive one, black sons of bitches."*

Eduardo laughed. "Don't exaggerate, either."

Mairena also laughed. "It's true. It's probably not convenient for you to remember."

"I'm not the one who said it."

"Don't be such a traitor, don't be a traitor to your own kind. A mestizo *said it and you're* mestizo*."*

Eduardo stood there deep in thought.

"What's the matter with you?" Mairena asked.

"Nothing, nothing, I was thinking about how, even with all that hatred you have piled up inside, you're not all that bad. I've slept with my door open many times and you haven't come in to kill me."

Mairena embraced Eduardo, who immediately reciprocated. They drank and laughed, and their laughter got louder and louder.

Eduardo came back from his memory of the South Bronx. He finished painting the wall. It turned out perfectly. He climbed down the ladder cautiously, balancing himself with one hand and holding the paint can with the other. He put his tools away. After packing and checking carefully to see that everything was as it was supposed to be, he changed out of his painter's clothes. It was his last day there. His two-week gig had come to an end, unless Lincoln Center suffered further deterioration and Charlie sent him back. Everything was tidy, except for the explanation he'd give Mirian as to what his job on Broadway had been.

32

New York awoke more lit-up than usual. It wasn't because the sun had decided to get up earlier; no, it was because flames had consumed a small underground social club in the Bronx. A Cuban lover had played at pyrotechnics to brand history with one of the greatest feats among love stories.

Just like many other New York City clubs, Happy Land opened its doors at the usual time to men and women who had made it a place not only for dancing to a Caribbean beat and sharing a few drinks, but also, and mainly, to look for new friends, swap stories of joy and sadness (mostly the latter) with old friends, whether on the city streets or in the cold or under the sun beating down on construction projects; to hear each other talk about the loves they'd left behind in their homeland, about their cousin who dreams of living in New York, about the letters from family members or about those who forget to write even one, about the strangeness of a noisy, alien city or the food they still can't get used to, about wanting to go back home with a few extra bucks in their pockets.

In between dancing and conversation, one subject stood out; a man protested indignantly to a woman, "Why did you abandon me?" The shouts got louder and the victim of unrequited love was kicked out of Happy Land. The incident was immediately forgotten and the partygoers kept their conversations and rhythm going without the slightest suspicion that the indignant, jilted man was prowling, listening to a masochistic and inciting song that advised a man to go all the way for a woman's love. The Cuban man felt possessed, not by the devil, but by blind jealousy, because the dancing woman wasn't his, but someone else's.

That's why the Cuban immigrant returned from the nearest gas station, after buying a dollar's worth of gasoline. (By that time he'd gotten over his jealous rage, but he'd made a public threat to his loved one and, if he didn't carry it out, this would mean that he wasn't who he said he was.) He emptied the gas can in front of the only exit and, as if that weren't enough, closed the iron door, and proceeded to throw a match that would light up the darkened Bronx street. He patiently headed toward his hovel, where he knew the police would track him down in no time flat. He could have escaped, but didn't want to, because he'd fulfilled his duty and had to finish fulfilling it by going to jail, resigned but satisfied to imagine his loved one dancing and melting on the hellish dance floor. His plan was so bad that one of the four survivors was his beloved.

Inside, the panic was immediate. The immigrants didn't quite understand what was going on as the flames invaded the tiny place. The flames swept up everything in their path, and the bloodcurdling screams of men and women joined in something like the sound of an off-key orchestra: the last looks they cast among themselves were filled with terror and good-byes; desperate bodies trampled each other in search of an exit, in search of a breath of air that wasn't contaminated. In a matter of minutes everything was left in silence; only the crackling of the flames reached its highest expression. Inside lay the eighty-seven immigrants. Some were asphyxiated, others charred to a crisp. The smoke and substances the burning things gave off apparently became toxic vapors, deadly and instantaneous, for people were found with glasses still in their hands.

Eduardo and Casagrande made their way through the crowd. They weren't able to get far because of the barriers the firemen and police had set up. Casagrande took several pictures of what had been Happy Land. Many wept; you could hear the screams of people asking about their family members, about those who hadn't come home. The bodies were transferred to a government building close to Happy Land. Desperate people, carrying photos of their family members, begged the authorities to let them in so they could identify their deceased. Eduardo and Casagrande met up with Leo and Javier and unintentionally formed a foursome.

Casagrande, an outstandingly cruel man, came close to getting lynched on a corner by a group of Hondurans. They'd have beaten him senseless if Eduardo hadn't intervened. He calmed them down and asked them to forgive him. Because the majority of the deceased in the fire were from Honduras, Casagrande had announced, "The *gringos* burned this place to get revenge because you people set their embassy on fire."

That Sunday was sadder than usual. Javier was silent. As was his habit, he had ingested cocaine and marijuana, but this time the effect was different. He didn't talk about not going back to Honduras. No one needed to say a thing, his sadness was clear. Javier had lost two friends in the fire. Most of the victims were Honduran and most of them were *Garífuna*, the blacks from the Atlantic Coast.

33

Eduardo felt jealous, restless, irritated almost to the point of being furious. It was a week after the Happy Land tragedy and Mirian hadn't called. She'd not been concerned with what shape he was in, with the fact that maybe by coincidence he'd been in that club.

His jealousy was picking up speed. Unable to make up his mind, he wanted to test her and see what day she would finally call him. The hours went by and other phone calls came in, minus the one he longed to receive. Elizabeth, the American to whom Casagrande had introduced him at Maribel's house in Queens, called him; Maribel called him; he got a call from the Colombian writer; from a Bolivian musician; from a Dominican painter. In short, many people called to make sure he was all right and that neither he nor any of his family had suffered losses in the fire.

Casagrande laughed in the living room with Julio, a Chilean missionary he'd met the night before at a photo exhibition on Salvador Allende's fall in Chile. He was a young man, about twenty-five, but his beard made him seem older. He was soft-spoken and deliberate in his speech, whether it was about something as insignificant as the weather or asking for a glass of water. Casagrande liked the missionary a good deal, and because he was having trouble finding a place to stay, Casagrande invited him to spend the two weeks in his room. He told him about the people who lived there, especially Eduardo, who he wondered about, because for some reason he hadn't gotten up and it was already midday.

Eduardo had never had insomnia like he had that week. He imagined Mirian making love with another, and tormented himself. He felt like dropping all his plans, his struggles, his nightmares from the twelfth floor, like casting his virtues and defects out, body and all.

Eduardo got out of bed, furious. He'd always been jealous, but not with Mirian, she hadn't given him that sort of grief until now. He trusted her faithfulness, her love, blindly. He tried to tell himself that there was something wrong with the phone line in Honduras. To test it, he called; the phone rang normally and, before anyone could answer, he hung up, feeling even more bitter than before.

Casagrande introduced him to Julio, the missionary, whom he had to put up with for two weeks. Eduardo didn't feel up to laughing at Casagrande's jokes. He made a superhuman effort to be courteous to the missionary, who shyly tried to find out what was on Eduardo's mind.

"What's the matter with you? You're in a weird mood," Casagrande asked him.

"Mirian hasn't called me. Who doesn't know that Happy Land burned down and that most of the people in there were Hondurans? I don't know what's going on, maybe she's become a whore already. Are they all like that?"

"You're imagining things, *huevón*. You want to settle your doubts? The telephone's right there. Call her, but don't get frustrated over hearsay."

The missionary agreed.

Eduardo dialed the number, which he knew by heart, to exhaustion. The little worm appeared on the other end. It couldn't touch the ear, though, because it came face to face with a furious eagle.

"If I hadn't called you, you wouldn't have called me. Don't you know about the fire? Don't you care about what might have happened to me?"

"I knew you were all right," the little worm said. "I was going to call you over the weekend."

"How could you know I was all right?" The eagle got angrier by the second. "Make up another lie. What's his name, who is the son of a bitch?"

"*Cariño,*" the little worm smiled, "don't be silly. I didn't call you because I saw the news reports."

"Yeah, the news reports. So what?" The eagle held its breath. "Up to now no one has the complete list of the deceased. How could you have known I'm all right?"

The little worm smiled again and the eagle felt that smile tickling his ear.

"I saw the news and most of them are *Garífuna*s, and I know you don't hang out in places where blacks hang out."

Not only did the little worm tickle the ear and descend the miniature snail-shaped staircase, the spiral, to settle into its nest, it also made the eagle, which at first had threatened it via satellite, feel microscopic, bacterial.

34

The memorial service for those who died in Happy Land took place out in the open in Van Cortlandt Park, even though the winter was not altogether over. A stage and sound system were set up. Attendance was sparse, despite the service having been advertised in the papers. The Honduran flag was raised next to the U.S. flag. The Honduran national anthem was sung to the weeping of many men and women. Casagrande took photos no one had requested. Several leaders of the Honduran community spoke. A warning was issued so that the Happy Land tragedy would help keep people from visiting social clubs that operated without a license.

In Honduras, the mourning spread nationwide. The bodies were brought home in several planes. When they arrived they were draped in the Honduran flag. It was a homecoming for the Heroes of Poverty, the Martyrs of Hunger. Thousands of family members of the victims traveled to the capital city and to San Pedro Sula, the cities where the bodies landed. The family members of more than one hundred fifty thousand Hondurans living in New York were filled with grief, because while many of them had no kin among the deceased, in the future they might be the ones greeting the casket of a family member.

Mairena, the black man from the Atlantic Coast who stood at medium height and had pronounced African features, left the circle of mourners and headed in the direction of the group in which he'd spotted Eduardo. When he got there, he greeted Javier and Leo, and before anyone had a chance, he was introducing himself to Casagrande.

"Just what I was telling you," Mairena said to Eduardo. "Most of them were *Garífunas*."

"They could have been some other group," Eduardo replied.

It was not often Casagrande was at a loss for words. He couldn't conceive of not understanding, of being out of tune with any topic. Admitting defeat to himself, he asked, "What does *Garífunas* mean?"

"They're the blacks who live in Honduras, on the Atlantic Coast, in Belize and in other places in Central America. As far as we know, they're a mixture of Carib Indians and African maroons," Eduardo explained to him.

Casagrande addressed Mairena.

"So one could say you're *Garífuna*."

"Yes, I'm *Garífuna*."

Javier lamented, "I lost two friends in the fire."

"It's a tragedy," Leo commented.

"And most of them were *Garífuna*," the *Garífuna* said.

"It was an accident, Mairena," Eduardo said.

"An accident, yes, but why did most of them just happen to be *Garífuna*? That goes to show you the marginalization we're subjected to in Honduras as we are here, like anywhere you go. Is there no future for the black race?"

"Why so resentful?" Casagrande asked.

"I lost a lot of friends, and some family members," Mairena said as he looked down. "It's not that I'm resentful, just a little sad because when they handed out colors, I got this one."

"You're not being fair," said Eduardo. "While it's true that most of them were *Garífuna,* it's because of your own situation, you don't like to mix with us. You hold your parties, your meetings, and everything else in a tight group. No wonder somehow you took over Happy Land."

"Let's say it was, say we did take it over; look at the sort of place, the sort of dumps we have access to."

"Well," said Casagrande, wearing the expression of a City College professor, "I don't think it's exclusively because you're black. There are also poor whites."

"Some day I'd like to go to bed with a white woman," Mairena said melancholically.

Eduardo patted him on the shoulder. "Count on it."

"That's what I'm saying," Mairena recoiled, "someone else always has to play a part in it, some damn *blanco* or *mestizo*."

Eduardo was amused. "You're unhappy about everything. If I told you that you were going to bed a woman, and not necessarily a white one, using your own charms, you couldn't handle it, you're so bashful."

"I'm too black," said the *Garífuna*.

"None of that," Casagrande interrupted, "it's a matter of language use. You can't deny a lot of people are against interracial relations, but some of us are for them."

Mairena still disagreed. "You're an example, Eduardo. How many women did you bed when you lived in my apartment? Tons of them, among them two white women. And why? Because you're not black. You're what's known here as a Latin lover."

Eduardo smiled. "No, it's not just because of that; it's because I can talk, I'm not bashful, and, well, I'm beautiful."

Casagrande laughed. "Upstart *bananero*."

"The truth is you've always had good luck with women. Remember in high school? You swept through the place."

Eduardo put on his sheepish face. "Yeah, I know. But I'm tired. Is it the same for everyone once you're over twenty-five? I'm tired of so many naked women in front of me. I know an infinity of naked women. I've tasted the nakedness of Latinas, Europeans, Americans and you know what? They're all women."

"Looks like you've tried them all, except black women," said the *Garífuna*.

Eduardo chafed. "The truth is I haven't. I've never had the chance. Once I was close to making love with a black model, an African who'd lived in Paris, who I met here in New York. I would have really liked it. She was quite beautiful, quite gorgeous, but that night I was with a *gringa*."

"So you gave the white woman preference," said the *Garífuna*.

"No," Eduardo laughed, "no way. I left the white woman to be with her, but she was a very intelligent woman, very proud. She didn't give in, even though she wanted me."

"How do you know she wanted you?" Leo asked.

"I danced with her that night, and I felt her."

"So there haven't been any black women in your life?" the *Garífuna* asked.

"No,"—Eduardo didn't bother to conceal his slyness—"but if you have any sisters around . . ."

"A cousin," said the *Garífuna.*

"Can I count on her?"

The *Garífuna* smiled and nodded.

"So count on the white woman," Eduardo said.

"I thought you were tired of so many naked women in your life," Casagrande said.

"Yeah, but I'll make an exception. I'll do it to her with her clothes on. No, seriously, Casa, I want to be monogamous, get married and be faithful. I'm fed up with sleeping with bunches and bunches of them just to ejaculate. Maybe I'm getting better. I'm demanding respect from myself."

"Banana!" Casagrande laughed. "You're really taking this to heart."

"I would never be faithful," Javier said. "After what the Honduran woman from the southern U.S. did to me, I don't think there's a single woman who deserves my respect."

"No generalizing," Leo interjected. "They're not all Honduran women from the southern U.S."

"Did she cheat on you?" Casagrande asked.

Javier grew sadder than usual, even for him. "That would have been great. It wouldn't have affected me so much. The worst part was that I loved her and offered a struggle her puny intelligence never understood."

Casagrande took what he heard seriously. "That's right. That is sad. When one of the sides' ignorance is greater, it's sad."

"Yes," Eduardo commented, "your Honduran woman from the southern United States needed to dream. That's the way it goes sometimes, and a lot of us aren't made for women that don't know how to dream. The important thing, beyond the money and material things, is the dream, the ideas, so that you can love. At this moment I have the woman of my life."

"That's great," Leo seconded. "It's beautiful to find someone like that. Up until a while ago I was in that same stupid routine with various naked women. And it's troublesome. That's why I'm devoting myself to my studies and to a single woman, my *Dominicana.* I'm writing a book about Francisco Morazán. That's a thousand times more marvelous than sex with no love."

"I don't know much about these things," the *Garífuna* said with an undercurrent of resentment.

Eduardo tried to console him: "Mairena, Mairena."

"Are you always so venomous?" Casagrande asked.

The *Garífuna* was embarrassed. "I'm sorry. I'm the deacon of a church. Sometimes I forget and I do harm. I'm sorry. I really shouldn't be that way, not with my religious upbringing."

"We understand you," Leo said.

"Everybody has their baggage," Javier smiled. "This guy with the racism thing, me with the Honduran woman from the southern U.S. . . ."

"That's how it is," Leo said, "and I've got my great obsession with Francisco Morazán. Incidentally, do you all think Central America could still be converted to a single nation?"

"Let's not get serious," Eduardo advised them. "Besides, Casagrande isn't Central American. What does he know about Morazán?"

Casagrande protested. "Of course I know, *huevón.* How can you underestimate a survivor of the sixties? You weren't even born when I was hearing about Francisco Morazán."

Leo was pleased. "Good shot, Casagrande. We'll talk about it at greater length some other day."

"A few *Garífunas* fought with Morazán," the *Garífuna* said.

Leo seconded him. "It's true, there were some Morazanist soldiers who were authentic *Garífunas.*"

"Or *Garífunas* who were authentic *Morazanistas,*" said the Garífuna.

Casagrande nodded. "It sounds better that way."

Javier looked doubtfully at Casagrande.

"You can trust him," said Eduardo.

"It's about me, what's up?" Casagrande said.

"I want to snort; you do any?" Javier asked.

Casagrande jumped in. "What took you so long?"

"That's bad," the *Garífuna* said, "I'm going back to the others."

Mairena pulled away from the group and moved back into the body of mourners. Javier suggested they walk toward the grove of trees on the edge of Van Cortlandt Park, where they would be out of sight. They did just that: they went deep into the bushes. Javier took out the piece of tinfoil and snorted up, using the blade from a nail clipper. Eduardo and Casagrande followed suit. Leo didn't want any, arguing that he was a beer drinker, or in any case, a man for alcohol.

That Sunday was made gloomier by the gray, the cold and the reason for their gathering. There was an atmosphere of death. The sobs released by a few women as the priest offered a prayer for the Happy Land martyrs echoed all the way to the grove of trees.

Leo talked about his New York experiences: the fury and the gloom and the feeling of impotence that possessed him when the U.S. invaded Panama. He'd cried beside a friend and countryman. It was in the news night and day. Now, while Leo would not defend any matter related to drugs, it was also true that he'd suffered because of that invasion. He, a revolutionary *Morazanista*, felt defeated by that invasion, and immediately afterward came the fall of the *Sandinista* government in Nicaragua, all of which ripped him apart and was driving him irrevocably into the league of nihilists, a league to which Casagrande somehow belonged. Casagrande was apathetic on political matters. He would vote only when he heard that there was a candidate who liked bananas and apples, played the saxophone and would celebrate his victory with rock music. He had traded in his long-standing political sympathies for photography and for writing songs he'd record some day. He kept a few things from the sixties: music tapes, a few books, the bohemian in him, and the lifestyle of the intentionally jobless and expenseless, which he'd learned down to the last jot and tittle in Abbie Hoffman's *Steal This Book*.

As soon as Javier snorted the tiniest amount of cocaine, it became impossible for him to distance himself from the past.

He was returning from the Mississippi River to torture himself over that woman who accounted for his fourth marriage before he'd even reached thirty. No matter how good a man Javier tried to be, it wasn't enough to keep her from going back to her reality: to sleeping with one man and waking up with another, to seeking refuge from herself, as if she were an obsessive collector. With that woman came destruction for Javier, who never again knew peace, and all struggles with any life circumstances whatsoever ceased to matter to him. Because of his education, his intelligence, he realized that he was sinking, yet he would do nothing to avoid it, nothing to reach out for a life raft.

He snorted again, offered Casagrande and Eduardo another toot, and went far away from where they were, back in time.

He practically relived the scene where he experienced the worst murderous impulses of his life. He was living at his in-laws' with his wife. In the daytime only he and his mother-in-law were left in the house, which was why he locked himself up to create future investment projects for Honduras or to read, only going out for the basics, trying not to stumble into his mother-in-law, because as soon as she saw him, she'd throw out snide comments. She'd say to a wall, "Wall, food is so expensive!" or she'd talk to a refrigerator, "Refrigerator, do you think a jobless bum who dreams about becoming an important businessman, un hombre de negocios, *can provide for a family on dreams alone?" She'd stand in front of a dishwasher: "Dishwasher, do you think that shadow that's walking over there might be a man?" Then she'd remember her religious calling and hide in her room to pray, on her knees, before an enormous sanctuary consisting of the greatest variety of insecticides ever assembled on the face of the planet. There were portraits of enormous cockroaches showing signs of having died under torture, some missing legs, others eyeless and missing antennae. In the middle of all the pictures of mangled cockroaches was a big poster of Franz Kafka, also covered with a few quartered cockroaches on the verge of death. The mother-in-law was repenting for having spoken to these objects, and began praying, reading the Bible, and promising, as an offering for her disobedience, to sacrifice a half dozen cockroaches in a twenty-four hour period.*

At that point, Javier was already crucified, and lemon, not wine, was falling on his wounds. That morning he knew he had to get out of that house. He was on his way to the bathroom, and the mother-in-law was cooking. The lard was sizzling in the skillet and he saw himself grabbing her by the hair, pushing her face all the way down into the searing lard. He heard her cry, picked her face up and was horrified to see it peeling off, falling off like an abandoned ice cream castle in the desert. He got to the bathroom and the stream of piss fell smack in the center of the bowl, producing a noise that competed quite deliberately with the crackling of the lard. He thought about how far he was taking it, and reprimanded himself for his homicidal urges. The stream kept going a few seconds more, and her failing, thawed-out face swimming in the toilet bowl passed through his mind. He imagined her letting out a cry for help, which the sound of the toilet's flush drowned out. He imagined his mother-in-law's last desperate attempts to catch her breath, the dim gurgle, the yellowness of the coffee drinker's piss covering everything, sinking her, putting the final touches on her before he slowly pulled the flush lever. He heard the lion's roar magnified acoustically by the torrent of water that would sweep her away into a whirlpool, the little fragments of her face sinking into the plumbing and blending in with the legless cockroaches, with the stinking hairs of a smelly, deodorant-less armpit, with the morning-after spittle of drunkards.

It made him happy to imagine the little fragments of eyes, mouth, eyebrows and tongue crying for help, trying to grab on to some piece of metal jutting out from the pipes, or to some cobweb of hair that had stuck to the iron, the little fragments of mother-in-law's face screaming for help at a canoe-shaped Kotex, or at an object the shape of a submarine hurtling implacably toward the mouth of the sewage waters. He came out of the bathroom. The mother-in-law was still hunched over the frying pan. He struggled with the inner force that urged him to carry out the aforethought and quickly passed through the kitchen, to moor himself to a book in his room that would make him oblivious to the witch casting her spell over crackling lard. He passed by so quickly that he didn't hear the mother-in-law: "Frying pan, do you think there's someone interested in stealing whatever we leave for our daughter's inheritance?"

Back in Van Cortlandt Park, Javier pulled out the tinfoil again and prescribed another toot. Casagrande and Eduardo seconded him. Leo shook his head in disapproval of all excess. They leaned on the shrubs and stayed there in silence.

Eduardo bought a mansion in Beverly Hills, right next to other movie stars. His relationship with a famous actress had fallen to pieces, and all because the beautiful but brainy woman wanted to get married. He was willing, but she didn't accept his proposal that they spend half the year in the U.S. and the other half in Honduras. The famous actress, who'd never visited a Third World country and wasn't interested in doing so either, was soundly against it. She spread a map before her beloved Eduardo Lin and searched for Honduras in Asia. When she couldn't find it there, she searched for it in Africa. Eduardo was offended by the fact that his beloved could not even locate the country in which her beloved had buried his umbilical cord. The wedding plans were ruined, even though they'd announced their wedding date in the news, and despite his outdoing himself bellowing about how his would be one of the stablest marriages in Hollywood, and how instead of dancing a waltz, which was in bad taste because in his day that's what the fascists had danced, they would dance to When a Man Loves a Woman *on their wedding day. Because he so loved his actress, it was the right song to yell to the four winds.*

The wedding didn't take place, and he kept appearing in magazines as one of the most lusted-after bachelors. After the letdown from the broken marriage, he called one of his friends, who believed he had experience to spare in matters of man-woman, woman-man relations. So his friend Warren Beatty came over to drink some aged wine and give him lessons for survival in the complicated world of Eves.

Three months later, he was caught by reporters in a São Paulo romance. A Brazilian woman he met while on a brief trip to Paris, who Mel Gibson, another friend of his, was good enough to introduce to him, made him forget the marriage-off fiasco. She was indeed willing to live a half a year or her whole life in Tegucigalpa, but his intentions were to have a simple frolic in Brazilian territory.

Leo tapped him on the shoulder. Eduardo came back from Brazil.

"Where were you? You're laughing to yourself."

"I was far away," Eduardo replied, "very far from Van Cortlandt Park."

"That's the only good thing about coke combined with a little joint," Casagrande offered, "it sends you out of this cruel world."

Leo was sententious: "Even though in the long run it leads you to a worse one . . ."

Javier snorted the crumbs left on the tinfoil. "If you want some more let's go to my apartment."

"That's enough," said Leo.

"I have some beer," Javier reminded them.

So Leo echoed the rest of them with his *yes*. They slowly crossed the field, leaving behind the Happy Land mourners, who'd begun to disperse, besieged by the rain.

35

Eduardo got all the way to Ruth's apartment, in lower Manhattan. She was a blonde woman, originally from the outlying areas of New York City. She worked as a third-rate translator. She had met Eduardo in Queens, at a group exhibition of Colombian painters. His visit came as a surprise, because she'd invited him over once before and he hadn't accepted.

Eduardo knew she wanted him. The day they met she wasn't content just to hint at it, she actually said it to him in good English and underlined it in broken Spanish. She offered him tea. He accepted and, while waiting for the brew, entertained himself by gawking at some paintings.

When she reappeared, she placed two cups of tea on a little table in the living room. She came close to him and without much of a preamble, brushed her hand over his fly. He smiled and walked away to find his teacup.

"I didn't come for that."

"What for, then?"

"I was bored. I remembered I owed you a visit."

She insisted on stroking his fly. He knew it was the right moment to take the lid off on the reason for his visit.

"Fine, we're going to do it but on one condition."

"Use a condom?"

"Well, that's a given. No rubber, I don't get an erection."

Eduardo knew Ruth's curriculum: she liked Latino and Black men. It didn't take any huge offer to get her to bed. She was always up all night in bohemian bars or at parties to which she constantly invited herself.

"So?"

"I have a Honduran friend. He's real shy, and he confided that he'd like to go to bed with a white woman. Would you agree to do that?"

"I'm not the Red Cross."

"But you don't need to be to perform an act of charity."

She was taken by his sincerity and spontaneity. "What if I don't like him? For me to go to bed with someone it has to be someone I like."

He knew Ruth wasn't very demanding. It would be enough for the aspirant to have a masculine sex organ, if that.

"I think you'll like him. He's a good guy. Still, we're not talking about whether you'll like him or not, but about whether you're going to do it or not."

She knelt down in front of him, as if to send a prayer to his fly. He understood the agreement.

Ruth ran him over. She cornered him against the closest wall and stripped him of his shirt. At first her aggressiveness scared him, then he realized he was dealing with a woman in need of a climax. He took the initiative and tore her teeny blouse in two; with her skirt still on, he pulled her panties down and his eyes and organ came across a bit of skin that was white in the extreme, sun- and techno-tan-free. It didn't matter to him, because he had neither the capacity nor the presence of mind required to pay attention to the details. Best of all, there he was, sticking his nose between two breasts that were snowy-complexioned but quivering like volcanoes in eruption. They tumbled naked onto the carpet in combat, a battle with no apparent losers or winners. She bit his neck, his erect little nipples; she hovered around his bellybutton and took it close to where he feared he might wake and find himself in a pool of semen, the result of unconscious self-gratification. He opened his eyes and he wasn't dreaming, but panting in the face of that reality, those lips like a safari gone astray in the desert, guzzling all the water down to the last drop and walking away from the oasis. The sign telling him he was a few short seconds away from reaching the goal and claiming victory made him shudder. She pressed down and then lifted, like someone grabbing a hose to water the garden. She opened the valve and let the liquid spread over her belly, turning his bellybutton into a little lagoon, then she turned it to her breasts, so he could rub it all over her as if he were discovering fire. And there he lay, exhausted, yearning to slip into a dream.

He stood up. Ruth was asleep on the rug. He went into the bathroom, pissed, admired himself from head to toe in the mirror, looked at his pronounced African features. The white orgasm still had him dazzled. He wanted to yell: "I am Mairena, *jodido*." His euphoria vanished as suddenly as it had come over him. He recalled that Eduardo was behind all that, that it had been Eduardo's conquest, that he, Mairena, was only doing it because Eduardo's words had persuaded the woman. And he felt stupid, ashamed. What had he gotten out of it? He thought about going out to look for his black *compañera*, not staying to sleep with Ruth as he'd planned to do. Never in his life had he so desired to be a deacon.

36

Casagrande conquered Julio, the missionary. Julio made it possible for Casagrande to distance himself from Eduardo and other friends. They were together day and night, and when they weren't, one would inquire of the other what he'd done in his absence. The missionary had never had a homosexual relationship until then. Still, he made his indecision over whether to be heterosexual or not clear to Casagrande, indecision which Casagrande, a long-time player in the Mexico and San Francisco Big Leagues, would not let go to waste. Through his attention, jokes, comments from any book he'd ever read about prejudices that shouldn't exist regarding love between men, Julio, the missionary, a weak man by vocation and in his own words wanting to try everything he could in this life, fell easily into the lulling web of the Mexican poncho.

The missionary had some theories on life that all the tenants in the apartment found really weird, except for Casagrande, who approved of the missionary's dream that a future without weapons would be more powerful for toppling dictatorships than the superiority of the human brain. The missionary was convinced that in the future it would be enough for human beings to have a massive chain reaction of thoughts about the death of a dictator or of some man who is harmful to humanity and he would die on the spot, because collective energy was invincible. The world would rid itself of warmongers, the greedy, the exploiters and in short, all men with no scruples. Then there would be a different world in which weapons had gone out of style and would be hanging in museums like a funereal memory of the times when humankind was still uncivilized.

Casagrande marveled at the missionary. Eduardo would listen, no longer as skeptically as the first time Beethoven's Fifth Symphony had reached his ears.

"So where were you on Sunday?" the missionary asked.

"I went with Eduardo and some other *bananeros* to Van Cortlandt Park for a tribute to those who died in Happy Land."

"It's ironic," said the missionary. "Happy Land, *Tierra Feliz*, those who died in *Tierra Feliz.*"

"It's possible," Eduardo said. "I think more and more seriously about leaving, and most of all now, when the fad is to do things in series. I don't want to be caught in Happy Land II."

"Banana Republic, if the Hondurans heard that joke they wouldn't forgive you."

"They would, they'd forgive me. You know Hondurans bad-mouth their country, the poverty, the delinquency, the corruption, but they say it and you can't reproach them. The problem is when a foreigner does it."

"Well, it doesn't seem like it." Casagrande stood up and took the coffeepot off the stove. "The *gringos* have told you many times, they've built a bunch of bases, and once I saw they called you their backyard."

"It's Communist propaganda," Eduardo said, without conviction.

"It's the world." The missionary poured himself some coffee. "Poor countries will always be the ones rich countries subject. How can a poor country deny it? The best thing would be if the powerful countries weren't so abusive, if they gave poor countries the chance to negotiate."

"Maybe if Latin America weren't so split up," Eduardo added.

"Split up, and most of the time run by leaders with no pride, lacking in principles, poor little robots that turn on for a couple of bucks," Casagrande added.

"What are you doing around these parts?" the missionary asked.

Eduardo flashed a smile in reply. "I want to be a famous actor."

The missionary took those words seriously. He looked at Eduardo carefully, as if he wanted to tell his future. Eduardo was ashamed.

The missionary nodded. "You shall be indeed, and you'll be very rich. I'll see you some day when you're in that place and I'm just going to say to you, 'My name is Julio, remember that fellow who one day in the Bronx, told you his name was Julio?'"

"I'll keep that in mind."

"He's talented," Casagrande said. "Too bad that's not enough."

"He'll make it," the missionary prophesied.

"Mirian will be coming soon," Eduardo informed them.

"The *bananera* couldn't take it any more," Casagrande said. "I think I'm going to like her just fine."

"Are you going to go back with her?" the missionary inquired.

"I don't know. It's possible. I know nothing about anything."

"Love is beautiful," the missionary added his approval.

Eduardo tested the temperature of the coffee on the outside of the coffeepot. He poured himself a cup.

"Too bad we refuse to accept that we love and that we like to be loved, all out of the damned fear of ridicule. If people were less afraid of ridicule, evolution would be further along. Because, when it comes right down to it, either everything is ridiculous or the ridiculous doesn't exist. Everything is ridiculous, because the only thing that changes is the point of view. For me, Casagrande is ridiculous in that poncho. Being a missionary is ridiculous. It's ridiculous to be a president and appear on national TV pretending to be serious. It's ridiculous to break your back for money. It's ridiculous to have no money. It's ridiculous for me to want to be a famous actor. It's ridiculous for me to live in New York when seventy percent of my life is in Tegucigalpa. It's ridiculous to be behind a desk, ridiculous to be the boss, ridiculous to be a worker, ridiculous to be a soldier and carry a weapon around. And so on, everything's ridiculous. All you have to do is settle on the right angle from which to perceive it. And it's also ridiculous to try and perceive the ridiculous."

All three laughed.

"It's a good theory, you ought to develop it. But do you love Mirian?"

Eduardo sipped his coffee. "Yes, much in spite of the ridiculous."

They were walking along Valentine Avenue. The missionary was the only one able to make Casagrande finally come to peace with his old enemy, Edgar Allan Poe. He entered Poe Park, not without some fear, and then went into the house turned museum. Before he went in he offered a prayer which, evidently, was in tribute, and begged for mercy before the plaque on the genius' house, which read, "Edgar Allan Poe wrote *Annabel Lee*, *Eureka* and *The Raven* here. And he began dying after the irreparable loss of his one and only love."

37

With the coming of April, the snow gave way to the flowers, and New York dressed itself in natural colors. Along with those flowers came Eduardo's favorite flower. At La Guardia Airport, Eduardo paced impatiently back and forth, checking the monitors to make sure that the flight from Miami was still on the list of arrivals. Casagrande, who had accompanied Eduardo, was bored and edgy at Eduardo's nervousness. Mirian had to change planes in Miami to get to New York. Again and again Eduardo had explained to her the risk of getting lost in the Miami airport. She listened, smiling, understanding his impatience and nervousness.

As soon as the arrival of Mirian's flight was announced, Eduardo and Casagrande went down to baggage claim to find her. Eduardo begged Casagrande to stay alert while he went upstairs again and posted himself at the exit ramp through which she would be arriving. More and more people walked by, and Eduardo began to wonder whether something had happened in Miami.

Suddenly he discovered Mirian in the crowd. She smiled at him. He didn't know how to act, what to say to her, what to do. He rushed up to her and he kissed her on the mouth. She, unaccustomed to kissing in public, blushed but didn't reject him. He sensed her embarrassment.

"This is New York. Even if it doesn't seem to make sense with everything they say about the dehumanization of this city, you can kiss in public here."

Mirian laughed. "It's as if I were hearing you yesterday, as if we'd never been apart. I love you, my philosopher."

"You're beautiful. Let's go down and get the suitcases."

When they arrived at the baggage claim, Eduardo spotted Casagrande. Casa came up and gave Mirian a peck on the cheek, as if he'd known her forever. She had said hello to him before over the phone, and there was always a story about him or by him in Eduardo's letters.

At seven in the evening, they found themselves riding the elevator to the twelfth floor of Valentine Avenue. Eduardo apologized for the dirty state of the elevator and explained to her that it wasn't precisely the most marvelous in all of New York City.

José, the subletter, as usual, was cleaning his sound system. He stopped when he heard Casagrande struggling with a suitcase, banging it against one wall and then the other along the length of the hallway. When they got to the apartment, they took the suitcases to Eduardo's room. In the living room, José, with his hand outstretched and pointing to a tooth which had once been made of gold, and to the hollow of another, which was ready to rot entirely, gave the newly arrived lady a friendly welcome. Mauro and Alfredo, the meek Ecuadorean workers, said their hellos and vanished into the living room in less time than it took to say hello. Rosa took a few minutes to appear, because even though on a tight budget, she never neglected her appearance when there was company. Mirian was there in the living room exchanging smiles and words with the tenants of the apartment she'd so longed to know.

Eduardo would have wanted Casagrande, José and Rosa to imitate the other two Ecuadoreans and vanish immediately into their rooms to leave him alone with his mate. Unfortunately none of the three seemed disposed to go to bed without looking over the new guest.

Casagrande came out with his traditional gallon of wine.

"Well, dear, welcome to New York."

Rosa reappeared with some glasses she kept under her watchful eye for special occasions. José, a hardened drinker as long as the drink wasn't a threat to a single *sucre* out of his pocket, showed his pleasure as he took the lead in opening the gallon jug.

Eduardo and Mirian couldn't stop looking at each other. He stroked her hands, drew his lips to her ears, and hugged her. Casagrande, an indiscreet person by birth, couldn't keep his comment to himself.

"I swear, Banana Republic, I've never seen you so happy."

Mirian guffawed when she heard that they called her lover "Banana Republic." He laughed, too, and thought about the fact that he'd never told her about the nickname he'd been given.

"Do you know what he calls you?"

"What?"

"La Bananera."

She smiled. "Well, Casagrande, I won't leave without getting my revenge."

"Are you hungry?" Rosa asked Mirian.

José, who'd come into this world with the sole purpose of figuring life out in *sucres*, cleaning and stroking his electronic appliances, and ordering a woman around without ever allowing her the possibility of showing off her friendliness or intelligence, said, "Don't ask dumb questions. If you're going to make the food, make it, and that's it. If they eat, they eat, if they don't, they don't."

Fortunately, Rosa had Casagrande on her side, a man who, due to his hormonal preferences, as he himself used to say, identified with women. As he served himself a drink, Casagrande said to José, "What's the matter with you, *huevón*? Stop talking to your woman like that. You go cook. All you do is clean that television set. Aren't you ashamed to be so in love with things?"

José felt ashamed indeed. She lowered his head, and his poverty of language and lack of boldness made him reply in a tone of reverence. "Casagrande, don't be like that, Casagrande."

Casagrande told Rosa that it wouldn't be a bad idea for her to cook something light. She agreed in good faith. His words and body language had the magic to please people. Everyone in the apartment followed Casagrande's orders without protesting, perhaps because of the way in which he gave them on the one hand, and on the other, because he was about twice as old as Rosa and José, and came just short of being twice as old as Eduardo.

Mirian watched Casagrande attentively. She prided herself on her ability to get to know people through their gestures more than their words. She had an intuition about Casagrande's human qualities, but there was something in her thoughts that made her wrinkle her brow for a few seconds.

"Some friends of ours," Casagrande said to her, "have prepared a welcome party later."

The creep said it, Eduardo thought. He was worried. The party was at Maribel's, a woman he'd slept with in a threesome with Elizabeth, who would most probably be there as well. And the possibility of Andrea being there wasn't remote, since they were all friends. What should he do? Should he tell Mirian in advance, let her know certain things? Casagrande had pushed him into the labyrinth and then rescued him by changing the subject.

"So what can you tell us about Honduras?"

Mirian was getting ready to respond when she was interrupted by José, who'd been in agony from the time Eduardo had been unable to answer a question that was vital to his daily existence.

"How's the *lempira* against the dollar?"

"Five *lempira*s and a few *centavos*, I don't know exactly."

"It's a much stronger currency than the *sucre*," he said, rejoicing.

"Why does that make you happy?" she asked.

"Because sometimes I feel selfish, stingy. And I know I'm right about this, because if I treat you to beer or to dinner or something, it's thousands of *sucres* I'm spending, but you only have to spend a few *lempiras*."

"Go to sleep," Casagrande bullied him.

Mirian was wearing her permanent smile.

"How long have you been living here?" asked Casagrande.

"Eight years." José lowered his eyes.

"And at this stage in the game, *huevón,* haven't you learned that the currency in this country is called the dollar? You live here, that's the currency you make your wages in and that's the currency you have to spend. Forget your miserable *sucres*."

"You're mean," Mirian said.

Those words made José's eyes swim like two tiny lagoons.

"Put some music on, José," Eduardo said to him.

Rosa appeared with a tray full of french fries and three kinds of sauce. Casagrande was serving a fresh round of wine. Julio Jaramillo announced himself through the speakers.

At ten, Eduardo dared to let out the first fake yawn, which no one noticed. Mirian was listening, concentrating on a story of human survival in which Casagrande had been involved in Guadalajara, Mexico. For the third time that evening, the Julio Jaramillo cassette repeated itself—*si yo muero primero es tu promesa sobre mi cadáver dejar caer todo el llanto que brote del sufrimiento.* By then, the weeping no longer came from the stereo but from José, who was soaking Rosa's dress unconsolably. The torrents of tears over her legs were so great she got wet and excited in the deepest part of her. Mirian forgot Casagrande's adventure with a start; José's open sobbing transported her instantly from Guadalajara to New York. Eduardo smiled at her.

"It's nothing, love. That's the way it is here. A few days ago a dozen Ecuadoreans were weeping here. And it was all Julio Jaramillo's fault."

Rosa turned off Julio Jaramillo and said, "I think it's better if I take him home."

Eduardo seized the opportunity for a second yawn. "It's late, I'm tired."

Casagrande, whose hobby was indiscretion, said, "Yes. It's late. Good night, Mirian. And don't oversleep."

38

As Eduardo and Mirian walked up the Avenue of the Americas, Eduardo stopped to point something out to her. She was happy to see the Honduran Coat of Arms displayed on a telephone pole along this famous avenue. Eduardo was giving Mirian the busman's tour of midtown Manhattan. Before going into the Empire State building, they'd visited the United Nations Building. A pistol with a knot in the barrel as a symbol of peace or the eradication of war caught Mirian's attention. Skeptical as always, Eduardo warned her that monuments wouldn't be enough for there to be peace on the planet; the human brain would have to improve. They visited the Empire State Building, then Battery Park. Eduardo felt as if they were on camera, just like that, hand in hand as a light drizzle fell and "New York, New York" played in the background. She asked about every little thing, forgetting that he wasn't the inventor of New York. In Battery Park they bought tickets for the ferry ride to Liberty Island, where the Statue of Liberty is located. Eduardo felt a bit tired, but Mirian was tireless. She wanted them to go all the way up the endless spiral staircase to the Statue's crown. When they came back from the island, Eduardo suggested they go to the top of the World Trade Center, where she could watch the transition from day to night in the Big Apple from atop one of the tallest buildings in the world.

After Mirian had made the third lap around the observation deck of the World Trade Center, Eduardo insisted they sit down for a drink and a break. He couldn't figure out where she had gotten all her energy. He smiled to himself thinking about how only James Bond would be the perfect companion for such a tireless woman. Mirian sat beside him without taking her eyes off the Great City, which was beginning to come awake with all its lights, looking like a giant with a million eyes slowly emerging from its slumber. Mirian was entranced. Eduardo asked if they could go back to the apartment and, anticipating her resistance, reminded her that they needed to rest a bit because that night some friends of his and Casagrande's were throwing her a welcoming party to the city of skyscrapers.

They had rested for only an hour when Casagrande knocked on the door. Eduardo woke up. Mirian hadn't slept at all, she hadn't even rested on the bed. She had devoted that time to carefully inspecting everything in the bedroom. Eduardo immediately noticed some annoyance in her, and his memory went into automatic, taking a photo of the past in search of any hint of something he might have left out that she wouldn't agree with.

Finding absolutely nothing, and feeling free of sin, he asked her, "What's the matter, *cariño*?"

Mirian lifted her eyes up from the desk and flashed him a look through her mussed hair. She raised a hand to show him a little piece of red aluminum foil. He came close and carefully observed the object.

Understanding nothing, Eduardo asked, "Uh-huh, so what? It's a piece of trash."

"No," she replied emphatically, "it's a piece of condom wrapping."

Eduardo smiled, knowing that only Mirian had been in that room with him. "But *amor*, that's absurd. I swear, I couldn't tell you where that piece of wrapper came from. It's so small, you can't tell what it is. Besides, other people have lived here before me. It's possible it's a piece of condom wrapper, but what can I do about it?"

He walked over to her, stroked her hair with his hands, and kissed her. Mirian felt the sincerity in his touch. He wasn't lying to her.

Casagrande knocked on the door again, and this time he raised his voice for them to get a move on.

The party was at Silvio's, the Colombian writer's house. The location had changed at the last minute from Maribel's house at Eduardo's request. There were a dozen people waiting and more were expected.

Eduardo introduced her to the host and his wife, and they in turn introduced the guests who didn't know one another. As he did at every party, Casagrande flashed a sly look around to spot the boy that would keep him company for a night of platonic love, because—according to him—after his relationship with Julio, the missionary, he was going back into retirement.

Javier and Leo appeared out of a half-dark balcony and came up to Mirian with the familiarity with which you approach someone from your own country abroad. They introduced themselves and asked about Eduardo, who'd strayed into the kitchen to request the best of attention for the woman who brought him sleepless nights.

From the kitchen, Eduardo heard a happy, loud voice which he immediately recognized. Andrea entered the apartment like a woman who knows she's beautiful. Without asking anyone, without the least hesitation, she went straight to Mirian.

"You must be Mirian, right? It's a pleasure to meet you. Eduardo's told me a lot about you," and she gave her a kiss on the cheek, which she repeated on Eduardo's cheek as he approached.

An hour later, they were all in a sort of uncircular circle, discussing the image of Latin Americans in the United States.

"Who knows," the host said, "the thing is, all they spread about Colombia is the drug issue, holdups and guerilla warfare, that is, everything related to violence. They forget about other aspects of our country. I imagine it's jealousy. In Colombia we have a bit of everything: a vast culture, artists, emeralds, oil, great forests, oceans, mountains, in short, a bit of everything, which is why they say, *What Nature doesn't give you, Colombia won't lend you.*"

"But *ché,*" said a skinny Argentine, "you know very well we aren't lacking for anything either, except that in the process we've had a bit more bad luck than you people. We've had one too many dictators and military coups. If it weren't for that, *ché* . . . ."

Casagrande, gone from Chile for thirty-two years and unable to forget a fraternal and apparently motiveless grudge against Argentines, imitated a *gaucho* and unleashed his ironic humor. "But of course, *ché*, you know we never lost the war over the Falklands; we just ended up in second place."

After the laughter died down, an American said, "The same thing happens with countries as with cities: We always feel proud of the place we come from and look down on others. Look at us here, after all these years the division between North and South isn't totally mended."

Javier felt called upon to offer an emergency opinion. "There's a reason for that. How can you compare the South to the North? No way, you can't do it. I'll stick with the North."

"Let any Southerner present raise his hand and speak up," yelled a Colombian poet.

A thin, blonde woman with a long, pleated skirt, yelled out, "I heard that just fine. Who wants to start the Civil War up again? It must be some Communist."

"What's your name?" Javier started. "If I'd known you in the South and you'd paid attention to me, I'm sure I would hate the North."

Glass in hand, the woman stood in the middle of the circle. She spun around like a model and said, "My name is Renata. I'm from New Orleans, I'm single, and I studied Hispanic American literature, which explains my good Spanish and my modesty. I'm from the South, but I love *Nieva York*. Is *Nieva York* in the South?"

Her performance, as much as her saying *Nieva York,* provoked an outburst of laughter.

"It's *Nueva*, Renata. Not *Nieva* York, *Nueva* York."

"No, no, it's fine like that," said Javier. "*Nieva* York means it's winter in New York. She's good with language. She synthesized it better than any of us. *Nieva* York means snowy New York."

"How about *Neutro* York?" asked a Bolivian musician, whose presence up to that point had gone unnoticed.

"*Neutro's* from neutral," Andrea replied, "which means that New York is neutral, which is like saying, New York belongs to no one or to everyone."

Mairena and his wife had arrived, and they now approached the circle. Eduardo was happy to see them and, without thinking twice, yelled, "Negro York."

Mairena began laughing heartily as he moved to find a place in the circle. "It sounds pretty. That's what this city should be called, 'Negro York.' Well, we'll re-christen it some day."

"Nazi York," Leo said.

"That comes with the neutral stuff," Mirian replied. "If it's neutral, that means anyone from pacifists to Nazis, from conservatives to Communists can live here, and so on."

"How about Never York?" Andrea asked.

"Those are the people who came to New York to pursue dreams they never fulfilled and who leave cursing the city, saying they'll never return: Never York."

Andrea blushed. Something was wrong. One of the guests, consciously or unconsciously, asked Andrea to dance, even though there was no one else dancing. Eduardo took advantage of that to dance with Mirian, and as they danced, he kissed Mirian's ear.

Mirian asked to go out to the balcony, but they were intercepted by Casagrande calling for Eduardo. Eduardo sensed that he should go alone and gave his place to Leo to keep Mirian entertained until he returned. Leo understood and immediately asked her what she thought about the possibility of Central America becoming a single nation, large and powerful, in the future. Those topics fascinated Mirian, and everything seemed fine.

In the kitchen, Casagrande and some other guy were smoking a joint.

"She's taking you to the balcony, *huevón*. That's why I called you. She's going to ask you about it, *jodido*."

"About what?"

"Eduardo, my actor, you're so näive. She's going to ask you if you slept with Andrea. That's where she's taking you. She suspects something."

"You think so, Casa?"

"Of course, *huevón*. We homosexuals know more about women than you machos do. We're closer to them. She's going to ask you about it. And she'll probably tell you it's just curiosity. She understands your situation as a single man here, that sometimes women are the ones who do the provoking . . . Deny it absolutely."

"I don't like to lie to her, Casa."

"Do you love her?"

"Like no one else, Casa."

"So protect that relationship. Women, even when they know certain things, would rather hear you lie to them. That makes them vain. They know you don't want to lose them. In that sense it's not lying, it's part of the occupational hazards of loving, *huevón*."

"Thanks, Casa. But I love her and if I love her I ought to be truthful. I'm going to tell her, Casa. I shouldn't lie to her."

Casagrande closed the door to the kitchen and prepared to dramatize the story he was going to tell.

"Okay, you over there, *huevón*. How can you lose your way with the lights on? She takes you to the balcony. Once there she'll say to you, 'What a lovely party, the people are so beautiful!' And you'll answer, 'Yes, they're all special.' She'll point out to the subway, and then she'll say, like she's talking to the train: 'Who's that girl, what does she do? She's very beautiful.' So are you going to pretend you don't know who she's talking about? That would be your first big mistake. Because it's obvious that Andrea and Mirian are the two most beautiful women here. She'll spell it out clearly: 'Andrea.' And you'll answer with an 'Ah, yes.' Which will end up giving you away. She'll draw close to you and say half-smiling, 'Did you sleep with her?' And you'll look at the subway, you'll sigh, and you'll remain silent. She'll know, she'll come close and stroke your neck, making you believe she understands you. And to clear you of the situation, she'll say in her melodious little voice, 'How many times?' You'll believe in that thing they call maturity, which is really one of the greatest human follies and hypocrisies. And you'll answer, 'I don't know exactly, just a few times.' And it will scare you to see that her reaction is to kiss you on the lips and caress you. You'll feel big and powerful, haughty and vain. Suddenly she'll let out a little cry: '*Ay*, my earring.' You'll look at her ears and, indeed, there will be one missing. She'll lean over and point to the area beyond the balcony. You won't see a thing, but the illusion of the lover performing an act of daring will make you see something shiny, and you'll lean over the wall, more than half of your body leaning into space. She'll grab you by the feet and you'll have just enough time to hear her say, 'Son of a bitch, ' and she'll push you from the seventh floor. You'll fall on your face and end up splattered like marmalade. We'll hear your scream flying downward, blending in with her make-believe cries of pain. No one will notice that she's missing an earring. You'll be dead and won't be able to accuse her. They'll take photos of her, they'll ask her questions and she'll say, 'It hurts me deeply that my future husband made such a drastic decision. He committed suicide because he dreamed of being a famous actor and saw that time was passing and he wasn't making it. He committed suicide out of disappointment. God keep my beloved in glory.' And she'll cry on the screens, and they'll feel sorry for her. In a few months she'll write a book about your suicide, and she'll exaggerate things about you. She'll talk about your sexual preferences, she'll say you always showed signs of schizophrenia, she'll say the worst things possible. And her book will be a success, and she'll have fame and fortune. And you'll be in Hell for two reasons: for not having fulfilled your dreams on Earth and for being stupid. And Satan, as punishment, will make you read her book out loud over and over for the rest of eternity."

On the balcony, Mirian commented on how pretty Queens looked, and Manhattan in the distance. She congratulated him for all the special people he had as friends. She raved about Leo's intelligence. She thanked him for being so measured with his drinking that night. She hugged him and kissed him. Immediately after the Judas kiss came the expected:

"Did you sleep with her?"

"With who?"

"Don't play the fool."

"With Renata, the Southerner? I just met her today."

"With the *colombiana*."

"There are a lot of *colombianas* at this party."

"With Andrea."

"Are you kidding?"

"Yes or no?"

"Where do you get this from?"

"It's simple: yes or no."

"No."

"I don't believe you."

"Don't believe me."

"I swear to you, it's just feminine curiosity. She's very pretty. If she were ugly I might be upset."

"I said no."

"I know the answer is yes. It's just that I want to hear it from your lips."

"Were you a witness?"

"No."

"So?"

"You can tell."

"How can you tell?"

"She blushed when you said the thing about people who dream of doing something in New York and fail."

"I didn't notice, I didn't see her. It's possible she blushed. She wouldn't be the first person not to have her dreams come true in New York. Blushing is nothing, some people commit suicide."

"But did you sleep with her?"

"Mirian, let's drop it."

"I promise you I won't get upset. You're alone here, and I'm no fool. I would understand, you're a man, you need sex more than we do."

"Even so, Mirian: no."

"Really?"

"It's true, but if you keep harping on the subject, you're going to make me notice her, and then maybe the accusation will come true."

"Estúpido."

Leo, who at that moment had come out on the balcony, saw and heard the slap. He smiled and returned to the living room.

"Control yourself, Mirian."

"Why do you say that?"

"So we can talk about something more interesting."

"It's interesting to me."

"Not to me."

"Seriously, *cariño*, I understand, it's just curiosity. How about Casagrande, is he homosexual? He seemed it from the first night I met him."

"Let's go back inside. Yes, he's gay. What's the difference? He's a good person."

"I knew it from the first day."

"Let's go back. So what's the big deal, it's not a crime, as far as I know."

Of course, among Hondurans a slap on the cheek can't stay a secret, with the aggravating factor that the slaps multiply, and Leo turned one into three. Mairena, Javier and Casagrande were laughing in a corner, to everyone else's envy and curiosity. Mirian and Eduardo rejoined the group.

"How do you feel?" the hostess asked.

"Fine, thank you," Mirian smiled. "I wasn't expecting so much."

And the song with which Eduardo took trips to the future began playing. He took Mirian by the hand and they were the only couple dancing. Eduardo told her that he would have liked to have composed and sung that song, "When a Man Loves a Woman" for her, and she congratulated him on his good taste.

In the corner, the record was becoming endless for Javier. He wanted to cover his ears. Casagrande guessed what was bothering him and couldn't avoid inquiring about what was making him restless.

"That song," Javier replied, "that song's from the South. They sing it and scream it just like Down South. I hate that song."

"Don't be a boor," Leo scolded him, "it's beautiful."

Eduardo danced slowly. He translated the song into Mirian's ears and imagined the film director telling him he was doing the dance scene perfectly; he looked natural; he took his partner gently; he said things to her and smiled; his breathing was just like it should be when a man is with the woman he wants; and the film was coming out perfectly because they really seemed like they were in love. The song ended and the film ended, and entangled between fiction and fact, he told himself it didn't matter, the important thing was that he loved her.

Mirian got rid of Eduardo to converse on her own with whomever pleased her. She floated around until she fulfilled her aim. Andrea was looking through a window towards the subway station, which in Queens is an elevated platform. Mirian approached her.

"Why are you so alone?"

"My *compañero* didn't come along," she answered spontaneously.

"What a pity!"

"Yes, he didn't guarantee he'd come. That's how it is here. There are so many places to go, and the distances from one place to another are so great, you have to stay put in one place."

"Have you known Eduardo for a long time?"

"A few months. He's a good guy and very handsome. Congratulations."

"Thanks."

"How long are you staying in New York?"

"Three more weeks. Though I'd like to stay the rest of my life."

"I advise you not to. A month is fine, then routine sets in and you get homesick for your country and your people, and that's a constant nightmare."

"Other people have told me the same thing."

"It's true. I think it's the same everywhere. The problem isn't the cities; it's being a foreigner. As much as you may want to be strong and say you don't miss your country, you're consciously or unconsciously thinking about going back for good some day."

"It's possible, I've never been out of my country for more than a month."

"I envy you."

"Because of Eduardo?"

"That too," Andrea smiled. "Come on, let's go join the others, or they'll think we're conspiring."

When Eduardo saw both women smiling as they walked through the living room, it seemed for a moment that he'd been the mythological man who had held the world on his shoulders.

"That's enough," Casagrande said, "you're going to give yourself away. You don't behave like a good actor."

No one was interested in dancing. They only wanted to talk and drink. Others vanished into the bathroom or the kitchen to do drugs.

The get-together would have been perfect if the Bolivian musician hadn't verbally assaulted Honduras.

No one paid attention to him except Mirian, the controversial student of journalism, who retorted, "It's the height of cynicism for a Bolivian to speak badly of a country like Honduras, because we both live in two of the poorest and most backward countries in the hemisphere." She feigned thoughtfulness. "Well, it isn't your fault, *boliviano*; it's part of your very backwardness."

"Hondurans are to blame for the failure of Central American revolutions. They're built on strong bases," the Bolivian Marxist laughed sarcastically. "Strong army bases, that is."

Furious, Mirian was about to strike down his argument when Eduardo interrupted her. Casagrande piped up that it was getting late, that they should be getting home.

39

Mairena is thinking as he reclines on the living room couch about why he did it, about the fact that he saw Eduardo at the party and hadn't had enough courage to call him aside and tell him how bad he felt. He'd fulfilled that years-old dream, to sleep with a white woman, spread her white legs, suck on her white breasts, bite her white cheeks, but he wasn't able to see the color of her soul. Mairena loathed himself. He couldn't have fallen that far, not he, Mairena, who'd been to school, to high school; he, Mairena, who studied a few years at the University; he, Mairena, who neighbors and family members had labeled as intelligent and a person of exemplary good will; he, Mairena, who'd studied the Bible and other sacred books; he, Mairena, who'd been promoted to deacon for his exemplary behavior.

He needed to confess, to speak to the priest, to ask for Eduardo's forgiveness, to leave that world of whites, which had no room for him, nor did he want it to have room.

He scolded himself for the injustice, because he hadn't looked for the woman in Ruth, for the human being, but for a piece of white meat, as if he were taking meat from any animal or from several animals, dead meat, and sculpting a woman's body out of that meat and painting it white and giving it a bit of life, not so that it would live but so that it would move to his rhythm. He hadn't gone to bed with a woman but with a skin color, and he did so not for pleasure, much less for love, but out of the human stupidity of comparison. He didn't talk to Ruth, didn't draw her thoughts out, didn't talk with her about anything, just took her, used her, raped her, and lied to her afterward. He said he'd stay all night and didn't. He's gotten his ejaculation out of it and didn't care whether she'd been satisfied or not.

Mairena had left on tiptoes like a thief, leaving her exhausted and asleep on the floor, naked, as if she'd fallen in battle. When she awoke she probably looked for him, but Mairena was far away in other dreams, and she felt revolted, humiliated, like an insect. Mairena knew that would happen and was happy for the pain he'd bring her, the state of humiliation she'd be subjected to when she opened her eyes to a voiceless and bodiless Mairena, like a ghost from an erotic dream. He would be laughing that same evening, reaching a second orgasm with his wife, with the black woman he loved, making fun of Ruth's whiteness because of the grand feat he had achieved.

This same Mairena reflected the next day and begged Heaven for forgiveness, but it wasn't enough to keep that night from stealing his peace, dogging him three weeks later in nightmares. He, that same Mairena, would not be in this state, he sensed, had he not gone to bed with her, had he thought of her as a person and not as a color, considered her his equal, not a piece of white meat that he ordered and painted and gave a bit of life to just for himself. He had transgressed against three people: against Ruth, against his wife and against himself. Mairena did not want to be Mairena; he wanted to be someone who was less of a cretin, more human. There he was in his South Bronx apartment, inconsolable.

Mairena got up from the couch and went outside, walked a few blocks, and reached to the destination he'd thought about on the couch. There the priest asked him what his problem was. Mairena did not answer, but the priest had enough experience to discover the inner whirlpool Mairena was carrying around inside him, a whirlpool made of nails, sharp tins, glass shards, thorns, with an inner core of salt and lemon. The priest challenged him to confess. Mairena consented. This same Mairena told the priest of the piece of meat with which he sinned, not for sex, but because he'd been looking for a color and not a woman.

Mairena returned to his apartment, feeling much better. He would feel a little better with each passing day. The priest had not only offered him forgiveness but told him to stop feeling sorry for himself, because it had been a test from Heaven, and that whirlpool of garbage inside was a sure sign of his great repentance. After that experience Mairena would be more humane than ever.

Mairena was finally content. The woman he loved, a person like himself, was the only one for him.

40

It was a week after Mirian's departure and Eduardo had not yet recovered. Twenty-five percent of him was still in the Big Apple, possibly less if Mirian was pregnant when she left. Feeling lazier than he usually did on Sundays, Eduardo called Javier and decided to pay him a visit. Casagrande had left early to teach his private photography class. Eduardo walked unhurriedly along Valentine Avenue, crossed Poe Park, stopped in front of Edgar Allan Poe's house, and thought about the writer's sad, cruel life. With that, he had no desire to go any further. He saw no sense in struggling for greatness if it only meant suffering such a miserable life. For some, like Poe, that was the price. Poe knew how to pay it, but Eduardo knew he was not as brave as Poe. He went down the stairs to Kingsbridge Station and sat down on a bench to wait for the D train. He waited patiently, knowing how slow the trains ran on Sundays. He tried to imagine the future, but it was impossible: the present clamored for his presence. The present or the immediate past.

He remembered Mirian two days before her departure at the goodbye party Casagrande had put together at the Colombian writer's house. Mirian had given the party a special touch. She wasn't going to swallow the Bolivian's barb; she'd find some way to get revenge, and that's just what she did. Casagrande announced that at Mirian's goodbye party those who wrote for a hobby could bring their texts, because there would be a household *peña*. Casagrande sang and read Beat poems, the Colombian writer read a short story, and the Bolivian musician read a melancholy poem about Bolivia, where the purest air in America could be found. Mirian took the floor and said that since

Eduardo wasn't a writer, she would read something in his place, because she had had a few small items published in Honduras.

The Bolivian threw out a cruel joke asking whether any Hondurans knew how to read—writing would be asking too much. Mirian, fully aware of the bomb she was carrying, smiled feigning friendliness. When silence fell, she introduced her piece, saying that she'd been inspired by the welcome party, for which she thanked those who'd taken the initiative to put it together. She also thanked people for the good-bye party. She requested that if someone felt uneasy, to please say so after her reading, but to please not interrupt her. Mirian had that divine gift for quieting the masses. She began reading.

BOLIVIA: THE POOREST ON THE PLANET?

As far as we know, it's said that the poorest on the planet are three, in strict alphabetical order to avoid offending sensibilities: Bolivia, Haiti and Honduras. There may be others in the world, undoubtedly—Somalia, for example. But it happens to be located in Africa, and they've taught us that in Africa there are only jungles, swamps, natural dangers or freaks of Nature. In the classroom they only told us about wild animals, elephant stampedes, ferocious tigers, famished lions, serpents as thick as sewage pipes, pygmies, savage tribes who walk upon thorns while carrying long rods that are not quite spears. No one told us that there were countries there, that the barefoot black runners were as human as we are, that those same blacks were people with traditions, joys—and grief, most of all because of the rights that had been denied them throughout history. No one told us that they had thoughts. No one told us that around the time that a little Bolivian musician was born, an African named Nelson Mandela was taken to prison for defending the rights of his own and had only recently been freed, when the little musician was close to thirty. No one told us about apartheid. No one told us anything, and for us Africa was always a huge swamp or a jungle full of savages who were able to resolve their nations' problems thanks to the prowess of a white man named Tarzan of the Apes. So, because of all those things mentioned above, we won't look for a country, much less a poor country, in Africa. Some other day we'll discuss Asia, a land of little yellow men with slanted eyes.

I know Haiti thanks to a Pan American Life documentary, and it really didn't make you want to go there; the camera didn't hide the barren earth, and the narrator said that only five percent of the country was forested. The rest is a desert in the middle of the ocean. Haitians have had to deforest their country because their ignorance, and their needs, have forced them to do so, among which is their need to produce coal, energy. Fish have become scarce; you won't see any for miles around, except for tiny sardines along the Haitian coasts . At four in the morning, Haitian women have to get up and carry enormous jugs on their heads to haul water. You can see them pulling it up from wells, from holes, from whatever's at hand.

The Haitians, in spite of it all, still dance, even if it's to the beat of a ramshackle band with a cardboard box or tin cans for drums. Their paintings are alive: little houses scattered everywhere, a festiveness painful to the eyes, little birds and trees, a thousand colors. In spite of it all, you see their white teeth or the hollows of what had yesterday been teeth, but in both cases you see them smiling. Probably because when they look back on the misery into which they've sunk, when the sadness of seeing no way out brings them down, they turn their backs on their immediate reality and unconsciously create another reality facing the ocean. From the shore they look at the ocean, they see beyond it and imagine a fairer world.

Honduras is, undoubtedly, the country I know best, simply and plainly because that's where I'm from. The water in Honduras isn't scarce. To the contrary, it's abundant, except in the capital city, in Tegucigalpa. In the summertime you have to get up early for water before the rationing starts. Despite the fact that the country's been neglected, it's not yet deforested. And we're learning to protect and defend our forests. There are beggars but not yet to an extreme. I won't mention the endless number of positive points because this article would be unfair: it's about the country of the person who wrote it. So I'll limit myself to saying that we have the essentials: rivers and two oceans, the Atlantic and the Pacific. That is to say, we have two windows on the world. That should be enough.

As for Bolivia, I don't know what to say. What can you say about a country that has no ocean?

When the Bolivian heard the ending, he became furious and murmured something in that under-the-breath tone Bolivians have, evidently a muted insult. Mirian, who was dumbfounded by his reaction, suddenly felt remorse, which some time later would make her an avid student of Bolivian history and culture.

In an attempt to change the subject, she said, "I love Neuro York."

41

Mirian's return to New York was two weeks away, and Don Jonás did not begrudge her the expenses he'd incurred so his daughter could go back to visit Eduardo. She looked revitalized to him, content, inspired about her studies and devoted to her family. James Bond could be mentioned freely, as well as Superman, Batman, and any fictional character, from comic books or from movies. Doña Rosaura thought that finally, after so many years, they could be totally happy. Ricardo, her other son, had written to her from a faraway port. His ship had been in port for a week and, according to the letter, he'd found his calling in life. He would come back to his country when he had enough savings to dedicate himself to business. That afternoon Mirian had also invited Fernando, Don Jonás' oldest son, to have dinner at home after so many years of distance. Mirian's idea in inviting him was to bring peace to the family, which Doña Rosaura eagerly accepted.

When Fernando arrived, Doña Rosaura herself came out to greet him. He embraced and greeted her with a kiss on the cheek. Don Jonás stepped forward. He would have wanted to embrace him and tell him all the things you say spontaneously to someone you miss, but the meekness of someone who has committed a major transgression kept him from doing it. In the absence of courage, Fernando hugged his father and said a few words that shook the old man's inner foundations. Mirian hung around his neck and kissed him again and again.

In the dining room, Doña Rosaura didn't spare a single detail to make her remorse clear to him in easily decipherable language. While Fernando was absorbed in talking to an enthusiastic Mirian, Don Jonás sat there staring at him as if by reflex, as if to return to an unforgettable past. Fernando exuded sincerity and self-possession in all he said and how he said it. Mirian told the story of her trip to New York, of how impressed she was with the metropolis of all metropolises, and of her wish that everyone would get to know it some day. Doña Rosaura was all over herself with her attentions, offering them a napkin, more coffee, cream, turkey, whatever there was on the table. Fernando was intelligent enough to get the message. No one brought up topics that might stir up unpleasant memories. Fernando talked about his five-year-old son, up to then Don Jonás's only grandson, and about the progress he was making in his university studies. He was about to graduate from Law School, but was already practicing at a friend's firm. Later on he'd dedicate himself to politics; he was fed up with traditional parties which, according to him, never paid attention to the people's needs, but were nevertheless still in power on the eve of the twenty-first century. He said he would join one of the minority parties to find out what new proposals they were offering. Don Jonás smiled as he listened to the language of his budding young politician.

After dinner they moved into the living room to enjoy a special dessert and uncork a bottle of champagne in good cheer. They laughed at each other's stories. They re-read Ricardo's recent letter out loud and passed around a photo of him hugging a very homely port city woman in a swimsuit. The evening couldn't have been better.

The next morning, when breakfast was over, Fernando said he had to go. He might be late for a study session, but it had been worth it to stay over and sleep in his old house. Don Jonás asked him to wait until Mirian finished fixing herself up so she could drop him off at his place. That morning Don Jonás, accompanied by Mirian, would pay one last visit to the psychiatrist, who'd suggested a final appointment so he could measure the progress made by his patient in the big city. They said good-bye in front of Fernando's apartment. Father and daughter continued toward their destination, guided by the prudent driving of James Bond's ex-student.

The psychiatrist greeted Mirian with much deference and, in the same manner, took Don Jonás's hand.

"This time," the doctor said, "more than a medical appointment, it will be a conversation among friends. Your father already told me about your trip, your return, and I don't think you have a problem at all. What's more, I don't think you ever did have a problem that we could call serious. You're something of an artist, and since when is a psychiatrist enlightened enough to understand an artist? I think never. In my latest reflections I've come to the conclusion that we psychiatrists are good for some people, but not for artists; in fact, we need to consult artists, and we have to accept that. Maybe what you missed in your childhood was communication. Your fondness for spy movies and novels, especially the ones about the Cold War, stunted you, because among spies a word too many can mean death, which is where your mutism, your self-absorption came from, and your love for James Bond. Of course, you found your accomplice in him, the same complicity you had with your father, coming from you but not from him, as it should have been. Now that it's cleared up, you both look a lot better."

"Yes, the communication I've established with my daughter, thanks to you, makes me feel different, happy. Even my relationship with Rosaura has finally settled down."

"It's true," Mirian said, "it's been positive for everyone. I feel so good."

"Yes, it's been good for me, too," the psychiatrist said, and he cut himself off before he could finish. He was going to mention that after Mirian read the article "Bonfire of the Multitudes," about the burning of the U.S. Embassy in Tegucigalpa, his ambition had subsided. He was no longer passionate about becoming a rich man at all costs. Nor did he believe that in the future he'd be extradited. No, he'd decided to be comfortable with the earnings from his profession and one legal business or another, all of which he owed to Mirian's article. The doctor preferred to keep his secret to himself and changed the subject completely.

"Tell me about New York."

Mirian needed no prompting. It was her favorite subject of the moment.

"It's a beautiful city, huge. To me, it's the modern headquarters of literature and art."

"How about Eduardo?"

"He's fine. He wanted to come back with me, and I wanted him to as well, but he had to be strong to keep struggling a little longer."

"How about his job on Broadway?"

Mirian smiled. She remembered the night he mustered the courage and confidence to tell her about the repairs to the Lincoln Center wall. She couldn't hold back her laughter. Now, she thought, a little lie to the psychiatrist, who would then lie to others, couldn't be a crime.

"He quit. He read the screenplay and thought it was unethical to work in a piece that denigrates Latinos."

"Great!" the father interrupted. "You hadn't told me about that, Mirian."

"Yes, it's admirable, but to be sincere, doing that closes doors for him," the doctor said.

"What does it matter!" Don Jonás said resolutely in defense of his integrity as a Latin American. "If they close doors for him over there, he has me here. He's not going to starve to death."

"Thanks, Papá," Mirian started, and thought about how a small lie can sometimes bring large benefits.

"Have you kept up your writing?"

"Yes, I wrote a little something about Bolivia in New York."

"What was it about?"

"Nothing that would offend anyone. It was about the purest air in America."

"Very well, so what are you writing now?"

"At the moment, nothing. Still, from tomorrow on I want to dedicate myself to writing something about the subway, the New York subway. The train is a world of its own in New York. I rode it every day at different times. I can tell you that in the morning the train is like bedrooms on wheels; people finish sleeping on it. At noon, or really from nine in the morning to three in the afternoon, it's like a library on wheels; people read newspapers, magazines, books in the greatest variety of languages you can imagine. Lots of people are in the habit of carrying something to read when they go out. We should copy that habit here. From five in the afternoon to seven in the evening, it turns into the place of the exhausted; people don't want to talk, there's a lot of bad moods and bad smells. You can see the exhaustion in the faces and the desire to get home. From that time until ten in the evening it's pleasant; people want to laugh about anything. They don't read, but it's easy to strike up a conversation even if you haven't met someone before. After that, the train's a place of terror, frightening: Drugged-out people, drunks, delinquents—and some well-to-do folk on their way back from parties or night spots—but at those times it's horrific."

"Amazing," the doctor said, "I've always been astonished by your powers of observation."

"Me too," the father added smugly.

"Well," the doctor said, "I want us to make this final. There's one last thing, but I'm not sure I should talk about it."

"What is it?" Mirian asked, intrigued.

"No, forget it, you probably shouldn't know about it," Don Jonás said, anticipating what the psychiatrist was about to reveal.

"No, no, don't worry about it, doctor. I imagine you mean the time they kidnapped me, the day Agent 007 saved me." She laughed at their expressions of amazement, and continued. "I knew it. The day they planned it, I overheard my father."

The doctor and Don Jonás, who were stunned at first, ended up laughing.

42

"It couldn't have been a dream, it was a revelation. I can tell the difference between an everyday dream and a revelation," Casagrande said.

They were waiting for the curtain to go up on a play called *The English Only Restaurant* by a Colombian writer, Silvio Martínez Palau, which the Puerto Rican Travelling Theater was producing as part of its summer season. The play was set in a Latino restaurant in Queens, where speaking Spanish was forbidden because a campaign had begun to make English the only language you could speak in the United States, with the transparent objective of eliminating Spanish, according to Hispanics. They were on Central Park at 64th Street. A good number of people had showed up early to get a front-row seat.

"No, Casa, it's just a dream."

Casagrande looked at Eduardo and shook his head. Javier, who was more serious than the matter warranted, pondered it and said:

"I believe that it's a revelation, Casagrande, but not a revelation that you should leave New York, or about there being a war in the making. It has something to do with the great love you feel for Julio, the missionary. He was in the dream, wasn't he?"

Casagrande gazed intently at a group of stagehands who were setting up the portable stage.

"No, my experience doesn't tell me that, it was a revelation about a catastrophe: either an earthquake in New York or a war. Whatever the reason, my duty's to leave New York."

"Earthquake," Eduardo repeated. "Don't scare me, Casa."

"Don't worry," Javier smiled. "The *gringos* who are opposed to all the immigrants here, especially Latino immigrants, made that up, and since they know we're superstitious, they exploit it and spread those ideas."

"Javier may be right, the dream is probably just a manifestation of your anxiousness to be with Julio, your love."

"The missionary," Javier added.

"No. It's not that, even though it's true that I was getting used to the little boy, and he's really tasty," Casagrande smiled, "but no, I've had those short-lived loves before. Seriously, it's a revelation, we have to get out of this city."

"So what if it were an earthquake or a war? I don't gain anything by leaving New York. If it's a war this could be one of the final theaters, and if it's an earthquake, no matter where I go it's going to kill me, because I love so many people here, their tragedy immediately becomes my own, and it might be worse."

Casagrande half-closed his eyes.

"Listen up: you *Banana Republics* could be right. You *bananeros* are intelligent, and the most beautiful part is you're very human. After meeting you, I think I'd like to get to know Honduras. What's Honduras like?"

"If you like us, well, we're a reflection of our country. Honduras is like us, no more no less: intelligent but lacking opportunities; full of projects but without the money to make them happen; with a bad reputation because people don't know us personally; we're not lazy, it's just not worth working if you're not well paid; a bit quaint, which we take not as a defect but as a virtue, because that may very well be the birthplace of humanism. What else can I tell you?" Eduardo concluded.

Casagrande laughed.

"Write it down, *huevón.*"

"I never heard a better description of my country!"

"Talk to me and you'll hear more things like that," Eduardo said, "and I'm forgetting another one of our virtues: modesty."

"What good does modesty do?" Javier wondered.

Casagrande fixed his gaze on the stagehands again, who were about to finish setting up the stage.

"Modesty does exist, it's when you play the fool but deep down you know you're superior. Immodesty is what doesn't exist. Some say immodesty is when someone says: 'I can do it.' If you can do it, that's not immodesty, it's capability; the theory of immodesty was made up by the incapable, with the aggravating factor that they're envious."

"Good one, Casa," Eduardo yelled. "I see *chilenos* aren't that dumb, they really can converse with *hondureños*, which isn't easy."

"And speaking of *bananeros*, what happened to Leo, the *Morazanista*? That boy's intelligent. We spoke a long while at the party, the party for Mirian, this guy's torment. Leo's good people, he knows a lot."

"Haven't seen him for days," Eduardo said.

"Haven't seen him?" Javier inquired. "I thought you knew already. Leo left New York."

"What?" Eduardo was exasperated. "He left. He did it to me again, the sonuvabitch. Where'd he go?"

"To the Dominican Republic, to Puerto Plata. He got a Dominican woman pregnant and they decided to get married. She's a university professor, she's got some money according to what he told me."

Eduardo complained: "So why didn't he call me at least? I'm going to end up hating him. When he left Honduras he didn't say good-bye, when he left Tegucigalpa for La Ceiba he didn't say good-bye either. I thought he might have shaken off that carryover of underdevelopment here in New York."

"He warned me you'd get like this, but said it was better if he didn't say good-bye. It was hard for him not to say good-bye to you, but he said telling you would have been worse."

Casagrande muttered something to himself.

"These *bananeros* are so sentimental."

Eduardo exploded.

"So what! What's wrong with being sentimental? Isn't sentiment what's missing in this son of a bitch world?"

"I'm sorry, *huevón*, take it easy. You have the right to get angry."

"I should probably get out of here too."'

"Is Mirian taking you away?"

"You've got all the luck. Sometimes I wish I had a magnet of my own in Honduras. If the woman from the South had been someone else . . ."

"There are others," Casagrande advised him, "but you've lost your vision. If you'd set it up right from the outset this situation would be entirely different; some are made for success, others for failure. Many times divorces come from that: one of the two wasn't prepared for success. And it's not a matter of being prepared, but of predestination. Therefore, if you're predestined to be a successful man and you marry a woman predestined to failure, there will be circumstances, no matter how much you resist them, that will separate you irrevocably, because success wasn't for her, success comes only to those who own it, unlike failure, which comes to those it has to come to and can also come to some of the successful ones who drop their guard. I think you were predestined to success, but her destiny to fail was stronger, or more pronounced, so strong that it affected you. In that sense you strike me as a successful man who dropped his guard. Perhaps a woman you could love and who might love you was waiting for you ahead, but you were a coward and let yourself falter midway."

"I wish I'd known you earlier, Casagrande," Javier said sincerely.

"That's good, Casa. And that's probably how it is. It's possible; before Mirian I had a girlfriend who I was going to marry, and at the last minute the wedding didn't take place: circumstances made it impossible. Now I have an explanation. Dina wasn't born for success."

"So what became of her?" Casagrande asked.

"She married an *ex-contra*, from Nicaragua, who stayed in Honduras after the war. It seems the fellow was kind of off his rocker. He'd get up at midnight pretending to shoot a machine gun, throwing grenades, laying mines. One of those nights, in his midnight warrior fever, he got it in his head that Dina belonged to the Cuban secret police, she was a Communist, and amid the machine guns, bombs, and airplane sounds he made with his mouth, he threw her headfirst from the second floor. Dina didn't die, but she's committed at Santa Rosita, one of Honduras' biggest psychiatric hospitals."

"How sad," Javier commented.

"It was her destiny," Casagrande declared.

"Maybe not," Eduardo said.

"Yes, yes it was," Casagrande declared again, "because she had you and lost you."

"I don't have any wealth, Casa."

"I do," Casagrande smiled, "I have me."

Javier agreed. "Great!"

"Yes, I have me. I've had me all my life. That's my wealth: I've never been interested in material wealth, even though I've had that too, but those aren't the riches that concern me, I prefer the wealth of the spirit. People need to understand that, even though we're not the majority, there are people who aren't interested in money, who don't chase after it, people for whom the basics are enough to take care of our needs, and we dare say we're happy."

"I'm ashamed, Casa."

"Why?"

"Because I'm here, I dream of fame, of becoming a movie star, and when you dream of that you dream of money. Though in all sincerity, up to this day I believe I've never been interested in money but in acting."

"That's fine," Casagrande said. "It's fine to try whatever you wish to try, but don't get bitter if you don't get it. What's bad is to lose sight of your happiness over something as insignificant as fame. I prefer prestige. I don't believe you aren't interested in money."

"And you shouldn't be ashamed," Javier offered, "on the contrary, you should be proud because despite coming from a small, poor, nameless country, you've put your luck on the line by playing with the big shots and that alone's more than enough, not just for you but for every Honduran. What does it matter if you get there or not? What matters is that one of our fellow countrymen has been bold enough to dream big."

"Thanks, Javi, thanks," Eduardo smiled and blushed.

"I don't know how far you want to go, but in all good faith I hope you make it. Julio said you'd make it."

"The missionary's very spiritual, that's true, he told me so personally. He could have been ambiguous, for starters because I should ask myself: where do I want to go?"

"Hold on," Casagrande smiled, "let's get closer to the stage, the play's about to start."

43

José the subletter was drinking alone in the living room. He was listening to Julio Jaramillo, lying in an easy chair, his eyes fixed on the ceiling. On the little table in the living room he had a half dozen unopened beers, and four empty cans. Without a word to anyone, discreet to the point of boredom, Rosa had bought tickets for her daughter and herself and had gone back to Ecuador. José found out about it late at night, at ten, the time at which Rosa had asked the neighbor to hand him a note, which only said, "I'm leaving with my daughter. We're fed up. You can stick your electronic appliances and your *sucres* up your ass."

Eduardo came home, opened the front door and was greeted in the hallway by the sounds of Julio Jaramillo. He suspected José was home. He went to his room to drop his work bag off and then headed into the living room.

"How could you possibly be drinking all those *sucres*!"

"All you and Casagrande know how to do is turn everything into a joke," José said, creasing his brow.

Eduardo ignored him, grabbed a beer and, as he popped it open, said, "Can I drink this handful of *sucres?*"

"Look, I told you, please stop kidding around. I just finished thanking God that Casagrande left ten minutes ago, and now you come in."

"Seems like God didn't pay you much attention. I bet you offered to pay him in *sucres* if he'd leave you alone, but he's used to getting paid in dollars."

José turned the volume up as far as it would go on his sound system. Eduardo sat there in an easy chair, laughing. Julio Jaramillo invaded all of Valentine Avenue. After a few minutes, José turned down the volume.

"Look, Honduras, some *gringa* called you, some girl named Elizabeth. She left her number for you to call her back. She said it was urgent."

Eduardo thanked him. He stayed in the living room to make the call, and after talking for a few minutes with Elizabeth he hung up, turned to José and said, "So I made a mistake. There must be a crisis in Heaven: they're taking devalued currencies. God heard your prayers, in spite of the *sucres*. I've got to go out right away."

Elizabeth was already at the Village café where she'd told Eduardo she'd wait for him. She was drinking coffee.

"You're on time," she said to him.

"You're more on time."

"What?"

He often had problems with Americans who spoke Spanish but didn't know how to use the *vos* form of Central American dialect.

"No, I meant to say that you're more punctual."

"No, don't use *tú*, I like to hear you using *vos*. Just speak slowly because it's hard for me to understand, not always, just sometimes."

"Understood."

"You remember how much we talked when I called you to find out if you'd had problems with the Happy Land thing?"

"Of course."

"I told you I might get you something, and it might work out. Look, a friend of mine is the friend of an important director's assistant. I told this friend of mine about you, my friend spoke to the assistant's friend, and by chance he mentioned it to the assistant, and it seems the assistant's friend heard his friend talk about a new movie they're about to start shooting and so my friend's friend mentioned you to the assistant, and he was interested. He wanted to see your headshot, your resumé. So that's what happened. He looked at your resumé, which is excessively poor compared to the competition's, but your look caught his eye, and he wants to see you in person. It's not definite, but he's the assistant to an important director, and just seeing him in person is a big step."

The unexpected news made him happy. "Yes, I know it isn't easy, but no matter what happens I'm very grateful to you."

"Good luck."

"Thanks, Elizabeth."

"Look at this café, or at all these restaurants around here: All of the waiters are actors and actresses looking for a break. The simple fact of working in these restaurants is already an accomplishment. Others aspire to be waiters, and even being a waiter in these restaurants isn't easy; the competition's stiff, they give you certain tests to fill out, and there are a lot of requirements."

"Yeah, I know all about it. According to what they told me, directors and other people like that come to these restaurants, and if you're a waiter you might have a chance."

"That's how it is. Do you believe in luck?"

"A bit. I'm a well-read man, which doesn't allow me to believe in it totally."

"Well, you should believe in it a little more, because when you see this agent, you're going to need it, and a lot of it."

A week later Eduardo walked happily out of the assistant's office. The agent had Eduardo read out loud to hear how his English was, made him model full-front and in profile, asked him to gesture in sadness, happiness, worry, disinterest . . . and the assistant took down his address and telephone so he could notify him of the time and date of his audition.

That night at Elizabeth's apartment, Eduardo, Casagrande and Maribel celebrated with drinks and marihuana. They wanted to have sex, but Eduardo indulged in some premeditated drinking to get drunk and avoid getting an erection, so that in his dreams he could embrace Mirian.

Two days later the front-page headlines proclaimed: "Iraq Invades Kuwait."

44

That winter threatened to become the cruelest in New York history. The rumors of war had reached a fever pitch. Some prophesied that it would be the last and final war. It was said that petroleum would run scarce, so there would be no central heating. People who were far from the frontlines would suffer the effects because ice storms would be unleashed on cities. In New York a few million would perish from the lack of heating in the implacable cold. People on the streets, at their jobs or in schools expected to suddenly hear a whistle above the skyscrapers and to have barely enough time to hear a missile, or several missiles, explode. More than a hundred thousand members of the U.S. Army were sent to the desert; others were on the way and the recruitment rosters were getting longer. News reports and conversations all revolved around what came to be known as The Gulf War. There was fear of terrorist attacks in the principal cities of the United States. It was said that the Iraqi army was made up of fanatics and was therefore indestructible, and that with the alliance of Iran, Syria, Jordan and other countries, they could join forces and defeat the Allies. It also became a matter of speculation that Communists from the ex-Soviet Union owned the Red Army and would take advantage of the war to support Iraq and in turn abolish *perestroika* and all its reforms. A few religious zealots saw the end of the world coming in that war.

One morning, Eduardo notified Charlie that he was going back to Honduras in a few days. Charlie, always a man of few words, accepted the news and told him they'd only work until midday, to get together with the closest among his employees to give him a little good-bye party in the office. Considering Charlie's background, that statement seemed like a miracle.

Some hours later Charlie and four of his trusted workers were preparing a barbecue in Eduardo's honor in the backyard of the building. Charlie bought a good amount of beer and several bottles of his favorite drink, Georgi Vodka. Eduardo hadn't forgotten that Casagrande had invited him out that Friday for a pre-good-bye. The real good-bye party would be that Saturday at Maribel's house. When Charlie found out, he asked him to call Casagrande and tell him to come to the barbecue. Which is what he did.

They put some office chairs out on the patio. Charlie was drinking vodka on the rocks, but you could very rarely tell when he was drunk. Robert, Eduardo's Texan foe, only drank one beer and was off, not without first saying to Charlie, "Seems like Hollywood don't want any Hondurans. He finally woke up."

Eduardo answered, "No, Tex, you'll never get anywhere; as a designer, you have no sense of humor. Let me give you some news to make you happy: I'm coming back in a few months for an audition."

The Texan started hurling insults, but Charlie gestured for him to leave, since he'd already announced his departure.

"True?" Charlie asked, when Robert disappeared.

"True. I would have had it two months ago, but they postponed it because of the war. When everything's ready they'll notify me in Honduras. I'm happy. They've showed some sort of interest in me, because I got them to pay for my trip back."

"That's very nice," Charlie said.

Leroy, a black man from Alabama, said, "Eduardo, talk a little Spanish. I like hearing Spanish."

Eduardo complied with his request: *"Así que vos sos el token*?"

Leroy tried to repeat it but only managed to produce a babble like the religious language they call "speaking in tongues," which takes over some people in religious ecstasy. He added in his black Alabama English, "I couldn't make out a thing. What's it mean?"

Charlie didn't understand either, and was interested in the translation. So Eduardo repeated it for him in English.

"So you're the token?"

Charlie laughed. Leroy quickly agreed and laughed uproariously.

According to Charlie's explanation to Eduardo some time ago, *token* refers to when there's only one black or Latino on a job. If there's only one, he's the *token*, because by having him you can prove that the employer doesn't practice racial discrimination. This is also applicable to films, television, plays and almost everything else; you can't be without your *token.* But in New York City the coin you use to pay for a subway ride is also called a *token.* Still, Charlie didn't hire Leroy as a *token* but as just another employee. It so happened he was the only black man to have asked him for a job, even though his office was close to Chinatown, next to Second Avenue and Houston Street, not too far from which there is a project where mostly African Americans live.

"That's right, I'm Mr. Charlie's favorite *token.*"

Casagrande arrived. "So how is it, Banana? You've got all the luck when it comes to people throwing parties for you."

"Only English allowed," Charlie said as he hid behind a smile.

Casagrande excused himself and greeted them one by one, including the three workers who were cooking the barbecue a few yards away from them.

Charlie didn't speak Spanish, but he understood a lot, which is why he asked Casagrande,"Did you call him Banana?"

"Yes, *Banana Republic* . . . that is, *The Big Banana*."

Charlie almost choked on an ice cube. There was nothing he found funnier on this planet than jokes about countries, as long as they weren't about the United States, naturally, and much less about New York City.

"Eduardo's taking off," Casagrande said, "because he's afraid of a winter without heat."

Charlie seemed worried. "Yes, it's dangerous, even though we have the strongest army on Earth and the most advanced weapons technology."

"That's precisely why," Casagrande said, "Iraq was weaned on arms from the U.S., the Soviet Union and other countries during the eight-year war against Iran."

"It's dangerous," Charlie repeated, "but it was more dangerous when the Soviets were in power."

"They still are," Casagrande said. "They might join the fight."

"No," Charlie laughed scornfully, "it's like they don't exist. They have an economic crisis that's choking them. They have to do what the U.S. tells them to do."

Leroy, who was preparing the barbecue, stepped in closer to hear about the topic of war. "After what happened in Viet Nam, I'm afraid of getting involved in a war with any country, no matter how small it is."

"No," Charlie said, "the Viet Nam thing won't repeat itself. Our army acts with lightning speed nowadays. Look at what we did in Grenada, in Panama, we had almost no casualties on our side."

Charlie's point of view seemed too easy for Eduardo.

"Grenada and Panama are tiny. They have no resources and no war experience. Iraq's different."

"But the methods we're using over there are different."

"I hope there aren't too many innocent dead," Casagrande said with an undercurrent of resentment that Charlie picked up.

"War is war. There will always be innocent dead."

"Like in Panama?" Eduardo asked.

"That dope pusher had to be removed from the presidency no matter what it took. We saved the Panamanian people."

"Never," Casagrande said, "the problem there was a personal problem with Noriega, and you showed your ineptitude by bombarding civilians. A single man turned you into murderers once again, because in Grenada . . ."

"Maybe you're right," Charlie chugged the vodka, "but the important thing was to capture the dope pusher, and that's what happened."

Casagrande was irritated.

"If one innocent dies, just one, it's one too many."

"I think the barbecue's ready," Leroy said.

"I'm hungry," Charlie added.

While they went off to get the plates, Casagrande took advantage of being alone with Eduardo.

"I don't like it here. Let's go."

"No, let's stay. It's important to hear this part out. If you feel bad, just think of our *gringo* friends. Fortunately they don't all think like Charlie."

They stayed in the office until late that evening. Charlie, an old man who had experience talking to foreigners, sensed that the subject of war was threatening to kill the barbecue. So they talked about other things.

Once Casagrande was a little drunk, he tried to start up the war conversation again. Charlie avoided it with smiles and questions that had nothing to do with combat scenarios. Thanks to all that, a good-bye party that had begun questionably came to a happy ending.

On the twelfth floor, a minute away from Edgar Allan Poe's house, on Valentine Avenue, in the Bronx, in New York City, State of New York, United States, on the floor of the apartment living room, they found José, the subletter, sleeping off a drunken stupor worthy of the books; the Julio Jaramillo record played over and over again. In the refrigerator, a dozen completely untouched sixteen-ounce beers were waiting for them and, what was most surprising, a torn-up ten dollar bill was on the living room coffee table. As they drank the dozen beers, Casagrande and Eduardo, who were no experts in finance, tried in vain to figure out how many *sucres* José had torn up.

45

January's heat in Tegucigalpa belies the fact that December is barely over. The heat comes from above, rises from the soil and blows in on the wind from the desert. Absolutely nothing matters anywhere in the country. Tegucigalpans swear the city's never been so suffocating, they swear it is an apocalyptic warning of the end of the world. The Allied armies have given Iraq an ultimatum to pull its troops out of Kuwait. Everything's ready in the theater of war. The men in arms are waiting for the order to fire. The black body bags, a hundred thousand of them, are already in the desert to repatriate U.S. and Allied casualties. The calendar speeds ahead and Iraq does not retreat.

As the countdown begins, people's excitement grows. Eduardo thinks that people are not so much sad or worried as they are festive. There's something to talk about everywhere you go. The pro-Iraqi and pro-U.S. factions argue in restaurants. Most of the population seems to be celebrating. Maybe the only ones who are worried are the car owners. The Honduran government has taken advantage of the war to raise the price of fuel five times above its normal price. People say that once the war starts it will go up more, and thousands of cars in Honduras will not be able to leave their garages. Many will be stranded without fuel on the streets and will be abandoned there. People will go out to their jobs at one in the morning, in huge groups to protect each other, and will come back home, still in groups, at midnight. There will be no taxis or buses. Maybe only the president and a few wealthy men will ride in their cars. After a few years go by, you will have to pay to even see a car, to remember a time when there were plenty of them.

War depresses Eduardo, makes him lament having been born. He imagines the screams of the injured, the loneliness of the fallen in combat, the grieving mothers in the United States, the grieving mothers in Iraq, the family members in mourning in America, the family members mourning in the Middle East, even before it happens. For him there are no winners, only losers: the planet Earth will once more suffer the defeat of warring against itself. He cannot sleep, and would be less able to do so if Mirian weren't by his side listening to him, keeping him company in his fears, feeding his hopes that it's all probably a bluff, that not one missile will be launched. She says that and more, thinking that a half-lie can't be a sin.

He would give it all up for there to be no war. At that moment he doesn't want any trips to the future; he doesn't want to be famous, or to have money, or prestige. All he wants is for there to be no war. If, by giving his life, he could put an end to war, he'd gladly lay it down. War makes him suffer, makes him ill no matter how faraway. Something unexplainable dwells within him: there's not a philosophy around that can persuade him of the need for war. He detests the fact that a few arrogant men from one side or another decide on a war that will affect millions. He dreams about there one day being wars of higher intelligence: wars over language, metaphors, irony, ideas. By that time there will be so much intelligence that you won't get to the point of physical aggression because the loser will also be intelligent, and the winner, because he's a more intelligent winner, won't gloat over his victory, but will seek reconciliation. By that time blood won't flow over the Earth, nor will prefabricated chemicals flood the lungs, nor will mothers cry for their children. They'll only demand that they study more for some future confrontation. Losers and winners will be happy. Dignity will reign on the planet.

Mirian asks him to go out with her to the movies, to a swimming pool, to some place where they can get their minds off the war. It's all the same. The war isn't in the Persian Gulf, it's in his brain, in his heart. The long-awaited day comes: people chant the countdown the same way a crowd chants at a KO'd boxer who's trying to get up again. Eduardo loathes that mysterious human condition that pulls men toward self-destruction like iron to a magnet.

The war has begun. Thousands of planes bombard Iraq. By the second night, eighteen thousand tons of bombs have fallen from the Iraqi skies. In Kuwait, oil wells have been set afire.

When Iraq surrenders, he feels a bit calmer. Not much, but enough to keep him from faltering. He thinks about the broken eardrums of thousands of Iraqis. He imagines what that multitude of dead would look like if they were exhibited on a giant table and put up for sale to interplanetary carnivores with a passion for human flesh. He imagines the selling of a thousand heads, two-hundred-fifty feet, two thousand pounds of liver, a hundred hearts, five thousand eyes, three thousand tongues, three hundred gizzards for the intergalactic dogs. "Scrape those faces off good; they still have hair on them. Give me twenty thousand pounds of roast, and take my address down. Let me know when the next major slaughter's going to be. It doesn't matter what sort of slaughter, but we do prefer when it's from natural causes: earthquakes, hurricanes, seaquakes, you know? But if you don't have any of that, we'll have no choice but to take the other sort. After all, what matters is the meat. The problem with war meat is that sometimes it has too much lead or gas and it's a lot more work for us to clean."

On the twelfth floor of one of the buildings on Valentine Avenue, in the Bronx, in New York City, Casagrande and José drink as they talk. The other tenants, Mauro and Alfredo, had left a month earlier, in search of a way to join the Army so they could obtain citizenship after the war.

"Don't leave, Casagrande," José's voice implored.

"I have to go. Last night the bombing began. I had a revelation about this war, and my duty is to go to San Francisco."

"If you don't want to, you don't have to pay me, but stay, Casagrande."

"I'm sorry. I'm leaving tomorrow. Are you going with me to the airport?"

The conversation is cold, lacking Casagrande's usual sense of humor. Just like Eduardo, the war hurts him; he hurts for people no matter what nationality, what color, much less their sexual preferences. He's gotten fed up. He can even acknowledge, for the first time in his life, that he is growing old. Baghdad, that cultural relic which belonged to no one in particular but to all of humanity, hurts him. And the dehumanization is turning it into ashes. There will be no more flying carpets, no Aladdin's lamps, only nightless days. You can forget about *The Garden of Earthly Delights*.

The next day Casagrande leaves for San Francisco. He is still half-drunk, and on the way to the airport he thinks about how he will fortify himself with a good dose of vodka during the flight.

Three months later, Mirian is content. She knows that Eduardo will never be able to recover altogether from the war, because she also knows that he's one of those special people who, even if everything around them and concerning them is all right, will never be totally all right because they do not suffer from things that concern them alone. She feels better because the whole family will be traveling to the beaches on the Atlantic coast for a few days. Eduardo did not turn down the invitation; for some time, he had wanted to get to know Trujillo, the port city where the Spanish conquerors first landed.

46

Towards autumn Eduardo returned to New York for his audition. He found a New York that had already started to forget the war. A few small businesses had gone broke and others were about to close. The rents came down drastically, thanks to the recession.

Eduardo stayed at Valentine Avenue, at José the subletter's place, who he'd called from Tegucigalpa, and who told him he could stay as long as he needed to; it was José's treat, he would charge him absolutely nothing. José had learned to smile; he'd recapped his worn-down gold tooth and filled the hollow of its neighboring rotted-out tooth. He was living with a Puerto Rican woman who'd taught him to live in dollars, as much because she was imposing and possessive as because she'd never known any other currency on her enchanted island. She didn't understand the least thing about exchanging dollars for *sucres*, which, by the way, she still hadn't learned to pronounce, calling them *surques*. He'd met the Puerto Rican woman in the Government Bar on Jerome Avenue in the Bronx, where she worked as a waitress. At first she didn't pay him any attention, until one day José was involved in an incident designed to awaken the coy Puerto Rican woman's heart. José punched Javier Solís' "En mi viejo San Juan" thirteen times on the jukebox. A Mexican fellow, who got fed up with the repetition, threatened to kill José if he played that song one more time. The waitress interceded on his behalf and asked the Mexican to leave the premises.

The night he arrived, he stayed in the room that had belonged to Casagrande. It would soon be November, and that first day of November came to mind when he and Casagrande, both desperately broke, looked for any way to make money. That was what made them decide to sign up for the New York Marathon, the biggest in the world. More than twenty-five thousand athletes from all over the planet were participating, and the prize consisted of ten thousand dollars and a Mercedes Benz. Eduardo Lin, The Big Banana, ended up in the twenty-four thousand, six-hundred-seventeenth position, while his colleague, Casagrande, the athlete in the black poncho with more than a half century of life and drinking, took last place, ten hours behind everyone else. He was able to make it to the finish line thanks to the fact that, whenever the opportunity presented itself, his panted humming of Tony Bennett's "I Left My Heart in San Francisco" kept his spirits high.

He also recalled the day he'd left for Honduras. Casagrande was helping him pack, giving him advice on how to live his life, repeating his greetings and kisses for Mirian, and cracking jokes which that day seemed more than cruel, because neither one of them revealed an inkling of a desire to laugh.

"Casagrande, I'm giving you my television set. I'm giving you this radio. I'm giving you my books—read them. I'm giving you these extra tokens I bought. Don't go jumping the turnstiles, because it's not the sixties anymore."

The Colombian writer showed up in his car to take Eduardo to the airport. Casagrande refused to go. They embraced.

Casagrande tried to smile, but when he saw Eduardo's eyes, he said, "Don't be a pansy, Banana."

Eduardo's eyes met Casagrande's. "What happened, Casagrande? Did you spill some wine in your eyes?"

They hugged again. They stood there, hugging. And something as unexplainable as esoterism itself overcame them both.

On the third day after Eduardo's return to New York the audition took place. The assistant saw him and, by good fortune, gave him an advantageous place in line. When his turn came, he felt neither sad nor happy, neither dreaming nor present in reality; he was just there, going through the door where the famous director was waiting for him. He didn't need the assistant to introduce him; it was enough to see the unruly beard, the long hair, and a forehead that reminded him of Poe.

He got excited. Eduardo Lin was shaking hands and smiling with the great Steven Spielberg, who'd invited him to take a seat.

"Eduardo, what a pleasure. How was the trip?"

"Fine, just fine, thank you. It's an honor to meet you in person."`

"Thank you."

"I never miss a single movie of yours."

"Thank you."

"No one told me it was you, and I never imagined it would be, either."

"Yes, I prefer it that way."

The famous director-producer asked him questions about his life, his country, his dreams and hopes. Spielberg watched the movement of Eduardo's lips as he spoke, the gestures, the words he combined with them, the harmony of the breathing, and whether he blinked rhythmically. He showed him a Van Gogh and pointed out a Picasso on the opposite wall so he could see his profile.

"You'll stay," Spielberg said to him, "you're the one I need."

His heart skipped like a little rubber ball bouncing down a staircase to infinity. He was speechless. He needed oxygen. He excused himself with a bow of his head and pinched himself. Leaning over his desk, Spielberg tweaked one of his ears as if he wanted to turn him into another Van Gogh. Eduardo yelped so loud that he convinced himself he was in possession of reality.

"It's incredible, I made it, I made it!"

"We know that already," Spielberg told him.

"Could you write me a note certifying that I made it?"

"Of course." Spielberg got on the computer and wrote it. Then he reread the document and signed it.

"You have no idea how I feel."

"I can imagine."

"Yes, forgive me, I know you have a good imagination."

"That's not why I said it," Spielberg smiled, "I said it because I can really imagine how happy you are."

Spielberg waved his assistant over.

"We're keeping him. Send away everyone who's waiting."

"No, don't send them away," Eduardo cried.

Spielberg coughed. He stroked his beard. He shifted his gaze, signalling his assistant to leave them alone.

"Why?"

"Because all I wanted was to make it, and I did. I'm a born actor. I love acting. I've spent my whole life acting."

"So, precisely," Spielberg said, unable to recover from the shock.

"I'm not interested in fame or money, but in acting. To act from day to day as I've been doing. I act when I walk, when I laugh, when I talk, you know? At every moment. The one thing I was really missing to feel like I'd made it was to know whether I really know how to act, whether I stand out as an actor. And I've managed to come as far as you, no less than the *maestro* Steven Spielberg, and that means I do it well, I'm good at it. That's enough, Mr. Spielberg. Get someone else to play the role you want me for."

Spielberg, elbows on the desk and running his fingers through his hair, thought, *Either this guy is an incurable idiot or he's a genius.* He asked him, "Are you serious?"

"I've never been more serious, Mr. Spielberg."

"It sounds incredible to me. You should think it over carefully."

"I've thought about it already. What I want is to go back to my country, tell my future wife that I renounced . . ."

Spielberg interrupted.

"Do you think she'll take you after you renounce this?"

Eduardo hesitated for a second, but a memory gave him back his certainty. "Yes. She spent many years in love with James Bond."

After Eduardo told him the whole 007 story, Spielberg thought he was the one dreaming.

"Keep going. And after you tell James Bond's ex about turning this down, what then?"

"To keep acting, Mr. Spielberg, just like I've been doing. Start a business for me to act in, act when I go sightseeing, have children acting, act when I talk, my whole life acting, die acting, you know what I mean? Because for me the Planet Earth in its totality is like a huge stage on which we all perform, except there are horrible, bad, regular, good, very good and excellent actors, as you've told me I am. So the Earth is the stage, and infinite space the great curtain, and behind the curtain there will be unexplainable lives, gods perhaps, who applaud or boo our performance."

"All of that seems very intelligent, of course, if you take the Shakespeare out of it. That thing about the stage isn't yours; Hamlet said it five hundred years ago. Nevertheless, turning this down seems incredible to me. Do you write?"

"Not really. I just think. I'd like to write but I've never done it."

"Would you venture to try it?"

Eduardo mulled it over for a few seconds. "Possibly."

"So write what you've told me, try doing it in that special way you have of seeing the world, a story. Tell your life story. Then send it to me. If you need money, I can give you some now. If the story doesn't appeal to me or doesn't do me any good, you don't have to pay me back."

"There's just one problem."

"What?"

"I can try to write, but it would be under a pseudonym."

"That's not a problem."

"Yes, because the pseudonym will be a woman's name."

Neither Spielberg's intelligence nor his intuition failed him, and he immediately thought that, if it were to be written, it would be written by James Bond's ex.

"That would be formidable," he said.

"Why do you say that would be formidable? It's just a change of name."

"That's exactly why."

"Why, Mr. Spielberg?"

"Listen, get it in your head, often a name is enough to give life another dimension or to thoroughly change a story. Don't forget it: a single name. And from now on, don't call me Mr. Spielberg. Call me Steve."

Outside the office, the Colombian writer and Elizabeth were waiting for him. He showed them the note signed by Spielberg, and they yelled for joy and congratulated him. They told him they had to celebrate.

"Listen, *pelao*, that's far out. With Spielberg, no less. Oh, my God!"

Eduardo wasn't speaking. He looked mentally retarded. They chalked it up to the huge excitement, and they took him to the closest restaurant so he could clear his mind with a couple of beers.

Inside the office, Spielberg called his assistant and asked him, "Do you think a war can affect someone even if they're far away from it?"

"If they've got family in the war, sure."

"What if they don't?"

"I don't know, it's hard to answer. Why do you ask?"

"When I saw this young fellow who just left, he struck me as intelligent, but I had a hunch he'd been affected by the war."

"The one we just went through?"

"Yes, of course. It seems to me that's where he got the thing about acting wherever, because after all we live on a stage."

"It's possible, but he was in Honduras when the war was going on, and I don't think he has any family members who fought in the desert."

"Maybe he thinks of all humanity as family. Yeah, that's it. Call him at home before he goes back to his country and tell him if he ever changes his mind, to look for me. He's young, he might need us."

That night at the Colombian writer's house, everything was happiness after the triumph of the Honduran, or rather *Latino*, actor. The guests congratulated him one by one. That same night a few women who'd rejected him on other occasions, more than insinuating, offered themselves to him. Eduardo called out to the Colombian writer, telling him they needed to speak privately. The writer took him to the bedroom. There Eduardo told him about his quitting, about how he saw the world as a stage. The Colombian writer, a nihilist by birth, an irreverent man by vocation, embraced him tightly and guffawed.

"It's only eleven. What do you think about telling the guests at twelve sharp? I'll turn the music off and you and I will stand up front. I'll say it and you watch the reaction. This party will go on until daybreak."

At the appointed hour, the Colombian writer turned off the music. He issued a call to silence, saying he had important news from Eduardo. The guests thought it might be a thank you for their well-wishing and a promise to do even the impossible not to let them down in carrying out his duties as a well-known actor. Those who thought they were closest to him: Elizabeth, Maribel, Laura, the Puerto Rican poet, the Argentine, and the Bolivian (who'd forgotten past grudges and had even sent Mirian his congratulations for her excellent article on Bolivia), took front-row seats. The writer offered the statements just as Eduardo had expressed them to him. It was as if Niagara Falls had descended on that living room in the middle of winter. And silently, one behind the other, all the guests left the party. They left Eduardo, the writer and his wife in the living room. The wife, after finishing a cigarette, complained of exhaustion, and vanished into the bedroom. The two of them remained, actor and writer, silent and drinking booze.

"Don't feel bad, *pelao*, there's a price for that sort of philosophy. It's not within reach of every human brain."

"No. My quitting doesn't make me feel bad. I wanted to do it. It's more the fact that they don't understand me. At this moment I act, I am my own director and producer, and I'm not charging them to watch me. That's the bad part: no one wants to watch me."

"You have one spectator. I'm on your side. One is a number, and Pythagoras said the elements of numbers are also elements of things, and that determines whether things are in harmony. In the abstract sense, one is the essence of unity."

Eduardo smiled.

"It would be two with Casagrande, and I couldn't care less about disappointing Pythagoras."

"Should we call him? He called me and gave me his number. Wait, I'll get the phone book."

The writer spoke first and explained the situation to Casagrande. When the telephone receiver was close to Eduardo's ear, the yell was audible: "Hey, Banana, now I have no doubts: you're a genius, you bum. Remember what we talked about? The important thing is to get there. Still, to be sincere with you, I was looking forward to the day when I could walk into a movie house and see a poster featuring 'The Big Banana.'"

Casagrande told him he was teaching photography at a small college and giving private classes at the pretty house he was renting outside San Francisco. He invited Eduardo to come spend his honeymoon there; it would be an honor to have him at his house.

The writer and Eduardo didn't sleep. They extended the party, just as they had agreed, until the morning light broke. Then they slept until noon. They had lunch at a Queens restaurant, because the writer's wife refused to cook, and the writer offered to take Eduardo to the airport the day he left.

47

"My name is Roger Moore. My mission: Central America." Those were the first words that Mirian heard out of Roger Moore no longer playing James Bond, Agent 007. The TV news reported that the ex-Agent 007 was in Central America and that he would visit the countries of the isthmus one by one, including Honduras, of course.

Mirian was happy that her old flame was coming to visit her. At first she seemed delirious. She rubbed her eyes, touched herself for signs of a fever, and shook her head in an attempt to wake up. She was awake, and Roger Moore was on his way to her country.

The ex-007 came to Honduras, where he visited schools and hospitals. He lay the cornerstone for a health project, inaugurated a potable water tap in a small town, and was seen, scissors in hand, cutting a white ribbon to christen a social project. He also appeared at a hospital giving a months-old, sick, malnourished girl a flower. Roger Moore's face betrayed the chill it caused him to find himself on the other side of the screen. He saw and hugged children, unlike any movie star or athlete or politician would, in earnest. From his glossy eyes you could tell that his encounter with the children of misery had marked him forever. It seemed impossible for him to believe that so much calamity, so much human isolation really existed. In his travels throughout Central America, he suffered, what's more, he spoke in such a way that you could feel the guilt he carried for having been so indifferent to humanitarian causes in the past, because seeing a news report about a faraway country with photos of the misery was never the same as actually living it, as being practically immersed in it. That's how Roger Moore felt when he walked the narrow unpaved streets, lined with shacks like animal shelters, small tin shacks, cardboard shacks, in short, houses made of garbage.

When Central American journalists asked the ex-Agent 007 why he'd decided to work for the UNICEF film arts project for a year in return for the sum of one dollar, he replied, "When you've gotten so much from society, you're obligated to give a little back, and if it goes to the children, so much the better."

Because of his movies, because of the violence unleashed in them, and above all, because of the arrogance it took to paint the country he represented as the indestructible possessor of total and perpetual supremacy, Roger Moore did not enjoy the sympathy of a great number of Central American intellectuals. Still, in the press conferences and private interviews he gave, Roger Moore was clever about distancing himself from Agent 007, his actor's work from his private life, and proved again and again that behind James was Roger, a man of flesh and blood, of sweat and tears, of sadness and joy, capable of being moved, a man, plain and simple.

Mirian looked for a way to meet Agent 007. As an experienced spy who'd graduated from the Cold War school, she made her calculations carefully, and managed to get herself elected by the university to attend the press conference and cover the charitable acts James Bond would perform.

In Tegucigalpa it was impossible for her to see Roger Moore, because he was constantly surrounded by so many people, between fans and bodyguards. She had to wait until the agent visited the second capital of Honduras, San Pedro Sula, which was where they'd assigned Mirian.

The news of Agent 007 in Tegucigalpa brought out many admirers who tried to meet him, to see him even if only from a distance. His statements to the press revealing the agent's other side garnered him new admirers, which is why Roger Moore drew a larger following than his screen roles had already given him. The agent's arrival was talked about from the lowest social stratum to the highest, from the riffraff to the intellectuals.

Mirian visited the Hotel Copantl Sula, in the city of San Pedro Sula, which was where she would stay until she could meet up with Agent 007. As she rode the elevator absorbed in her thoughts, remembering Eduardo, thinking of how excited she would be to tell him she'd met Roger Moore, she took no notice of the others riding next to her. Suddenly, as if by reflex, she raised her eyes to see a man staring at her, right at that moment. The impression was so great she came to the brink of fainting.

As she tried to half-pull herself together, she exclaimed, "Roger Moore, James Bond, Agent 007!"

Roger Moore, unable to explain it to himself, playfully pretended to pull a pistol out of his waist and stuck his index finger in her side. She smiled, and that smile amused him. Before the elevator could bring the agent to his destination, she explained to him that she was a journalist and needed to talk to him. The agent, a gentleman, invited her to join the group surrounding him.

Wearing a fine white jacket and a pair of binoculars hanging around his neck, Roger Moore visited schools, hospitals and community centers in poor neighborhoods. They invited him to play soccer on an improvised field, built out of the sheer desire to play, and he accepted good-naturedly. He played for close to ten minutes with players from the National Soccer League and street children. After that day, the humble field was baptized the Roger Moore Sports Complex.

He completely impressed Mirian when he spoke on an improvised tribune in one of the many poor places he visited. Close to two hundred women, old ladies with many children and ailments, listened to him. Moore was talking about the need to support each other, about the struggle to be carried out in order to come out ahead in matters of first priority. To the rhythm of the agent's words, the murmur of the ladies began growing stronger. Suddenly, Roger became aware that the murmur had turned into a full-throated wail, a wail through which they out and out asked Agent 007 to help them, to help them right then and there. It was a sort of multitudinous cry for James Bond to multiply the loaves and fishes. Not until that moment, over the course of his entire tour, had Roger Moore felt exhausted, useless, incompetent. In the face of that, the only thing he could do that was less self-conscious than he himself was to lift one of his hands to his forehead, raise his gaze skyward, and say indignantly, "I wish I were God, ladies, so I could help you."

On two occasions his son, Christian, offered him water, but he rejected it because he'd offered it in public. It was his special water, which he never drank in public unless he was undercover. He said it made him feel ashamed that life had to be that way: he had special drinking water so it wouldn't get contaminated, and the people in the places he visited had no water, not even contaminated water.

A journalist, the mayor of the city, Mirian and other people accompanied Agent 007 to Las Cuatro Rosas, a bar, where they talked for many hours. The agent drank Salvavida beer, from the Honduran Atlantic Coast, and told stories about his private life.

One thing that was hard for Mirian to accept was that Roger Moore, as he appears in films, is a dangerous Don Juan, but in his other life, he's a married man with three sons.

The days the agent spent in Honduras as UNICEF's guest to the Press Awards ceremony for journalists who promote children's causes helped Mirian endure Eduardo's new absence, and shorten the time until his return.

The day the agent left, he smiled at her because they'd talked a lot during those days, and he'd liked that restless young lady who told him about New York and her future husband who dreamed of becoming a movie star. He drew close to her and gave her a kiss on the cheek, leaving a red rose in the palm of her hand. Once the plane had taken off, a happy Mirian drove off in her red car to put the red rose in water, to smile smugly, thinking about how, if she had to choose between James Bond and Roger Moore, the human being would always come in first place.

48

Eduardo used the week he had left in New York to visit a few of his remaining friends, people like Mairena who neither belittled his quitting, nor saw it as an heroic deed. From the first day he arrived, he'd been trying to reach Javier. Finally someone answered and told him that Javier hadn't lived there for a long time. Mairena could tell him nothing of Javier's whereabouts.

From the time he met Ruth, the white woman, Mairena had undergone a metamorphosis, which had turned him into a man dedicated to his family and spiritual life. He'd taken a different stance regarding racism. He didn't stop fighting it, but now it was across the board, no matter where it came from or what color it wore. As the established deacon he'd become, he had no need for extramarital affairs. He loved his wife and they were expecting a baby. In his free time he studied Martin Luther King. He thanked Eduardo for what he'd done for his life by getting Ruth for him. Eduardo could not accept his gratitude, arguing that it was an act of circumstance which he had no way of knowing might have a positive outcome for Mairena. Eduardo let him in on certain secrets of his private life, such as the fact that he hadn't begun to worry about the blacks' situation until after living at Mairena's. Mairena didn't resent him for it; his intelligence and kindness overcame that small barrier. Maybe true friendship hadn't begun budding between the two until then.

A day before leaving, Eduardo walked through Manhattan. He went to greet Charlie in the morning, but didn't tell him about having quit, though he did show him the note signed by Spielberg. Charlie had changed a lot; he had a new point of view toward Latin Americans and workers. His friendship with a Honduran writer who'd lived in his building for some time had helped him find fresh points of view. Leroy, the token, the black man from Alabama, had disappeared and taken several power tools with him. Robert, the Texan, was gone. Eduardo made a copy of Spielberg's letter on the office copy machine and left it for him, signed right next to Spielberg's signature; before he handed it to Charlie, he contemplated what he'd done, and it seemed to him those two signatures looked very well together: Steven Spielberg and Eduardo Lin.

Afterwards, he walked along Canal Street, the main street in Chinatown. He strolled through the Village, went into a café and admired the actresses who aspired to be movie stars. He went to 14th and Union Square to buy things for Mirian, and then headed toward 34th Street with the same purpose.

At five in the afternoon he found himself at Grand Central Station waiting for the subway, the 4 which would take him to 161st and Yankee Stadium, where he would get on the D to Kingsbridge, to Poe's house, close to Valentine Avenue. He was in no hurry to get through the crowds at Grand Central station. He was distracted, when suddenly he thought he heard a familiar voice. He searched around for the voice and could not find where it was coming from. The voice repeated itself: *After all, I love Honduras, that country's beautiful, my country, I'll go some day,* and Eduardo knew it was Javier's voice. He made his way through the crowd, following the barely audible monologue. *I already forgave the Honduran woman from the southern United States. Besides, the South is pretty. I like the South. Some day I'll go back to the South* . . . as Eduardo struggled to make his way through the train stops, he managed to hear the monologue: *I love jazz, I love blues, blow is divine, may God take the woman from the South to his glory* . . . Eduardo knew who was delivering the monologue . . . *I love the blues, stand by me* . . . Eduardo followed the monologue to the subway car, but he was too late. The door closed in his face. From the window of the train he finally saw Javier with a beard, in rags, knew in his own little world. The train pulled away and Eduardo that his great friend had become a homeless person, a beggar, with the neutral insanity

Casagrande had spoken to him about. Eduardo's eyes began to flood over, he couldn't help it. He cried in the middle of that multitude and no one seemed to realize it. It was as if he were crying in a foreign language. He stood there in the crowd, alone. Under different circumstances, he had stopped to watch some homeless person he didn't know, and felt some sort of short-lived pity for them. Now it was different: this was someone he knew, a friend.

That evening he called Mirian collect in Honduras from the public phone close to Poe's house to tell her his arrival time and flight number the following day, and that he loved her. He also commented to her that he'd never before experienced the magic of calling from a public telephone without depositing a single cent, and that if she were to ask him to show the magnitude of his love, he would tell her that he loved her as much as he loved New York Telephone on that day, at that hour and at that precise moment.

Every step he took from the public phone in Poe Park to his place was like one drop of jealousy after another falling on him. With every floor he rode up in the elevator in the building on Valentine Avenue, the drops came down harder. When he got to the twelfth floor, the drops had become a downpour. He entered his room, drenched. He tried to convince himself he was being a fool. Perhaps 007's presence in Honduras didn't bother him so much as did the terrible circumstances of destiny, of esoterism, which would have Roger Moore arrive just when Eduardo was in New York, and the way that Mirian, who was an articulate person but clumsy with words when referring to Moore, had finally told him over the telephone.

He went out to the living room where he found José, who was enjoying some lively Caribbean music. In a search for some merciful fisherman to take the hook out, Eduardo asked him, "Do you know if Roger Moore is married?"

José, who had just graduated from his life in *sucres,* hadn't been to a movie theater in years, nor did he watch television in any language that wasn't his own. Maybe if Eduardo had said James Bond or Agent 007, José might have understood, but that name, the way Eduardo pronounced it, wasn't among the inventory of things that had invaded his ears during his lifetime. He tried to be courteous, to give an answer that, even if it weren't definitive, would somehow lead to the required answer. Serious, solemn and attentive, as he'd become in his new life, he said, "Look, I really don't know. But if you want to, you can call him. Don't even ask to use the telephone. You're my guest. Go on, go, call him and ask him."

49

From the little window in the airplane, Eduardo looked at Tegucigalpa, its small houses, its narrow streets, practically buildingless from that height, the mountains surrounding it like a secret city. Had he given up a different world for the sake of that city? Or was he really embracing a new philosophy in his existence? What would he get out of it? Early on he'd believed that his main aspiration of looking for a place among the big shots had nothing to do with wanting money, or wanting to boast about what they call fame. He had only wanted a platform from which he could be heard and set forth his ideals for a better world, against social injustices, against war, against the destruction of nature, against the evils that beset the world. What had become of all those desires for a platform? Had he committed the greatest mistake of his existence in getting there and rejecting it at the same time? If he were to be sincere and boil it down to its essence, what would his answer be as to why he'd come back? Where would he go first when he stepped off the plane at the airport? For whom was he desperate to come back? Undoubtedly everything he did and was doing had no other name than Mirian.

From the airport Mirian and Eduardo drove in the red car to a restaurant outside the city. They celebrated the reunion with wine. He told her about his quitting at the top. For a moment she creased her brow and got flustered. Thanks to his quick thinking, he realized that it must not have mattered to her, because had he taken it, he would have stayed over there and married a famous actress or model. Thus,

Eduardo Lin, not a word more to be said about it, belonged to her, and that seduced her into not condemning his actions.

"Did you see Andrea?"

"No."

"Yes, you saw her."

"No."

"I called her but they told me she'd gone back to Colombia."

"Poor little thing, I imagine that was the saddest thing that happened to you in New York on this last trip."

"No, not really. In fact, I'm glad she made that decision. She needed to go away. She has more of a future in her country. I told her I admire her.

"Do you know the saddest thing that happened to me? The fact that Paul Simon waited for me to leave to put on a historic concert in Central Park. They say he was marvelous. Are you still jealous?"

"No, not as much."

"So we can dance?"

On the restaurant dance floor, only one other couple was dancing. Mirian whispered in his ear, "I'm jealous of New York. When you're not around and I see a movie shot in New York, it makes me furious. I wonder who you might have walked down that street with, or whether you went to see a Broadway show."

"Les Misérables," he smiled. "Casagrande and I went."

"But even if it's just to the movies, I can't believe you'd go alone, even though I know you do. But you see, it's me being silly."

"Why don't you close your eyes and think about us on the beach I told you about, the one on the way to Long Island, where I told you *Jaws* had been shot. Imagine us there in bathing suits, running in the sand, hungry to make love, except it's not allowed in public places. Now think: about what? That's it, we're on East 59th Street. We're walking. I suggest we ride the tram, remember? And we take it all the way to Roosevelt Island. And up there, in the tram, you and I dance and the people surround us excitedly, and behind them, beyond the windows is that very beautiful Manhattan looking at us, surrounding us as we ride along in the middle of the East River. We dance slowly, the song I always dedicate to you, 'When a Man Loves a Woman,' and in the middle of the song we kiss and people applaud us. New York needs people to kiss more, and the song goes on: 'Spend his very last dime . . .'"

The song had been over a long time ago. They were dancing without music, to the amazement of customers and servers. That might be considered natural in other parts of the world but not in Tegucigalpa.

"That's so beautiful!" he says to her. "It's like I'd lived it. We've lived it," he added, and his voice without the music or any other sort of noise sounded deep and strong.

They realized they were dancing without music. They laughed and hugged and left the dance floor smiling at the surprised customers who replied with inquisitive smiles.

"You know what?" Mirian asked, "I think I really would like to be a writer. My ex-professors and colleagues always compliment me on my writing—those who aren't jealous, of course."

"As far as I'm concerned, you're already a writer."

"No, you're not getting me. I'm not talking about someone who writes articles and things like the burning of the embassy article, but books, novels, stories, I don't know, maybe even theater."

"Casagrande liked your articles. He said it was literature, and good literature at that. You have a lot of talent. I can tell you stories I know about. Yes, someone in New York asked me whether I wrote. He told me I should try it. But I was born to act."

"That's it, and you've made it. You got as far as you wanted to. What else could worry you?"

Eduardo half-closed his eyes as if trying to make out a ship in the distance.

"I don't know. I don't feel fulfilled. Whatever you see of me could be just appearances. I know I made it, because even the day after the audition Spielberg's assistant called me to tell me that if I ever changed my mind, to call them collect and they'd send me airfare, they'd always be willing to give me a shot."

"That's beautiful. That means you impressed Spielberg. I really want to be a writer."

"I love you. You're going to be my favorite writer. I'm going to give you a ton of ideas, things they've told me about. You'll write them and I'll perform them."

"When we get married, we should go live in La Ceiba, by the sea."

"Sounds good, but it would be better to divide our time between La Ceiba and New York. Don't forget I have an open offer from my friend Steve. It's November. Our marriage is a short time away, six months. We can look for a nice place in La Ceiba starting now. I have only one piece of advice for you."

"What?" she smiled.

"Actually two pieces of advice."

"The first one?"

"Don't write about war, any war. Not even anti-war books. It's useless; they don't add anything. In some book I read a father's advice to a distinguished writer: 'Don't write about war, any war.'"

"Why so sure? We could write anti-war novels."

"It's useless; they don't do any good. There will always be wars."

"That's exactly why they should be written, because wars do no good."

"Of course, I didn't think about that."

"How about the second piece of advice?"

"You're very romantic, well, we both are, and so what? As for your novels, though, they won't do any good if happiness reigns at the end. Most critics dislike happy endings. That's what they call pulp or fluff."

"I know. Why is that? People suffer so much in real life, at least in fiction they should give them the right to be happy."

He laughed. "How beautiful! Besides, it's true. It's a shame they don't understand."

He held her closer.

"I'm sure," he added before kissing her, "they won't forgive you for even a single chapter with a happy ending."